ROAD KILL

Gavin MacFadyen Suspense Series

JAN COFFEY

with
MAY MCGOLDRICK

Book Duo Creative

ENJOY!

Nikoo & Jim

[handwritten signature]

CHAPTER ONE

Northwest Connecticut
April 1997

WASHING down the Xanax with a long swig of vodka, Lacey felt like from now on, every day would be a Saturday.

She tried to focus on the joint she'd dropped on her faded jeans. With an effort that almost made her laugh out loud, she finally trapped it between her fingers and lit it. The acrid smoke curled down her throat.

As Lacey stared into the blue and yellow flames licking the wood in the bonfire, figures took shape with sudden clarity. People. Trapped there in the fire. A man and a woman, screaming at each other. The man's arm snapped out like the crack of a whip, striking the woman across the face. As she dropped to her knees, he kicked her in the stomach.

"No you don't, you *bastard*." Lacey reached into the flames to squash him. Her hand burned. She pulled back and stared at it. Her fingers were matchsticks—five of them.

Last week, she couldn't find a lighter in the bathroom. Well, she'd never have to worry about that again. She spread them out against the dark sky.

A scream down by the beach sliced through the edge of her consciousness. The matchsticks hissed and disappeared, and her fingers returned. She sat bolt upright. The moon was gleaming off the waters of Sherman Pond.

A skin-and-bones girl sat across the way, plugged into her Walkman, on the other side of the fire. Lacey remembered her name was Liz. She was rocking to some tune, and everyone else had disappeared.

There was that scream again, muffled this time. Lacey tried to concentrate on the laughter coming from the beach. It would be so easy to zone out again.

That girl Stephanie must have gone with them.

Lacey was only here because she'd run into Michael Phoenix and his friends at the donut shop. Those guys were all seniors at the high school. Stephanie was only a sophomore, like Lacey. But Michael had promised some good shit if she'd go to the door at the nice house and ask for Stephanie. So, she'd done it. No big deal.

That seemed like an eon ago. Lacey looked back into the fire. There'd been an Easter wreath hanging beneath the fancy brass lantern beside Stephanie's front door. Bunnies and colored eggs and purple flowers arranged in the woven branches. Her family never had anything like that. They'd never celebrated any Easter, or Thanksgiving, or Christmas. Holidays like that would mean there was something good in life. Lacey couldn't even imagine it. Not in their house.

As soon as Stephanie climbed into the van, it'd been clear she was hot for Michael. They hadn't even pulled away from the curb before she'd had her hands all over him.

The muffled cry from the beach again broke through the fog.

"Did you hear that?" Lacey looked across the fire at Liz.

Liz pulled her ear buds. "No."

"Where is everybody? I heard something."

"It's nothing."

Lacey's stomach got queasy. She really didn't know any of

these kids. Since moving to the area in January to live with her sister and her grandfather, she hadn't made any friends. These guys were older, and it was the first time anyone had taken her partying with them. Still, it was better than sneaking money out of her sister's wallet and buying the stuff.

"Sounds like somebody's in trouble."

"Aren't you from Chicago or someplace?"

"Cleveland."

"Whatever," Liz snapped. "Don't they party there?"

"Yeah, but that—"

"Just cool it. Your friend Stephanie knows what she's doing."

"She's not my friend."

"Better for you."

"But is she down there with all the boys?"

"I said, *cool* it." Liz threw her Walkman on the ground next to her. "Fuck. You really know how to ruin a good buzz."

The cries and laughter grew louder as Lacey struggled to her feet. The sharp pain in her hip shot straight down her leg. She'd left her cane behind in the donut shop. She didn't want it. Didn't need it.

It sounded like the boys were chanting. But another voice was drowning out the others. Her father's shouts. The crash of furniture. Her mother begging, pleading for him to stop. Lacey's head was spinning. She tried to take a step but couldn't get her bad leg to work. She almost staggered into the fire.

"*Sit* down," Liz snapped. "It's none of your fucking business."

Lacey could hear her mother screaming. *He was hitting her.*

"No!"

Lacey lurched toward the beach, but the girl cut her off. Her face loomed over her in the dark.

"I said it's *none* of your fucking business."

Lacey felt the prickly heat of panic wash through her, and she scrambled away.

Silhouetted by the fire, Liz was watching her go. "Yeah, bitch. Just keep going."

Lacey limped off, moving as quickly as she could through the dark woods. Pine branches whipped at her face and body. Missing a step, she went sprawling flat on her face. The smell of cold, damp earth filled her nose.

Lacey needed to get her mother out. She could see his crazed eyes, the rigid mask of rage stretched across his face. He wasn't stopping. He couldn't. Her mother was huddled against the wall by the stove. Next time he'd kill her, he screamed, going after her again. Lacey believed him.

Fear propelled her to her feet as she struggled against the pain in her hip and leg.

Lacey hobbled as fast as her feet would move. The cracked yellow walls of their kitchen vanished, replaced by darkness and the smell of night. Her breaths stuttered in her chest.

Suddenly, the trees thinned and she found herself standing at the edge of the lake. Across the way, a solitary red lantern shone at the end of a dock, reflecting a blur of deep crimson on the water.

The voices and laughter were clearer here—goading, encouraging, taunting—and on the beach she caught glimpses of Stephanie's white skin writhing amidst the dark shapes. One figure was standing back, watching the others. His cigarette glowed in the dark.

"*Stop*, you bastards," she shouted. "Let her go!"

Her cry did nothing. No one turned. The chants became louder. Lacey felt in her pocket for the cell phone and dialed.

"Hello?" Her sister Terri's voice was cool, calm. Like the coo of a dove. She would know what to do. Terri was older, smarter. She had just been accepted into the police academy.

"It's me. Lacey." Her tongue was a wad of cotton in her mouth.

The guttural sounds from the beach tumbled across the water. There was something nasty in the tone. Sick. Satisfied.

Lacey saw the dark solitary figure step forward, joining the others.

"I need help," she pleaded into the phone. "There's a girl here. She's—"

A scream cut through the laughter...and then there was silence.

Deep, thick silence.

And then only the sound of the water lapping the rocks at her feet.

CHAPTER TWO

Sixteen Years Later

"WE CELEBRATE the life that never dies and the love that lives forever. We celebrate that Terri's life with God is one without suffering or pain. It is an eternal life of joy and bliss."

Gavin MacFadyen leaned against the heavy wallpaper in the reception room and let the words of the minister drift past him.

They'd been partners for a dog's age. Hundreds of stakeouts. Scores of murder cases. He remembered every one. And he remembered how he used to kid her about the meticulous record-keeping she was fond of, the anal way she liked to organize their workload. Man, the endless arguments they used to have over nothing, just for the sake of arguing. He and Terri had been paired up for over ten years. He'd been on the force for ten years prior to that. That made him the senior partner, but he'd admit to anyone—except her—that she was better at the job than he was. She was tougher, meaner, more dedicated, and she made a habit of getting so deep into every case that it became personal.

Terri lived the life of a cop around the clock. That is, until her sister showed up at the end of this past summer. Still, the job never suffered. Terri was the best of the best. Thirty-eight years old. Too young to die. Way too young.

Some two hundred people, mostly dressed in uniform blues, crowded the funeral home halfway between New Haven and Westbury in a dead gray city straddling rusted train tracks and a murky brown river. Terri hadn't lived here, didn't work here, didn't go to church here. But the younger sister had arranged for the service to be held here. She'd chosen a place as isolated and off-track as she was herself.

Gavin's gaze focused on Lacey Watkins sitting in the front row. Chairs on either side of her sat empty. No friends. Nobody to hold her hand. The last one left of their family. Black knee-length skirt and black fitted shirt. Dark hair pulled into a tight ponytail. She just stared at a flower arrangement by the foot of the podium. No emotion showing. No tissues in hand to wipe away tears...real or pretend. From this angle he could see the mask of indifference that she wore like a second skin. He knew it didn't mean she wasn't feeling anything. It was just there. He'd seen the same expression on Terri's face plenty of times. It was a give-nothing-away look. On Lacey, it made her look like a beautiful statue. Untouched. Cold.

"We celebrate Terri as one who has gone before us and who will greet us again." There was a pause and a long moment of reflection before the speaker encouraged the crowd to repeat lines of prayers.

"Hey. Sorry, man."

Gavin turned his head and acknowledged the squarely built man who edged in next to him. Luke Brandt was a detective at New Haven PD. Gavin had retired this past year from the force to start his own private investigation firm, but that didn't stop him from staying in touch with the old crew.

"When did you get back?"

"Last night," Gavin told him.

Terri had died in a hit and run accident in Westbury a week ago Saturday. Gavin had been in Las Vegas going over the security arrangements with the management company for some concerts coming up at Mohegan Sun. No one had called him about Terri's death until he was back in Connecticut.

"When did you find out?"

"Last night."

"That's tough." Brandt shook his head with a frown.

Gavin had never been close with Luke. They both played their cards close to the vest. That's just the way they were built.

"How's the case going? Any leads on the car and the driver?"

Luke shook his head. "The Chief could tell you more about what's been done. But as far as I know, they've got nothing."

The service ended. Gavin saw Lacey Watkins stand up as a line of people approached her. Her response wasn't much different from before. A nod. A brief handshake. He saw her glance around once at the door, clearly impatient to get out.

"Sort of sad to lose Terri and have that one hit the jackpot." The detective stared at Lacey.

"Jackpot?"

"Pension. Life insurance. Savings. Everybody knew how Terri was about socking it away. Gotta be a pretty good pile of cash. It doesn't get better than that for a jailbird."

"Back up. Terri always said her little sister was a troubled kid in the wrong place at the wrong time, and she still did three years for it. Not exactly a jailbird." His flash of temper surprised him. Must have been for the sake of his old partner. Terri loved her sister. Gavin didn't think he'd ever seen her as happy as this past summer when Lacey agreed to move back here.

"I'm just saying it's a pretty sweet deal."

Gavin was in no mood to play defense attorney. He shrugged and walked away. Brandt obviously had never lost a sister.

He wanted to meet Lacey, convey his condolences. Terri had been keeping the two of them at arm's length. She'd even told him why. Too many one-night stands. She didn't want to have to shoot him in the balls when he got close to Lacey and started something. Gavin had no doubt Terri would have done it too.

A gaggle of uniforms surrounded him. Everyone knew him. They wanted to know what he was up to. Many expressed condolences to him. Marg Botto, the last girlfriend of Terri's that Gavin knew of, stopped him. Marg and Terri had parted ways last spring.

"It's not right," she said, holding it together. "I can't believe she's gone."

Gavin patted Marg gently on the shoulder and cut through the crowd. By the time he worked his way through to Lacey's seat, she was gone. But he saw the small purse left under the chair. He picked it up. Compact and light, the black case was easy to carry and obviously easier to forget. The main door to the hall was packed with people taking their time getting out. A side door was ajar, and Gavin caught a glimpse of fallen yellow leaves plastered to a cement walk.

He pushed open the door. A crowd was gathered in front of the building. The walkway snaked through some ornamental shrubbery and down to the parking lot behind the funeral home. Lacey was hurrying down the path. Limping.

He followed her. "Where are you going that's so important?"

Today was about Terri and there were a lot of people still here to honor her memory. A life worth honoring. Terri had been so consumed by the idea of helping her sister, of rebuilding their family. She talked all the time about Lacey and how she'd never had a fair chance at life. And how it was a miracle that they were being given another opportunity.

Lacey reached the car and yanked unsuccessfully on the latch. When it wouldn't budge, she banged on the roof of the car and her shoulders sagged. She hugged her middle, her head dropping onto her chest, her bluster crumbling before his eyes. Her body began to shake as she leaned onto the car.

"Shit." He didn't do well with women in tears. Uneasiness rushed through him. He felt like an intruder, watching her fall apart like this. And he was also an asshole for thinking that she didn't care.

The tap on a horn made her jerk her head around. Gavin realized he was blocking a car from going by. Lacey's gaze flicked over him, and she quickly turned away, brushing back tears.

He took his time approaching her. "Hi. You left this under your chair."

"Thank you." She reached out awkwardly and grabbed the purse, refusing to look at him.

"I was going to keep it, but I was afraid there might be a cop or two around."

The look she sent him was worth the wisecrack. Her eyes were green and they glistened like emeralds.

It was impossible not to stare. She had the same body type and facial mold as her sister. But there were many differences. The slant of her dark green eyes. The full lower lip. The soft line of her jaw. The pale skin. The slender column of her throat. His gaze moved down to the rise and fall of her breasts under the fitted shirt. The sudden wave of lust rushing through him was unexpected. And uncalled for.

"Gavin MacFadyen," he said, getting his head back into the moment. "I was Terri's partner at NHPD."

"Terri often..." Her husky voice faltered. "She often spoke of you."

"I'm sorry about what happened," he managed to say. "I was away. I didn't know."

She looked at the car. Gavin didn't want her to go yet.

"Are you okay? Is there anything I can do?"

A slight shake of the head. A few more tears escaped. She had the keys in her hand.

Gavin dug deep for some way to delay her. "Can I take you out for a cup of coffee? A late breakfast? Can we go someplace and talk?"

She shook her head and the beep of the car lock told him his time was up.

He yanked one of his business cards out of his pocket and offered it to her. He was relieved when she took it. He held her hand for an extra beat, waiting until she met his gaze again. Her fingers were like ice.

"Just call me if you need anything."

"Thank you."

Gavin opened the car door for her and gawked as the black skirt hiked up to mid-thigh when she got behind the wheel. He felt like he was back in high school, but it didn't matter. The buttons of her shirt strained, teasing him with a glimpse of a white flesh above a black bra.

She closed the door and started the car before he could come up with some other lame invitation.

There was no point in analyzing what had just happened. The woman was beautiful and vulnerable, and he was attracted to her. True, this was the first time they'd met, but he knew so much about Lacey that he felt he'd known her forever.

Heading back to his car, Gavin realized that he wasn't the only one watching her drive away.

Across the parking lot under a tree, an old man in a gray raincoat and battered fishing hat was staring at Lacey's silver Honda as it moved along the driveway to the street.

CHAPTER THREE

Westbury, Connecticut
A Month Later

LACEY WATKINS LOOKED through the viewfinder of her Nikon and squeezed the shutter release several times. A breeze swept through the branches of the trees above them, stirring life in the autumn woods. A falling shower of red and yellow leaves offered an ideal background for the shots as she clicked away. The tawny, black-faced puppy and the three boys made their way like tightrope walkers along the top of the stone wall. Every few steps, the dog stopped and barked an invitation to the two adults moving along the ground parallel to them.

"These will be the most non-traditional holiday pictures we've sent out," Michele, the young mother, said.

Lacey kept the camera up to her eye, watching and waiting.

She got several shots of the boys as they tried to jump hand-in-hand off the wall. Button-down shirts that had been crisp and white a couple hours earlier were now rumpled and dirty, the sleeves rolled up to their elbows. The boys' khakis had grass stains on the knees. Six or seven posed pictures were all Lacey was able to get before the excited puppy was leaping from one lap to the other, managing to imprint his muddy paws on the clothes of the nine-year-old and the five-year-old twins. The happy grins on the three faces tugged at her heart strings and Lacey's throat tightened. There were no pictures of her and Terri as children. What she had been left with was only what was imprinted in her mind.

She forced her thoughts to the afternoon ahead. She was booked with appointments into the evening and she'd spent far more time than she'd originally planned with this client.

"I got some shots you're going to love."

"When can I come see them?" Michele asked.

"We can schedule an appointment for tomorrow." Lacey unzipped her bag and started packing up her equipment.

"Awesome." Michele bent down in time to grab the puppy before he climbed into Lacey's camera bag. "Should I call you later?"

"That would be great. You can call Amy to set up a time." Hauling the heavy bag up onto her shoulder, Lacey glanced at her watch.

Amy, Lacey's part-time help, worked at a local adult daycare facility on Wednesday mornings and didn't get back until 1:00. Because Amy was blind, she was dependent on the van service which didn't always run on time.

Michele attached a leash to the rambunctious puppy's collar and walked with Lacey as they left the woods and started across a field toward their parked cars, the boys running behind them. "So, how's business going?"

"It's keeping me busy," Lacey said.

"I guess that's a good thing, considering everything." There was a polite pause. "I didn't know your sister personally, but I saw the article in the paper. It must be tough."

Lacey wasn't comfortable with wearing her sorrow on her sleeve or accepting sympathy of any kind. She'd learned those lessons early in life. Where she'd been, displaying emotion was a weakness. To admit vulnerability only made it easier for others to hurt her.

Lacey was saved from any more awkwardness by her cell phone. She dug into her pocket and answered it.

"I was late," said Amy. "You're late. And Jeannie Bond and her mom were early."

"I'll be there in fifteen. Tell them I picked up the proof for Jeannie's wedding album this morning, so we can look at the finished book together. While they're waiting, lay out the singles they thought they'd like prints of. It's the folder on the center of my desk."

A few minutes later, speeding along the country road, Lacey forced herself to take deep breaths to calm her emotions. Just the mention of Terri these days was enough to throw her off.

Five weeks. It would be just five weeks this coming Saturday. Terri had been killed in a hit-and-run while out on a morning jog. Gone. Just like that.

Only a couple of weeks prior to that, the two of them had been busy planning a future and rebuilding the family they'd been deprived of for most of their lives. It had been her sister's encouragement that had brought Lacey back to Connecticut to their grandfather's old house to make a go at stability. And it'd been because of Terri's financial support that she could buy Brett Orr's business.

She slammed on the brakes when the car in front of her suddenly slowed to a crawl on the narrow country lane. Autumn with its changing colors drew sightseers in droves to the rolling countryside, and Lacey arrived back at the house ten minutes later than she'd told Amy. She was relieved to find her client's car still in the driveway.

Lacey found them looking at the overgrown garden out back. Apologizing deeply for the delay, she led them into the house.

She squeezed Amy's shoulder as they passed the office area and headed for the small parlor beyond it.

A love seat, a straight back chair, and a coffee table filled the center of the room. The small sofa faced the fireplace and a flat-screen TV hung above it. Lacey had painted the walls a dark green, and the colonial windows had built-in shutters that could be closed to shut out the daylight.

Rather than taking over the building lease after buying Brett's Orr's business, Lacey had decided her grandfather's old farm house would be perfect as a studio. And it was. Aside from providing a quaint and homey space to work with her clients, she'd saved a ton of money by moving her equipment here.

She settled the two on the loveseat.

"I haven't had a chance to look through the proofs this morning, but we can still make changes." Lacey took the mock-up pages out of their plastic wrap and stacked them on the table before her clients.

She felt deep satisfaction as she heard Jeannie's mother gasp.

"Honey, you look beautiful. The wedding dress. The flowers."

"Mom, you were there."

"I know. But the whole day is a blur." They turned to the next spread. "And I love these captions."

"Lacey's idea," Jeannie smiled. "When it's all put together, it will read like a book."

Lacey grabbed her clipboard and sat back in her own chair, ready to jot down notes if necessary. In the age of Internet-based publishing, this kind of customer attention was quickly going away. Clients weren't willing to pay for anything extra when they could do it cheaper themselves. Personal service and word of mouth was the only thing that could give her business a chance.

Jeannie's mother pointed to a picture of her with her daughter. "You're amazing, Lacey. You even make me look good."

"It's not me. You *are* beautiful." Lacey was feeling good about how this job had turned out. This was the first big job she'd taken on since moving back to Connecticut, and Terri had even come along that day as her assistant, carrying the equipment bags and keeping her company. It seemed like ages ago.

Rolling the chair to the desk, Lacey fought the tightness in her chest. She didn't want to show any hint of the grief that was smothering her. She and Terri had spent most of their lives apart, but it had been Terri's strength that kept the bond between them strong. She'd always been willing to go to any length to help Lacey, whether it was during the three years Lacey had been in prison or when she had been half way across the country, wandering from some godforsaken dot on the map to another, looking for purpose in a purposeless life.

"Wait." Jeannie pointed to the center of a page. "*That's* not my wedding."

"My Lord, what is that?" the mother whispered in shock.

Lacey walked over to the table and stared at the proof.

The single, wide-angle shot showed a winding gravel road snaking through a grove of trees. Wet, autumn leaves lay scattered on the ground. Morning fog obscured the distance, and wisps of mist curled like claws around a fallen object.

She looked closer. It was a body.

The caption beneath the picture read, *Road Kill.*

CHAPTER FOUR

THE COUNTY DART League met every Wednesday night at six o'clock at the State Street Bar and Grill across from the new train station. Competition was fierce and drinks were cheap because of happy hour. Trash talk, predictably, was vicious.

Gavin had never been a regular in league play, but he'd subbed more than a few times over the years with the New Haven County police team. Even after leaving the force, they'd still kept his name on the subs roster. Today, Jake Allen had called him begging.

The semi-finals against the Middlesex County team had drawn a full house and the State Street Bar was packed. Even without practice, Gavin could hit the cork as well as any of them. Watching the other team throw, he realized tonight would be no different.

It'd been a while since he'd done anything like this. Anything that resembled having a good time. There was always his work. And then Terri's accident had thrown him off kilter. A few times he'd contemplated calling Lacey Watkins but then talked himself out of it. His motivation was twisted. And no one else would do, unfortunately.

Jake was talking to Luke Brandt. They were looking up at the board.

Luke shot a glance at Gavin. "Okay, big boy. Step up to the hockey and show us if you still got it."

Gavin pushed his beer to the side and stepped to the plank that marked the throw point. The Middlesex County team was huddled by the window, watching with feigned unconcern.

"One time, baby," Jake murmured.

Gavin looked down at the black Hammer Head dart in his hand. Its tungsten barrel was cool between his fingers. He sighted and raised the dart, allowing nothing into his vision but the narrow strip of green between the wires on the board.

"Game shot," he said in a low voice.

The cell phone vibrated in his pocket just as his hand flicked forward, but he didn't let it affect his aim, the steel tip of the dart splitting the gleaming wires and sinking solidly into the green bristle surface.

He turned to the cheers and high-fives of his team as he pulled out his cell phone. "MacFadyen."

Either the bar noise was too loud or the person on the other end was not talking. Running his own business with a handful of assistants who worked case by case required Gavin to be on-call twenty-four seven. He had an answering service for general questions and for potential business; his cell was only for existing clients.

"I'm looking for..." The voice was so faint that he could barely make out the words. Sounded like a child.

He tensed, feeling the sharp stab to an old wound. He motioned to Jake that he had to take the call, grabbed his jacket, and headed out to the sidewalk. It was already dark and the breeze coming off the harbor was cool. Because of the tournament, there was a line of cars parked all along the front of the bar. A half empty bus huffed and went past.

"Say that again," he said into the phone. "I didn't quite get it."

"Terri Watkins. I'm looking for Terri."

Gavin's spine stiffened and he gazed down the street at the red taillights of the bus. Terri's death had been in the papers and on all the local TV stations, but it was possible that someone who knew her could have missed it.

"I tried her cell phone, but it keeps going to her voicemail."

"How did you get this number?"

"She gave it to me. Last time I saw her. That was a couple of months ago. She said if I can't get her...to call you. Said you'd know how to find her."

Gavin wondered if this was the time to tell her that Terri was dead.

"I gotta get a message to her. It's really important. I'm in trouble."

"Have you called the police?"

"I can't." Panic edged into her tone. "She knows I can't. That's why she gave me these other numbers. I gotta fuckin' talk to *her*."

It wasn't uncommon for an informant to trust the handler and not the system.

Gavin didn't know anything about the cases Terri was working on before the accident. A couple of phone calls and he could probably find out who had taken over her files.

"Give me your name and a number where someone can reach you."

"Not someone! Terri." The girl's voice rose sharply. "Last time she picked me up she took me to the hospital. And she knows what they fuckin' did to me. This time is worse."

His sister Elsie's face flashed before his eyes and pain seared his skull. He rubbed the back of his neck, not going there now.

"Hey, man. You there?"

Gavin knew what this was. Prostitution—especially involving young girls—drug trafficking, and the usual extortion rackets were all in a state of flux along the shoreline right now. With so much of the Mafia old guard dead, in prison, or retired to their Florida estates, the new muscle had been moving in for the past couple of decades. The Black and Latino gangs were just the most visible players. Asians and Eastern Europeans had been positioning themselves, as well. They didn't care how young the girls were and this one had to be working in the trade.

But lately there was an even more brutal driver behind the street mopes, one who aimed at controlling all the pieces on the board. He was more ruthless than any of the old school players. Gavin knew very well what was terrifying this girl.

"Where are you? Do you need to get picked up?"

"Not me. My mother. And the twins." The girl was crying. "Last night, I took off and didn't show up like they told me. And now I hear they're going after my family. One fuckin' time I mess up. My sisters are only seven. Just tell Terri she was right about everything. Tell her I got what she wanted before. This time, I'll give her what she needs. I already have their list, the one my boyfriend took. But she's gotta help me. She's gotta get them someplace safe."

"Address. Give me an address."

She blurted out a street address in the Newhallville section of the city. "They're staying with my aunt."

"Your name?"

"Tell her Alisha."

"Last name?"

"No. Just Alisha. Terri will know."

"Can I have her call you at this number?"

"No way. I just lifted this fuckin' phone, but I ain't keeping it. Tell her to get the twins someplace safe and I'll call her. I promise. Please. I gotta go."

The line went dead as the door of the bar opened and two women stepped out, lighting cigarettes. Gavin walked away from them and dialed the Newhallville police substation, telling the dispatcher to send a cruiser to the address. But as he hung up, he already knew that wasn't enough. The cops would look for a disturbance, ask a few questions, and if no one complained, they'd be out of there in a couple of minutes. Newhallville was a tough beat, and the uniforms had little time for hanging around, even on a Wednesday night.

Calling the captain on duty and asking who'd taken over Terri's cases wasn't a quick answer either. He'd already heard from the guys inside how bogged down everyone was with the caseloads. They'd probably split up her cases. New Haven just kept getting tougher.

The desperation in the girl's voice grabbed him. He'd left the force six months ago. The fact that Terri had given Alisha his number and not someone else's in the department was puzzling. But she was one of the very few people in the New Haven PD who knew about his sister's murder. She knew he would help.

Jake shoved the door open. "Hey, you coming in? We're up next."

"I can't. Something's happening. I gotta run. Hold on to my darts. I'll get them from you later."

Gavin didn't wait for the verbal abuse that he knew would follow and made a beeline across the street to his car.

He had no business going there. He could have passed the message to Jake or Luke in the bar and let them check into it. Something in his gut, though, told him otherwise. Terri was a smart detective. In the years they worked together, he'd learned to read her moves, to respect her intelligence. He trusted her.

Ten minutes later, he was on the street of the address Alisha had given him. A black BMW sat double-parked in front of a triple-decker house. As he drew near, two men pushed their way through the door of the first-floor apartment and shut it behind them. The lights were on, but the blinds were down.

Glancing in the windows of the Beamer as he drove by, Gavin could make out at least one person in the car in addition to the driver. He didn't slow down, but went to the end of the block and turned left before redialing the station house.

"Yeah, this is MacFadyen again. Same address. There's a home invasion in progress. Two are inside and at least two outside in a black BMW."

After relaying the license plate number, he hung up. Two cruisers were being dispatched, but it wasn't going to be fast enough. His only chance was to go in the back door, but that was risky here. There were more pit bulls than swing sets in the back-yards of Newhallville.

Turning at the next corner, he parked next to a hydrant. From under his seat, he pulled out his Glock .22, loaded a clip, and slipped the weapon into the holster before clipping it on.

A moment later, he was cutting through the side yard of the house that backed up to the address. He ran along the wall of a garage at the rear of the property, then scaled a rusted chain-link fence.

The backyard was dark, except for a light streaming through a rip in the shade of a rear window. Going to the wall, Gavin pulled himself up by the sill and peered in. The bedroom was empty, but he could see bunk beds and girl's clothing. Posters with teen pop stars adorned the walls.

Mounting the wooden steps to the back door, he drew his pistol and tried the knob. Locked. The old door had a piece of plywood tacked over a pane of broken glass. Prying it loose, he reached inside, unlatched the door, and stepped into the back hallway.

The sound of people crying came from the front of the apart-ment. One woman was pleading, but a male voice cut her off. No one was in the kitchen, and he continued down the dark hallway toward the front room.

"I'm only saying this one more fucking time," the man threat-ened. "Where is she?"

"Please," she begged. "Just let the girls go. Please, they're just bab—"

The sound of the blow that silenced her drew terrified shrieks from the girls.

Gavin peered into the front room. A burly gangbanger was facing the woman, his back to Gavin. The two girls were huddled together at his feet. The woman who'd been struck was slumped in the center of the room, holding her bloodied face, another woman kneeling beside her.

A second thug was standing over them, holding a collapsible police baton in his left hand.

"Hand me that neena," he said, holding out a hand to his partner. "I'm tired of looking at these old bitches."

The front door swung open and another thug burst in.

"We just got a call, man. Heat coming. Grab them kids. Let's go!"

Looking past the girls, he spotted Gavin.

Gavin had no choice. There was no backing away.

Especially when the hood reached behind him and came up shooting.

Gavin fired back. He didn't miss.

As the man went down, Gavin aimed at the other two. The burly gangster spun around to fire, but ended up sinking to the ground as Gavin nailed him in the shoulder. The other guy ran for the door.

Gavin moved to the window. Outside, the multicolored flashers of a cruiser lit up the block. The BMW took off, only to screech to a stop at the end of the street as a second cruiser cut it off.

Gavin kicked the guns away from the men who were down and glanced at the two women who were now huddled with the kids by the sofa.

A patrolman came up the front steps, gun drawn.

"Jonesy, it's me. MacFadyen."

"Came as quick as we could. Jeez, Mac, what a mess."

Gavin stood by the door over the first man he'd shot, the blood pooling under the body.

"Ambulance?"

"On the way."

"Do you know him?" Gavin asked.

"Never seen him before."

Gavin crouched down to take the man's wallet out of his jeans pocket and flipped it open.

There, inside, was Terri's badge.

CHAPTER FIVE

HER LAST APPOINTMENT of the day. Lacey smiled, nodded, took notes, said what needed to be said, that photo—and the sick caption—blazing in her mind.

She finally escorted the clients outside to their car and stood alone in the dark, watching the taillights disappear down the road. It was only then that she allowed the sick feeling clenching her stomach to gain the upper hand.

"No. It can't be."

Her footing turned to quicksand. Hours of restraint gave way to complete collapse. Lacey crouched down, hugging her knees to her chest. Bile rose into her throat and she thought she was going to be sick. She closed her eyes, taking quick breaths. Her stomach churned, protested, but nothing, thank God, came up.

The photo. The country road. She hadn't gone to the site of the accident. Had refused to even drive by it, but from the police description she knew that picture was the place where Terri's body had been discovered.

Some sick bastard had staged the reenactment to get at her. Tears ran down her cheeks, soaking into the dirt. Chills coursed through her limbs, sharpening the constant pain in her hip. She

shivered violently, sitting there, exposed for an eon, as the coldness of the night seeped into her bones.

Finally, Lacey stood, took two deep breaths and brushed away
the tears. She had to figure out where that picture came from,
who had taken it. And how it had been inserted into the wedding
album.

Pulling herself up the porch steps, she was glad that Amy was
long gone.

The month after Lacey returned to Connecticut, Terri had
rented Amy the apartment in the renovated barn at the far end of
the property. They were neighbors and had become friends. Still,
Lacey wasn't ready to talk to Amy about this. Not when she still
had to wrap her own head around the reason someone would do
it. Not when she still had to figure out a way to keep the raw pain
of her sister's death from clawing her to shreds.

She paused inside the door, then locked it before going to her
office.

She'd uploaded the file for Jeannie's wedding book directly
from her computer onto the publisher's website. Opening the
directory now, she checked the folder and went through the
thumbnails of wedding photos.

The image was there, just as it showed up in the album—
which meant that the breach had been on her home computer.

Someone had been inside her home.

No. That was impossible. No one had touched her system. No
one could have accessed her files. The only one working here was
Amy, and she had her own special laptop. She couldn't possibly
have done it.

She opened the file on the publisher's website. Paging to the
photo, she stared at the caption. *Road Kill.*

Lacey sat back in her chair, fighting the grief ready to crash
through her thin barrier of control.

The flashing lights on the modem caught her eye and it got
her thinking. Was there a way to trace the intruder? She had a
wireless network that could reach Amy's place, and firewalls and

virus protection that came with the initial installation. She knew enough about the entire set-up to do her job, but nothing more.

She went back to the files in search of the date that was associated with the photo. That was when she noticed the folder of the same name under her picture directory. *Road Kill.*

Lacey's hand shook as she opened a slideshow of the contents. More images.

The first photo was of the same country road. Fog, but no visible body. The second photograph was a duplicate of the one inserted into the wedding album. And the next one... tied Lacey's insides into a knot.

The photo was a close-up of the body. The spandex running shorts, the white T-shirt with the blue and white logo, the dark curly hair tied back in a ponytail. Terri had spent the night before with Lacey in Westbury. She'd borrowed Lacey's clothes that morning for her jog.

The last photo was a close-up of Terri's face. Her head was partially buried in leaves. Blood and dirt smeared her face. Her green eyes were open. But she was dead.

This was no reenactment.

Lacey shoved the chair away from the desk, her stomach protesting the images her mind was trying to process. She couldn't think. Couldn't not think. And she couldn't breathe.

The autopsy report said that Terri had died of head trauma. Brain hemorrhage on impact. The local police told her that Terri's body had remained there for eight hours before being discovered.

She couldn't stop her tears. Invisible needles pierced every inch of her skin, digging deep into her, threatening to deaden what was left of her heart.

Terri had always been with her, embracing her. At the height of her misery, a thousand miles away, Lacey had felt her sister's arms around her. And now she could hear, echoing in her head, the words Terri had said to her every time she'd been knocked down in life. We're survivors, Lacey. The two of us are survivors.

Lacey batted away tears and turned from her desk. Through

blurred vision, she could see the basket still filled with sympathy notes on a side table. Going to them, she picked up the business card she'd left on top.

Gavin MacFadyen. Private Investigator.

His was one of the few names that Terri frequently mentioned over the years. A friend. Someone to trust.

She stared at the card. Nothing fancy. Just the essential information. She recalled the sincere dark eyes that made her believe he cared. But she also couldn't forget the stir of excitement and apprehension she'd felt for the few moments when she stood with him outside the funeral parlor. When he held her hand, she'd felt it. He was all raw muscularity and power. Authority and dominance.

The kind of man that made her to want to run.

A loud bang against the porch railing in front of the house set Lacey's heart racing. She dropped the card in the basket, grabbed the phone, and moved to the front window. The light from the house stretched far enough into the yard that she spotted the upended trashcan. Thursday mornings were pick-up, but rolling the barrel out to the curb was the last thing she'd been thinking about tonight.

Stuffing her cell phone into her jeans pocket, she grabbed the cane. Her once-shattered bones always picked the wrong moments to act up. She stepped out into the night. A fine, cold mist had started to fall.

Pieces of trash littered the ground. Hitting the cane against the railing a few times, she made enough noise to scare off any hungry critters. Seeing nothing, she righted the trashcan.

Hauling the barrel to the curb, she took deep breaths. The distinct smell of wet autumn leaves was still a new scent to her. This was her first fall living in New England.

The years in jail didn't count.

The leaves were slick under her shoes, the night mist cold on her face, leaves and twigs crackling into the soft earth.

Until she heard a sound.

"Who's there?" Clutching the cane tightly in one hand, she turned in the direction of the noise. A deep buffer of trees separated her property from the neighbor's yard.

"Amy?" she called out. "Is that you?"

Lacey's scalp prickled as a damp breeze came up. Someone was out there. Standing. Waiting. Silent.

She swept the cane around her and the hollow sound of it striking the trash barrel echoed through the night. Looking around her with apprehension, she snapped the lid onto the can tightly and left it at the curb.

Lacey hurried toward the house, leaning heavily on the cane. Damn it. She was more dependent on it now than she had been seventeen years ago, when she'd thought shattered bones and torn-apart heart were the worst things that could happen to her.

Now she knew better...

A shadow materialized from behind a tree. Cold eyes watched Lacey move up onto the porch, and stared at the door and lit windows long after she had disappeared inside.

CHAPTER SIX

"ALISHA MILLER. THIRTEEN YEARS OLD." His face grim, John Trevor read from the pages of the report in his hand. "The night Watkins picked her up and took her to the hospital, she had alcohol, marijuana, and crack cocaine in her system."

Gavin's former boss looked across the desk at him.

"She tested positive for STDs and told the nurse she'd been forced to have sex with five men that night." Trevor dropped the folder onto his blotter.

Gavin had come to the Union Avenue police station to fill out paperwork for the shooting in Newhallville last night. He was no longer with the NHPD so the assistant chief's sharing of this information was way outside standard department procedure.

"The girl was put in a group home after being released from the hospital," Trevor continued. "Couldn't stick there. Disappeared a week later."

"Why go to a group home?" he asked. "Why not to her mother?"

"Unsafe home. That was Watkins's recommendation too." Trevor paused, reading. "Let's see. DCF has been trying to yank the twins. The paperwork has been in the works for a while."

"And now Alisha's back on the streets."

Trevor looked at him sharply. "You didn't walk out that door too long ago, MacFadyen. You know there's only so much we can do for these kids. We pass them along to Social Services when we can, but it takes a miracle to get them out of this cycle before they end up disappearing into the weeds. We lost our street liaison in that last budget go-around."

Every city department was fighting for their scrap of shrinking funds. New Haven was no different. Crime rates climbed while funds for cops and social programs got slashed. It was pitiful, but it was a fact of life.

Gavin glanced out the window at the bright fall morning. Glistening leaves were swirling in the breeze. His sister Elsie had been fifteen when she ran away. And then no news, no trace of her, until her decomposing body was found in a ditch in Jacksonville, Florida. That'd been five months and ten days after she'd gone missing. The coroner's report said that she'd been dead for most of that time. The bastard who'd killed her was never found.

He looked back at Trevor. "What was Terri's involvement with Alisha anyway?"

"The girl is a part of a homicide case Watkins was working. Alisha's pimp was killed in a shootout. Naturally, they were part of the Bratva organization. Watkins was working on the girl, trying to gain her trust, but Alisha was scared shitless. She actually called the pimp her boyfriend. She was upset that he was dead."

Gavin knew Alisha was afraid from the thirty-second phone call. She had good reason to be.

Bratva's signature work, headless corpses washing up along the coast, had been established years ago when he'd been consolidating turf along the shoreline, muscling out the smaller players and taking larger pieces of former Mafia territory. The word was that executions were carried out by Bratva himself, but the murders could never be pinned on him. He was smart and ruthless.

Today, Bratva controlled virtually all of the drug trafficking, sex trade, and private gambling from Stamford to Newport, including the north coast of Long Island. Every gang and small-time operator in New Haven—from the Black Elm Street Gang and the Jungle Boys to the Latin Kings and the Mara Salvatrucha —either worked for Bratva or paid him tribute.

An FBI task force hadn't made any headway into his organization which could be because the guy was totally connected. And protected. By politicians, judges, and more than a few cops on his payroll.

"Watkins had been able to pin down Alisha enough to find out that it was Bratva's people that were gunning for the pimp."

"A little dissension in the ranks?"

"Your partner thought that the mope was trying to squeeze a little extra out of Bratva's till. Never a good idea with that guy. He had something damaging to the organization...maybe even to Bratva himself."

"And those gangbangers I ran into worked for the organization?"

"Yup."

The two thugs Gavin shot were at Yale-New Haven Hospital. The one carrying Terri's badge was in critical but guarded condition. The other one was listed as fair. And a lawyer was probably already camped out at the courthouse with a wad of cash, ready to post bail for the rest of the pricks.

"I don't suppose the two that can talk are saying anything about how they came to be in possession of Terri's badge?"

"I can't give you specifics, but I can tell you that Watkins was sticking her nose deep into Bratva's shit following up on the pimp's murder."

"So it could be Bratva that hit her."

"It's a possibility, but we don't have anything that supports that. I personally went a couple of rounds with those guys out at the Newhallville station. They were giving up nothing." Trevor leaned forward. "We're not letting it go, Mac. We'll find out where every one of these bastards was the day Watkins was killed."

"And their cars. There might be paint and glass evidence. What about the forensic report on Terri's clothes?" Gavin realized what he was doing and stopped. It was easy to start thinking like he was part of the team.

"Look, MacFadyen, we'll do whatever needs to be done. We haven't forgotten that Watkins was one of our own. But just so you know, we can't even assume that her badge was lifted from the scene of the hit-and-run. We don't even know if she had it on her when she went jogging that morning."

"Where was her weapon?"

"In her locker, here at the station. Why?"

"When she was off duty, Terri kept her badge with her pistol. She only carried an identification card tucked under her driver's license."

"Not this time. I'm the one who went through her locker after we heard the news. There was no badge there. She left it somewhere else."

If Gavin was going to point fingers, it was not going to be at the assistant chief. His instinct and his years of working with the man told him the guy was honest to the core.

Trevor leaned back in his chair. "The day after the accident, Lacey Watkins turned over whatever department-issued stuff she could find. She didn't have the badge either. She said she'd look for it once she got a chance to sort through the rest of her sister's stuff." Trevor closed the file on his desk. "I'll keep you posted on developments, but it all has to be off the record. Meanwhile, if Alisha calls you back, give her my direct number. I'll get her some help."

That was Gavin's cue to get out and he stood.

"Listen, Mac," Trevor said. "I know it's hard, her being your partner. But we're working it at this end. We really are."

On the way out, Gavin went down to the Investigative Services section to get his darts from Jake Allen. Weaving through the maze of cubicles, Gavin immediately realized he was the morning's entertainment. The novelty of him leaving the force and starting his own business had not worn off for these guys.

"Hey, Gavin. Are you hiring?"

"What the hell, Mac! You didn't get to shoot up the town enough when you were on duty?"

"These fucking retirees, always making more paperwork for us."

"Hey, MacFadyen. Is it true you're 'shooting' to be the next chief?"

There were a dozen other remarks. Gavin shook hands with the two section new-hires who were smiling at the ribbing he was getting.

"Christ, Mac. I thought we got rid of you," a sergeant called after him.

Jake Allen was on the phone and Gavin nodded to Luke Brandt, who swung around in his chair and nodded back. The two detectives shared back-to-back desks in a cluttered cubicle. Gavin spotted his leather dart case on Jake's desk.

"I see you've got a couple of new faces in the division."

"Yeah. I'm thinking those two rookies are glad you came in and took the heat off 'em," Luke said. "They've been getting hammered all week."

"Glad to oblige."

"What the hell?" Jake said in greeting as he hung up the phone. "You leave the tournament of the year to go messing with lowlife scum that are none of your business?"

Gavin shrugged.

"Can we count on you next week or are you going to take off on us again when the game gets hot?" Jake groused.

"Hit me up as we get closer and I'll check my schedule."

Gavin grabbed the dart case from Jake's desk, sucking in a breath when he saw the name on the file at the bottom. *Lacey Watkins.* What was that doing here? Her case had been handled in Litchfield County, not here.

"What's this here for?" he asked, looking from Luke to Jake and pointing to the folder. He yanked the file from the stack.

Jake glanced at the name, then grabbed it from him and tucked it under his arm. "I believe that would fall under the category of official business."

Luke just shrugged his shoulders.

"Okay." Gavin remembered how vulnerable she looked at the funeral. She didn't need more trouble. "Just thought you two losers might still need someone to keep you out of the doghouse, but whatever."

Shaking his head, Gavin tucked the dart case under his arm and headed for the door.

CHAPTER SEVEN

"I THINK we have everything we need for now." The young police officer tucked his clipboard under one arm.

Lacey stepped back as a second cop walked out. He was carrying a police department laptop with the files from her computer loaded on it.

"What does *for now* mean? Where do we go from here?" she asked.

"We'll do some checking and try to confirm that it's your sister in those photos," he said.

Lacey had told him a hundred times that it was Terri, but they weren't going to take her word for it before the State Police had their say. They still believed it could be a prank.

"If we have to take your computer, we'll come back for it," he added.

She rubbed her arms to try to ward off a chill that wasn't going away. "I want to know how that file got mixed in with my work and who took those pictures."

They'd gone over in minute detail at least three times where she'd been and who might have had access to her cameras and computer in the past week.

"It might be just what I said before," he said. "The Internet is like the wild west. It's the fastest growing area of criminal activity. Someone could have planted this through a virus or something. You never know."

She bit back her frustration. "Have others gotten this? Have you had any other calls or heard of anyone else complaining of the same thing?"

The cop shook his head. "Not yet. But that doesn't mean anything. The State Police have a Computer Crime Unit. If it's out there, they'll have heard about it."

Lacey wasn't feeling any better. She was already questioning her decision to call the locals. She should have contacted an expert. She thought of Gavin MacFadyen again.

"In the meantime, I'd be a little more careful about who you let use your computer."

Lacey looked up to see Amy standing in the doorway. She had on her coat and dark glasses. She was holding her white walking stick. Lacey had called her first thing this morning to give her a heads-up about what was going on. She didn't want her to be startled at the police activity at the house.

Although blind, Amy worked as a receptionist at a local health club, did a shift at the adult daycare facility, and put in a few hours a week running Lacey's home office. Amy was both independent and efficient.

"I'm walking down to the convenience store for some milk. Do you need anything?"

"I could use some fresh air too. How about if you wait a minute, and we can go together?" Lacey turned to the police officer as Amy left. "I work with professionals. I'm the only klutz around here when it comes to this kind of stuff."

"Since we don't know much about anything so far, we'll keep the lid on this for now. You don't need people reading about it in the *Westbury Times*," the cop said before heading toward the door. "Might not help with business."

She met Amy at the bottom of the steps. "Hey, did you fall?" Inside, she'd noticed dirt stains on Amy's knees and the sleeves of her jacket.

"I tripped over something on the way over. Something gross and definitely dead." Amy wiped the palm of one hand on her coat.

"Where? Show me." Rumors had been circulating of a pack of coyotes hunting in the area at night.

She followed Amy not fifty yards from Lacey's porch. The dead animal was beyond identifying. Gray fur and blackened entrails. It wasn't the whole animal, and it also wasn't freshly killed. It looked like something from the side of the highway. Nasty.

"What is it?"

"I don't know." Lacey shuddered. This was the second dead animal she'd found near the house in recent weeks. "Whatever it is, I'll throw it in the barrel when we get back."

A brisk breeze was churning up the leaves, sending them flying in every direction. Giving the carcass a wide berth, Lacey led Amy to a path through the woods behind the property. In a few minutes, they crossed through an old cemetery, a shortcut to downtown.

"So, what did the cops say?" Amy asked.

"Nothing. They had no answers. They took a copy of the file. Otherwise, they were totally useless," Lacey summarized. "But they were nice enough not to take my computer."

"I overheard him blaming me," Amy said when they had reached the paved lane of the graveyard.

"No, he wasn't. He was making a general statement."

"My laptop is networked with your system. Could I have somehow screwed up?"

"No. You couldn't. Regardless of what the cops say," she continued, "this is a lot more complicated than someone mistakenly downloading a file. It's ridiculous to think that an image can randomly insert itself into a customer file I was working on last week. Those are pictures of Terri. The caption was meant to hurt *me*. This is personal. Whoever it is, he's trying to get to *me*."

The air suddenly felt colder. The breeze was bending the gnarled branches of ancient trees. Only a few orange leaves clung tenaciously above them as they neared the edge of the cemetery. Lacey buttoned her jacket as a chill swept down her spine.

She couldn't shake the image of Terri's face, gray and lifeless, from her mind. Prior to seeing that photograph, she remembered her sister from the morning of the accident when she'd been leaving the house. Lively. As happy as she was capable of being. Bragging about the coffee she'd brewed being superior to the pot of mud Lacey usually made.

"I can feel you shivering." Amy's fingers touched Lacey's. "Are you cold? Do you want to go back?"

Lacey stuffed her frozen fingers into her pocket as they stood in the shadow of an evergreen hedge at a turn in the lane. The breeze had died and the place had become very still.

It had been Terri's wish to be cremated. They'd discussed the morbid topic twice on their long telephone conversations across the country when their grandfather was dying. Lacey always thought she'd be the first one to go, but Terri's ashes were now in the heavy ceramic urn on a dresser in the upstairs hallway that she touched every morning on her way down.

Suddenly, the hair on the back of her neck jumped to attention. She was being watched. Again.

Lacey looked around. Fifty feet away beyond the rows of gravestones, she saw him.

He always watched her from a distance. Never approached. Never said a word. She could never make out anything recognizable in his face, except that it was lined with age. She had no idea who he was. She saw him mostly in the cemetery. Perhaps he had a loved one buried here. He always seemed to wear the same gray raincoat and a battered fishing hat. This time, he stood under a tree and just stared.

An old feeling of defenselessness rushed back. Perhaps he recognized her. Maybe he knew of her past. She wondered if he'd been outside her house last night.

The truth stared her in the face. She was no longer able to ignore it. Lacey pretended that living in a different town in Connecticut, having a job, and minding her own business would be enough to make her invisible. But many in the area still remembered the horrific crime and there were a few who believed she'd gotten off too easy. It had only been a matter of time before connections were made and everyone would realize that Lacey Watkins was the teenager who'd been present when Stephanie Green had been raped and murdered.

And she had a sick feeling that Terri's hit-and-run was connected to the lakeside tragedy sixteen years ago. There were no accidents. Someone was punishing Lacey.

The knot in her throat was large enough to choke on.

"Lacey? Are you okay?"

She took a couple of quick breaths and forced herself to focus. She hadn't told Amy about her past. And Amy had never asked.

"I'm okay. I'm sorry. Let's go." She took Amy's arm, relieved that the man had left.

They walked for a while in silence while Lacey struggled to put one foot in front of the other. The pavement, lined on either side with graves, was a bleak reminder that she was the last one left alive in her family. Terri had been taken before her time. Now it was up to her. She had to be strong.

And find the bastard who had done this.

As they reached the cemetery's main entrance, a white sports car slowed to a stop. The passenger window rolled down, and even at a distance the smell of expensive perfume reached them.

"Hi, you two. It's too cold to be out there," the driver, Donna Covington, leaned across the seat.

Donna lived up the street and was the district manager of a chain of health clubs, including the one where Amy worked part-time. Smart, fit, platinum blond, she was one of those women who always turned heads. Lacey had decided early on to like her because Donna was even nice to misfits like the two of them.

"Donna, are you okay?" Amy asked, reaching out with her

stick and gauging the distance to the car. "We've been worried about you this last week."

"No, I'm fine. Just a nasty flu. Lots of fluids and bed rest. I'm back to normal."

Lacey vaguely recalled Amy mentioning that Donna had been absent from the health club.

"Where are you headed? Do you want a ride?"

"Just getting some fresh air," Amy answered. "Thanks, but we're fine."

"I saw the police cruisers in your driveway this morning, Lacey. Everything okay?"

"Someone hacked into my computer. Very upsetting," Lacey caught herself and stopped. An awkward moment of silence followed as she refused to offer any more information. Thankfully, her cell phone rang, ending that conversation.

"Watkins' Photography," Lacey answered.

"Lacey Watkins, please."

The man's voice was deep and had a familiar edge to it. And it took her a split second, but she remembered him.

"This is she."

"Hi, Lacey. This is Gavin. Gavin MacFadyen. We met at—"

"I remember." She took a few steps away from Donna's car, a small, tight knot forming in her stomach.

Nervousness. That's all this was. Just nerves at the level of authority in Gavin's voice that made her uncomfortable. He was a cop. An ex-cop. Cops and ex-cops weren't high on her list of must-have friends.

But there was something more going on—the sudden pounding of her heart, a warming in her cheeks. The mix of emotions was confusing. All last night and this morning, she'd been wanting to contact Gavin and here he was calling her.

"I've been meaning to call you." Gavin's voice lost its intimidation factor when she thought about how he'd looked at the funeral. "I wanted to see how you were making out and ask if you needed anything."

Her silence was painful, but she couldn't manage a single word. It was as if her brain and her mouth were both tongue-tied.

It'd been a long time since any man had affected her like this.

"So how *are* you doing?" he asked.

"Fine," she managed to get out, aware that Donna and Amy had stopped talking and were looking at her. So Lacey put more distance between them. "Actually, I...I was going to call you. Something *has* come up that I was hoping to get your opinion on."

"Do you want to get together?"

"That would be best."

"I have to be in Litchfield this afternoon to meet with a potential client. How about after that?"

"Yes, that would be great. Can you come to the house?"

There was a pause. "Sure. Does around seven work for you?"

She hadn't looked at the appointments Amy had booked for today. But it didn't matter. She had to see him. "Yes, that's perfect."

She should ask him if he wanted to stay for dinner. But that was too personal. She was tongue-tied over the phone; she could be in worse shape in person. But the nervousness was stupid. She had to think of him as Terri's partner and nothing more.

CHAPTER EIGHT

THE GRAVEL PARKING lot was situated beyond a long walkway, separated from the street by a small river. As Fay Stone crossed the narrow pedestrian bridge, she glanced into the black water. A streetlight cast a broken reflection on the surface. It was getting dark so much earlier these days. At the end of the bridge, two dumpsters overflowed with torn trash bags, broken glass and beer and soda cans littering the ground around them.

Fay had parked her old Dodge Intrepid under the only light post in the deserted lot. Unfortunately, the car was still there.

"What do I have to do for someone to steal this piece of crap?"

The mechanic's quote to do the brakes, get four new tires, and replace the water pump and timing belt was twenty-five hundred dollars.

"Have I mentioned today, car, how much I hate you?"

Fay yanked the handle and pulled open the door with a mighty, upward heave.

"A fifty-dollar bill," she said, throwing her purse and briefcase across the center console before lowering herself into the driver's seat. "I'm taking you to Bridgeport and leaving a fifty-dollar bill and the keys on the dashboard. That should make it worthwhile for some junkie."

But first she had to clean out the car. She definitely kept too much crap in here. Jamming the key into the ignition, she reached for the seatbelt.

It was only then that she sensed that someone else was in the car.

Before she could turn, the cord snapped taut around her neck, jerking her back against the headrest. Fay grabbed at her throat in a desperate effort to get her fingers under the cord.

She couldn't breathe. A sharp pressure was building in her head, and she twisted in the seat, catching a glimpse of her attacker. Recognition registered, but it didn't matter.

The killer yanked once more, Fay's bowels released, and it was over.

CHAPTER NINE

LACEY'S TONE this morning had made it clear that this wasn't a social call. Still, Gavin picked up a bouquet of flowers when his appointment in Litchfield ended early. He was glad he'd called her. He was even happier to know she'd wanted to see him. Her appeal hadn't diminished at all since that first meeting.

Plenty of women had walked in and out of Gavin's life over the years. His love life was no mystery. He was no romantic, but he knew how to woo them. He had needs like any other healthy male and he was good in bed. The Connecticut shoreline had its share of satisfied women who would attest to that.

But Lacey, for him, represented that forbidden fruit. The one that he'd heard so much about for ten years but was beyond his reach. She was no saint and she was wounded. And from all the conversations he'd had with Terri, he knew something special lay beneath Lacey's scars. He'd even come to know what made her tick. And what could hurt her. Still, he'd always thought there would never be an opportunity for him to know her personally.

But now he could.

Turning on to her street, he glanced at the time. Early. Five or ten minutes might be forgivable, but he was half an hour early. Westbury was one of those suburban towns that rolled up the sidewalks at sunset. There wasn't anywhere else he could go hang out while he waited.

He drove slowly past the house. It was set back from the road behind a grove of trees, but all the lights were on. Her silver Honda was there by the house.

He backed up the deserted street and started down the long gravel driveway.

Large paper bags stuffed with leaves were piled up against a garage. His headlights flashed on a painted sign displaying the name of her business with an arrow pointing to the front door. The railing on the porch appeared to have a fresh coat of paint. By the door, an oversized pumpkin and a bunch of gourds decorated a bale of hay. The house looked lived in, cared for. He was glad she'd decided to stick around at least for now. She'd always run before. She probably would again.

Gavin pulled around by her car and parked. Calling her number, he checked out the house. He'd been here many times and he knew the layout. The last time he'd been here, he'd helped Terri move furniture around after her grandfather died.

The house was set at a protected angle from the road, but from the driveway he had a clear view into the windows. None of the curtains were closed and he wondered if she was in the kitchen at the back of the house. The few pieces of furniture he could see were the same as before, but the walls had been painted. Large prints of photos had been newly hung as well.

The phone rang a few times and went to her voicemail. He didn't leave a message and hung up as his gaze was drawn to the second floor window. Lacey walked into a bedroom, obviously from the bathroom. In one hand she was holding a small towel against her body as she threaded the fingers of the other hand through her wet hair. Generous stretches of naked skin were visible. He eyed the smooth curves of her bottom. She picked up the cell phone off a shelf and, using the same towel, started drying her hair.

The phone slipped through Gavin's fingers as he admired

Lacey's body, the silhouetted movement of her breasts and the swing of her hair. She must smell like soap and perfume, and he could only imagine what her skin would taste like. God, he wanted to find out first-hand—

His phone vibrated in his lap—and it wasn't the only thing.

He tested his voice first before answering. "Hello?"

"Hi. Did you just call me?"

She leaned down, displaying her perfectly heart-shaped ass. He was disappointed when she straightened up and pulled on black underwear.

"Gavin?"

"Yes. I'm here. I called because I'm running early."

Her one-handed struggle with the bra was the best part of the evening. So far.

"You don't have to wait until seven. Drive over now. Where are you?"

He grimaced, looking up and trying to take his fill. "In your driveway."

The shade on the window came down with a snap. "Oh. Well, give me a couple of minutes to put myself together."

The phone clicked off.

"Please don't," he murmured. "Not on my account."

"Oh, my God!" Hyperventilating, Lacey stared at the closed shade. *Now he thinks I'm an exhibitionist too.*

What was she thinking? She wanted to start off making a good impression. Keep their interaction at a professional level. Getting naked was not what she had in mind.

As good as it sounded, crawling under the bed and pretending that he wasn't in her driveway probably wouldn't help either.

Lacey hurriedly pulled on her jeans and grabbed a green oxford shirt from the basket of clean clothes on the bed. Stupid of her to think she had plenty of time to take a shower and look decent after her last customer left. Peeking at her reflection in the mirror, she flinched at the beet red blush on her face.

"Crap. Crap. Crap." No amount of makeup could hide this.

The car door opened and closed. Her hair was wet, but she had to go down before losing what was left of her courage. Making him wait would only make things worse. She rolled an elastic band onto her wrist and went out into the hallway.

Going down stairs was still a challenge. Her nightmares of falling never went away...and with good reason. The operations seventeen years ago had left her right leg was almost an inch shorter than the left; that's what the doctors told her. Lacey thought the difference was growing.

"Be calm," she whispered, taking some slow breaths as she reached the bottom step. The front door lay ahead of her. Through the beveled glass panels, she saw he was already on her front porch.

Lacey stole another look at her reflection in the mirror near the door and pulled the wet strands of her hair into a ponytail. Wild green eyes, no makeup, flushed face... This was absolutely *not* the way she'd intended to look for this meeting.

Gavin was watching her through the panels and gave her a casual wave.

Heart racing, she unlocked the door, yanking it open. "Hi, I'm sorry."

"Don't be. I'm sorry for being so early."

Lacey couldn't look him in the face. She didn't know how long he'd been in her driveway or how much he'd seen. She stared at the flowers he held out to her. "Who are these for?"

"You."

"You didn't have to."

"This is nothing, considering the show."

Her eyes snapped up to his. "What show?"

"I was in Litchfield, discussing floral arrangements for an upcoming show."

Gavin MacFadyen had glittering black eyes and dark hair that was going salt-and-pepper at the sideburns. His face was angular and well-proportioned with a strong chin. He was squarely built and tall, a couple of inches over six feet. Damn, he was even more handsome than she remembered.

"I'd like to hear more about it," she said finally.

"Sorry, can't. Client privacy. I can't discuss any details."

She stared into his serious expression. He was being a devil.

At Terri's funeral, she'd been upset. The crowd attending had been a wall of dark suits and uniforms. She'd been impatient to get out of there when he'd stopped her in the parking lot, looking just like the rest of them. Well, sort of. The suit had been the same, but the look in his eyes...

And right now, in his leather jacket and jeans, he looked comfortable. Handsome. He had the air of someone stopping to see a friend.

"The flowers. I handpicked them just for you. At the grocery store."

Lacey was happy to take the bouquet and bury her face in it. The smell of lilies always tickled her nose—and it was a great excuse to cover her blush.

Of course, she only blushed more when his gaze ran over her face and down her body to her bare toes. She knew what he was doing. He wasn't looking for similarities to Terri as most people did. He was telling her he'd seen her naked. Lacey's body tingled in the most private places.

"Am I allowed in the house?"

"Oh, yes." She opened the door wide and stepped back. "Come in."

He paused by a pegboard in the hall and hung his jacket next to hers. His shirt stretched across the taut muscles of his broad back. His hair was longer now than it'd been the first time they'd met. Lacey caught a hint of spicy cologne and barely stopped herself from leaning in to take a deeper whiff.

"Place looks good." Taking a couple of steps, he perused her office and the parlor beyond the doorway. He turned around and did the same thing to the living room to their left. "Looks like you're settled in."

"Pretty much."

Facing her, he smiled. "You're wearing flower pollen on your nose."

She started to wipe it away, but he got there first. His callused thumb brushed her cheek then the tip of her nose. Lacey's heart beat so fast she was worried it might pop out of her chest. She was a coward and couldn't look into his eyes for fear of what she might see. What *he* might see...

"I should put these in water." She slipped around him, heading to the kitchen at the end of the hall. "Can I get you something to drink?"

"Sure. What are you having?"

He was right behind her. "I started a pot of coffee before getting in the shower."

She opened and closed cabinets, looking for a vase, trying to buy herself time to pull her scattered wits together. Men didn't usually have this kind of effect on her. Then again, she'd never dealt with someone like Gavin MacFadyen.

"Coffee would be great, thanks."

The flowers were beautiful, and she found the perfect vase for them.

"How do you take it?" she asked, taking two mugs out of the cabinet and pouring the coffee.

"Black."

He stood in the doorway, watching her with an amused expression on his face.

"What have I done now?" She wiped her nose, her face. "Have I got petals in my hair?"

"No. Not anymore anyway." He sat down at the kitchen table.

He was more manageable seated, thank God. She needed the break.

Then she put his mug in front of him and her nerves got shot to hell all over again.

"How's the business going?" he asked as if her insides weren't churning.

"It's good," Lacey replied, leaning against the counter, going for nonchalance. She prayed it worked. "Having a client base to start with is helping. I'm busy enough right now to pay the bills."

Gavin sipped the coffee, and it was impossible to miss the grimace on his face.

This time her blush had nothing to do with him seeing her naked. "Sorry. Terri always claimed my coffee was too strong."

"Undrinkable," he corrected.

"Excuse me?"

"She said your coffee could fuel a rocket to Mars."

"She was a wuss and so are you. You don't have to drink it."

"No, this is good. I have a lot of work to do tonight." He eyed the cup with new appreciation. "This should keep me up all night."

She opened the fridge and took out the milk, adding a dab to her cup. He extended his mug for some too. She took the sugar bowl out of the cabinet and put it on the kitchen table and pretended not to look as he reached over to add a heaping spoon to his.

There was history between Terri and him. Her sister had liked him. Trusted him. Lacey wondered just how much of their family's past he knew.

"You mentioned on the phone that you've been here before." She slid the flowers to the center of the kitchen table. The more obstacles between them, the more at ease she felt.

Gavin immediately moved his chair until he had a clear view of her.

"A few times over the years. Mostly when your grandfather, Walt, was still alive. He liked to have Terri invite her cop friends over to watch a baseball game and shoot the shit. We'd barbecue in the backyard. I'm also kind of handy with tools so I was a favorite whenever there were projects that needed to be done."

Lacey never really got to know Walter O'Connor very well.

But he was the only one who'd stepped up for her and Terri during the tough times. He'd never turned his back on them.

"You and your sister were pretty young when you moved in with him, weren't you?"

She nodded. "Terri came to live with him first. She was a senior in high school. I came a few years later."

Lacey took a deep swallow of the bitter coffee. She'd lived with her grandfather for only four months before she'd screwed up all their lives. Still, he'd put money in her jail account and sent her a letter once a week. No earth-shattering prose and very little news; just a few words to remind her that there were people beyond the razor wire who loved and cared about her.

"He had a soft spot in his heart for you." The dark eyes were studying her face too intently for comfort.

"I was a lot of trouble for him. I always wondered if he'd wished he'd never asked me to come east."

"That was never an option for him, considering what you walked away from. And he never blamed you for any of it. You were only fifteen."

Gavin knew too much. Lacey went to the sink, dumped out her coffee, rinsed out the mug, and refilled it. It was so much easier when people didn't know. She'd mastered living in a void. Move often. Never let people get close to you. Have no past. Don't plan for a future. That way, there was no sympathy, no doubts, no regrets. It was simply better not to *feel*.

They drank their coffee in silence for a moment. He let her get a grip on her emotions, saying nothing until she turned around.

"How are you doing, settling Terri's things?" he asked. "I ran into one of her neighbors last week who said no one has been to the apartment."

"I've been ignoring it. Hiding away, I guess." She shrugged. "I know I have to get out from under this rock and deal with all of it. Her life. The apartment. Her car is in the garage behind the house here. There's a mountain of paperwork." She took a deep breath; she'd been rambling. "I'm sure there are other things I've ignored. I keep expecting that she's going to come back and take care of everything."

Gavin nodded. "She liked to be in charge."

"It wasn't time for her to go so she had no plan for what needed to be done. You know, the way she always did."

"I worked with her. She was my partner. I know."

Lacey watched him nurse his coffee. Trust and friendship didn't come easy for either her or Terri. Their upbringing had made sure of that. Still, Terri called this man a friend. That was a feat on so many levels.

"Has anyone from New Haven PD contacted you?"

Lacey focused on the present and why she'd wanted to contact him. "I met one of Terri's bosses right after the accident to hand over some files she'd brought here the weekend she died. But do you mean since this morning?"

"Something happened this morning?"

"The Westbury police were here. Collecting information." She left her coffee on the counter and started for the door. "There's a new file on my computer. It has to do with Terri. That's why I wanted to see you."

He pushed the chair back and followed her.

"Someone hacked into my system and put it there," Lacey pulled a second chair up to the desk when they got to her office.

His legs were too long. His thigh was pressed against hers when he sat down, and she tried to pull back. There was nowhere she could go.

"Do you have a secure system?"

Lacey explained what she had, told him about the radius of her network, and Amy. Then she opened her directory and found the folder before pushing the keyboard and mouse in front of him. There wasn't enough air with him so close.

She stood up. Trapped against the wall by his chair and desk, Lacey motioned to the file. She feared she'd fall apart if she looked again at that photo of Terri's face.

"That's it. That folder, *Road Kill*. It's not mine. It has pictures of Terri. The day she was killed. But the cops who came over this morning didn't seem to believe me."

Her voice shook. Gavin's eyes were glued to the screen. A couple of clicks and he had the file and the pictures open.

Lacey didn't want to see them again, but her gaze involuntarily drifted to them, her throat burning.

His attention was riveted to the images, studying every detail. He enlarged them, getting a close-up of Terri's face. At the areas around the body.

Lacey looked away and blinked back tears, focusing instead on an unraveling piece of yarn on a shawl Amy had left on her chair.

"When did you call the police?"

His tone had changed. She recognized the cop's voice. Interrogating. Trusting no one.

"Last night. That's when I found the folder on my computer. But since it wasn't an emergency, they sent a cruiser over this morning. But it's even more complicated than that." She told him how someone had inserted one of the pictures in her customer's wedding book.

"There will be an electronic fingerprint of everything having anything to do with this file on the hard drive of your computer. Someone who knows what they're doing can give us a lay down of the whole exchange." His jaw clenched jaw.

"I want to compare these to the crime scene photos the police took. Is it okay if I email them to myself?"

"Yes. Do whatever you have to do." Lacey wished she could stop the tremble in her voice. She wanted to tell him how she suspected Terri's death was retaliation for Stephanie Green's murder. Sixteen years ago, everyone held her responsible. The teenager's family thought of Lacey as the criminal who'd lured their daughter away from home. The others involved had blamed her for calling Terri and later accepting a deal from the district attorney for a reduced sentence. Lacey had been a key witness when the other five had been tried on a score of charges.

All these years later, Lacey still felt like the outsider. Nothing had changed.

She couldn't say the words, but her sister was dead because of her. All of a sudden, she was freezing. Still, she didn't want to leave the room and risk losing this chance of Gavin helping her. She watched in silence as he emailed the folder to himself.

"This morning, what did the cops do?"

"Took copies of the file. I haven't heard from them since."

"The locals had a chance to seize your computer and take it back to the station, but they didn't."

"I asked them not to. My business is dependent on this equipment."

"Good. It gives us the green light to do some checking without interfering with an official investigation."

She looked at him curiously.

"I don't work for NHPD anymore," he explained. "But I have to steer clear of obstructing anyone's work. In my job I need them on my side."

"Then you *can* help me?"

"Definitely. At least, I can push for some answers about who's doing what on Terri's case. And I'll get these photos into the right person's hands."

She nodded. He stood up and she stepped back, her back coming up against the wall.

"Do you remember seeing Terri's badge after the accident?"

Lacey slipped past him and went around the desk. "No. They asked me about it. She came here the night before directly from work so she might have had it with her. I didn't find it in her bedroom, and it wasn't in her car either. I still haven't gone to New Haven to check her apartment."

"Would she have taken it with her jogging?"

Lacey shrugged. "I don't know. Actually, I don't remember ever seeing her badge. I couldn't tell you what it looked like. She never showed it to me."

With the exception of her sister, Lacey didn't have a high

opinion of people in uniform and Terri had known it. When they were together, they almost never talked about the cases she was working on.

"She had her wallet on her when she died," Lacey told him. "The police returned it to me after they found her body."

"Was anything missing?"

"If there was, I wouldn't know. I did notify the bank, so except for automatic bill payments, her accounts are on hold until I get around to...to taking care of things."

"How about her cell phone?"

"She'd forgotten to bring her charger. We have different cell phones. It had gone dead overnight. So, she'd left it upstairs next to the bed."

"Have you done anything with it, yet? Like closing the account or checking her voicemail?"

Lacey shook her head. "There's a lot that I haven't done yet. It's been easier to lose myself in the work and try not to deal with reality," she continued without any prodding. "I know...it's almost five weeks."

He rose to his feet and touched her on the arm. "You're doing okay. There's time for everything."

Lacey felt her knees go soft. His hand was warm and her skin tingled beneath the shirt. She wanted to lean into him, let him take away the chill.

"Have you had dinner? I haven't eaten yet. We could go out."

"No. No. I already had dinner," she lied. He had a way of knocking off her balance, making her mind stray. He was too attractive. Too much for her to handle. No way was she going to put herself in temptation's way.

She started for the door. "And I'm sorry I couldn't offer anything but my high-test coffee. I have so much work to catch up on."

He took the hint and followed her to the door. "I'll call you in a couple of days or as soon as I have some information. In the meantime, try to get somebody here to secure your network."

In the hall he took a card out of his wallet and handed it to her. Lacey didn't mention that she'd held on to the one he'd given her at Terri's funeral. She watched him put on his leather jacket and regretted pushing him away. But she was too nervous to have him stay.

"I know you run a business, not a charity." She leaned against the doorway to her office. "So, if you could let me know what you need as a retainer, I'll take care of it."

"Forget about it. Or we'll consider that coffee the retainer."

"No, I can come up with the money."

The touch of his warm hand cupping her chin silenced the protest.

"No more talk of a retainer. I want to help you because your sister was my friend." His dark eyes bore into hers. "And because I'm attracted to you. And yes, my invitation to go out to dinner stays open. And I'm not saying that it has to be a show and dinner. But dinner and a show has a nice ring to it too. Don't overthink it. I don't want to stress you out. Understood?"

The heat was back in her face. All Lacey could do was nod.

CHAPTER TEN

"Why did you stop?"

"There's a car coming out of Lacey's driveway." Nick Reilly answered as Amy flipped open her watch and feel the time.

"Seven thirty-five. He didn't stay too long."

"Who was that?" Nick asked.

"Lacey had her sister's old partner over tonight. He called her this morning to catch up on things."

"He's a cop?"

"An ex-cop," she said.

"Social call or business?"

"I think business," Amy replied. "Someone hacked into Lacey's computer. The police were here this morning."

Nick felt the heat rise up on the back of his neck. He used Amy's computer whenever he was over to check email or browse the net. "Did they talk to you?"

"No."

He should have been relieved, but a sick feeling lingered in the pit of his stomach. He didn't need any unnecessary attention from the police. Not while he was still on probation after that fight with a bunch of rednecks outside of Foxwoods earlier this year.

Black and adopted as a teenager by a local Irish Catholic family, Nick was the busiest carpenter in town. Everyone knew and trusted him, so he had jobs in the pipeline going out six months. That'd been before the mention of the fight in the papers. It was daunting how quickly his backlog was going away.

"Are we walking the rest of the way?" Amy poked him in the ribs.

"Hold on to your horses, miss."

Nick turned into the separate driveway at Amy's end of the property. Moments later, he stopped in front of the renovated barn.

"Home again," Amy said cheerfully. "Can you stay tonight?"

"I can't, but I can come in for a little while."

The pout on Amy's pretty face brought a smile to his lips. Nick had been at the end of renovating this barn for Terri and Lacey Watkins when Amy had showed up to rent it. They'd hit it off right away.

Amy was great in bed, undemanding, pretty, and totally independent, regardless of being blind. They went out once or twice a week, had sex afterwards, and went their own way the rest of the time. Their relationship was uncomplicated.

Nick came around the car and opened the door for her. "Getting out?"

Amy reached her hand out. He gripped it to help her.

"Hey, do you want to go to a movie next week?" he asked once they were inside the apartment. "The Waterbury Theater just set up that descriptive video thing."

She reached for his face with her fingers, then touched his lips and rose up to kiss him. "How can I repay such a sweet offer?"

"Definitely out of those clothes. Do you have any whipped cream?"

She smiled. "As a matter of fact, I do."

"Good. Get that, and I'll meet you in the bedroom."

"Where are you going?"

"I've gotta send an email," Nick told her. "I promised a client I'd send him the invoice for that job I finished this afternoon."

"Who's the client?"

"Judge Green."

Amy paused in the doorway to the kitchen. "A judge?"

"Yeah. At least, he used to be a judge, I guess, before some family tragedy. He's an old divorced guy. Used to live in the northern part of the state, but now he lives like a hermit on the lake by Black Rock State Park. Couple of miles down the road. Weird guy."

"How so?"

"In lots of ways."

"Like what?" she pressed.

"Like he wouldn't let me go inside his place to use the bathroom when I was working for him."

"What did you do?"

"I peed in the woods."

"That's it? That's being strange?"

"No. Of course not. There's more. Like...well, everyone tells me that he doesn't talk to anyone. That you can't *get* him to put two words together. So I go out there to do this job, right? And he ends up hanging outside with me, asking me question after question."

"What kind of questions?"

Nick shrugged. "About me. About my personal life. But also about Lacey and Terri. Shit like that. Like I should know everything about them."

Nick opened the laptop as Amy went to the kitchen. A second later she poked her head out again.

"What kind of a job did you do for him?"

"Fixed his deck. The boards had rotted through."

She leaned a hand against the door jamb. "Can I ask you one more question?"

"What?"

"Do you ever download files on my computer when you're checking email?"

He was quiet for a moment and then laughed. "Of course."

"Really?"

"Yeah, porn. Where do you think I get my good ideas from?"

"Oh. Well, in that case, get to it," Amy replied with a smile as she backed into the kitchen.

CHAPTER ELEVEN

GAVIN WAS past kidding himself that he was helping Lacey out of respect for Terri.

The two sisters had a few physical features in common, but Terri was taller, square-shouldered, and muscled from years of police training. She had developed the tough, masculine manner needed for the job. To Gavin, she'd been a partner and a friend. That would have been as far as it could ever have gone, even if she hadn't been gay.

Tonight, in Lacey's kitchen he'd discreetly tried to size the younger sister up. But the male in him had reared its very predicable head. The slant of her cheekbones, the deep green eyes, and the pale flawless skin only encouraged a closer look. She was feminine, delicate, beautiful. He'd felt the tightening of his ball sack that usually signaled *collision ahead*. And this was not helped by the lingering image of her naked body in the window.

But Gavin had been served up a double punch. First, his reaction to her, and then finding out why she'd wanted him to come by.

During his years with the New Haven PD, he'd looked at thousands of crime photos. He'd been at the scene of hundreds of homicides. But looking at the photo of Terri's dead body on Lacey's computer made him vaguely ill.

That was not a picture of the strong and resilient detective he'd known for ten years. This hit-and-run victim was not the Terri he knew. His partner was tough and astute and alert. She had no hint of *victim* in anything about her.

This lifeless corpse made a mockery of the Terri he remembered.

And some sonovabitch had taken these pictures and forwarded them to Lacey. They weren't police photos. He was certain of that. This was the action of some bastard bragging about his handiwork. It didn't even smack of hit-and-run to Gavin. That was the worst part. He recalled what John Trevor had said about the homicide Terri was working on. Bratva's name edged back into his mind. But why would someone like that have a detective killed and then send a picture to the sister? This wasn't his style. He might send pieces of the body, but not a photo.

Still, that didn't mean there weren't others gunning for her. Over the years, Terri had made plenty of enemies.

The police world was no different than any other. In New Haven, just like in other mid-sized cities, the line between the worlds of light and dark sometimes got crossed. Of course, there were good cops. But there were also bad cops. And lazy cops. And there were those who didn't stop until they prodded and poked and pushed to the very end of things—and sometimes brought about real change—no matter what good-old-boy establishment got pulled down along the way.

Terri was definitely one of those. She'd made a career out of intentionally stepping on the toes of the high-and-mighty. On either side of the blue line. Given the chance, more than a few of them would have gone after her. This only pissed him off more.

Gavin stared ahead at the dark, gloomy hills lining the high-way. He had to keep his feelings in check while he was at the house because Lacey was barely holding it together.

He knew the two sisters had survived a disastrous upbringing and both carried scars from it. Gavin had decided a long time ago that Terri's childhood had contributed to her mistrust of men. It had taken a long time for her to accept him as a friend and not just another male detective she worked with.

Whatever lack of trust his old partner exercised with other people, she made up for with the people she cared about. And Lacey was at the top of that list. Terri had been as much mother-figure as she was sibling. And he knew there was some degree of guilt behind it too. She had escaped their poisoned home early enough to make a change in her life. Lacey, on the other hand, had almost died at the hands of their father. Her limp was a visible scar, but Gavin guessed there were many emotional ones.

Sexual arousal or whatever other fascination he'd been feeling before walking through her door was nothing compared to the punch in the gut he'd felt once they were face-to-face. She was a very attractive puzzle. There were so many pieces to her. Striking, mysterious, humorous, timid, sexy as hell. But she lacked confidence and didn't seem to know how to pull her assets together to her advantage. And Gavin suddenly had the crazy notion that he was the man for her.

His cell phone rang, and for a second, he hoped that it was Lacey. Perhaps she'd changed her mind about going out tonight.

He was wrong.

"Yeah, this is Alisha. Terri don't answer her phone no more, and things keep going to her mailbox. I wanna leave another message with you. You remember me?"

"Of course." The girl's tone wasn't hysterical, as it'd been the other night. "Where are you?"

"It don't matter."

"Okay, I'm hanging up."

"No! Don't. I'm in Bridgeport. But tell her don't bother coming after me. I'm leaving in a few minutes. I've found a place I can go chill."

Gavin could hear a PA system in the background, announcing

the scheduled trains. The Bridgeport train and bus stations were right next door to each other.

"Is this a good number I can give her to call you?"

"Shit, no. I'll be dumping it in a sec."

"I don't think she'd be happy to hear that."

"Don't fuckin' matter. Just give her this message. I'm leaving her an envelope."

"What's in the envelope?"

"The list she wants. The one my boyfriend lifted and I never mailed like I promised. She knows what I'm talking about. I gotta go."

"Where is it? Where are you leaving this envelope?"

"I'll call her when I get where I'm supposed to go. I'll tell her where it is then. And tell her she better answer her own phone if she wants to know."

"Alisha—" Gavin was too late. The thirteen-year-old hung up.

Going somewhere else to chill only meant that she'd be working for some other pimp in some other city. It was frustrating as hell.

He punched in John Trevor's cell number. The assistant chief answered right away. Gavin gave him the information on Alisha's whereabouts. He intentionally held back what she'd said about the envelope. He had no idea what was in it or where it was. Alisha could give that information to whoever her new contact was.

"Did she tell you where she was going? Or what time she was leaving?"

"No."

"I'll call Bridgeport and have them pick her up."

"You're going to look after this girl, right? She can't go back on the street." Gavin knew how much it mattered to Terri that her informants were protected.

"I got it covered, MacFadyen. Don't worry."

"Another question before you hang up," Gavin said. "Did Westbury police contact New Haven PD today about some computer files that turned up on Lacey Watkins's computer? About someone hacking into her system?"

"No. I would have heard that," Trevor told him. "What's she doing now? Getting herself into more trouble?"

Gavin resented the attitude. "No, she's trying to help with the investigation of her sister's death."

"How?"

"The files were photos of Terri's corpse."

"Crime scene?"

"I doubt it."

There was a pause on the line. "She was out there for some time before they found the body."

"Will you check into it?"

"Because of town lines and where they found the body, the Staties have taken over the case, but I'll give them a call and see what's going on. Yeah, I'll definitely get into it. Thanks for the tip, MacFadyen."

CHAPTER TWELVE

A LINE of vending machines stood behind the Plexiglas doors leading out onto the train platform. Just outside, Alisha stared at the two little kids running back and forth in front of the candy, coffee, and snack dispensers. An old granny sat on one of the benches inside, watching the brats like a hawk.

Alisha wasn't going to leave the envelope for Terri unless she was sure she could get the message to her. But now that she'd talked to this Gavin dude, she guessed he'd let her know. He'd done it last night. Alisha was sure Terri would answer the phone when she called back because she'd been waiting for these papers forever.

After walking around the station, she had decided this was the only place the envelope would be safe. Bathrooms got cleaned all the time. The benches in the waiting area were too open. Trashcans got emptied. Anything left outside on the platform would get blown away by the wind. But here she had a chance.

The trouble was how she was going to slip it between the vending machines with these two pairs of beady eyes watching her.

Halfway down the platform, the teenager she'd lifted the cell from was going from person to person, asking if anyone saw his phone.

"It must have just happened. I was sitting right on that bench. I only closed my eyes for two seconds."

"Call your number," someone suggested. "Use my phone."

Alisha strolled off to a nearby trashcan and dropped the phone in.

She was already past the kid when the station speaker crackled to life. The incoming Amtrak train. "Washington, Baltimore, Philadelphia, New York to New Haven, Providence, Boston. Arriving in ten minutes."

More people came out the door from the elevator and stairs onto the platform. She checked the clock. The bus to Albany wasn't leaving until 10:00 from the terminal right next door. She already had her ticket and knew they would be loading at Bus Bay C. She had time. Still, she didn't want to walk that way by herself. There was a large parking lot behind the bus stop.

Somebody on the train coming in had to be going that way, she decided. She would wait and walk over with the passengers.

Alisha took the envelope out of her bag. Walking inside the vending area, she went to the machines. Immediately, the two brats attached themselves like ticks to her sides.

"What you buying?"

"I like Oreos."

"No, chips."

"*Get* back here." Granny's shout from the bench was like a whip, snapping the kids back to the seats.

Alisha pushed the envelope between the soda and snack vending machines. The paper slipped in and disappeared. For a moment, she worried that Terri might not find it.

She's a fucking cop, Alisha reminded herself. *Terri can do anything,* especially when Alisha told her where to look.

Leaning against a wall, she waited and tried not to worry about Albany. The friend she was staying with was eighteen. She'd already told Alisha that she wouldn't have to pay anything for food or rent the first month.

And that was way better than New Haven. There was nothing left for her here with her boyfriend dead. No one to protect her.

The people on the platform faced the train as it rumbled in. To her disappointment, not many riders got off. Those who did didn't hang around either. They all had places to go.

Alisha went with the small crowd. The platform stairs to the street were a popular way to exit, she realized. She followed, walking fast, pretending that she was somebody and had a family waiting for her.

Family. That really *was* pretend. Her mother only knew how to take care of herself, and she could barely do even that. Her sisters were much better off now that Terri was involved. At least, Alisha assumed Terri was. Alisha had heard through the grapevine that there'd been a shooting at her aunt's apartment but that no one in her family had gotten hurt. The twins had been taken away by the cops. That meant Terri *had* to be there.

The crowd thinned out more when they reached the street. Two preppy boys, one pulling a noisy rolling suitcase, were ahead of her heading toward the bus stop. Everyone else seemed to have rides or was parked at the garage across the street. Alisha followed the two boys.

The sidewalk was well lit. The traffic on the street was light. She accidentally kicked a can and jumped a foot. Looking up, she realized she could have taken the elevated walkway that ran right from the train platform to the buses. Instead, she was following these two morons.

It didn't matter. She'd taken the Metro North from New Haven to Bridgeport, and hadn't seen anyone she knew on the train.

They wouldn't be looking for her here.

A police car with *City of Bridgeport* written on the door was parked by the curb some thirty yards ahead. Two cops were sitting inside. She hurried to stay close to the preppies.

As she passed the cops, she kept her eye on them. They were talking, paying no attention to what was happening on the street. Alisha let out a sigh of relief when she got past them.

About twenty yards farther, an SUV with tinted windows pulled up next to her. By the time she realized what was happening, the passenger door had opened.

She recognized him immediately.

"No. Please!" she said, backing into the concrete wall behind her.

"Get in the car, Alisha."

"*Help!*" she cried to the two preppies up ahead. They didn't even turn around.

"Get in here," the man said, menacingly. "Now."

She turned around and started to run back toward the police cruiser, her arms flailing in the air like a wounded bird.

Before she got five steps away, she was caught from behind and lifted into the air.

"You fuckin' scumbags! Let me go." Alisha was shoved inside the SUV, and the door slammed shut.

One of the cops glanced up at the departing vehicle, but only for a second before turning back to his conversation.

CHAPTER THIRTEEN

A LONG SHOWER, herbal tea at midnight, a two-a.m. bowl of cereal, and intermittent periods of meditation, pillow hugging, pillow punching, and yogic breathing. Nothing worked. Lacey didn't get even a minute of sleep. Every bit of conversation she'd had with Gavin played back in her mind. His invitation, most of all.

It wouldn't be just dinner.

Lacey didn't go on dates. She didn't *do* relationships.

She was far from oblivious to the opposite sex. She knew men were attracted to her. But she wasn't flattered. She didn't do well with one-night stands. Over the years, she'd perfected the routine of putting up a wall before things got serious. She didn't want to get emotionally involved with men. She didn't trust any of them and she was not about to risk her heart and her life the way her mother had done.

But Gavin wasn't simply a stranger. They had a connection through Terri. And, man, she had to admit that she was attracted to him. And, for some reason, she wanted his approval. Perhaps *because* of Terri. He was the only human link she had to segments of her sister's life that she didn't know much about.

But dealing with Gavin would be complicated. And for that

reason alone, she had to keep their relationship on a professional level. She couldn't afford to screw it up.

But loneliness surrounded her like a shroud.

Terri had been the cheerleader in her life. In Lacey's darkest moments, her sister had always held the light that showed her the way. Now what did she have? There was no motivation to put one foot in front of the other to get through each day.

As daylight slipped grayly into her room, the clock ticked over to six o'clock, and she got out of bed. Pulling on an old sweatshirt and sweatpants, she went down to the kitchen. She made coffee and watched the brown liquid start to drip into the decanter. Turning away, she gathered up the piles of mail she'd had forwarded from Terri's address.

Since the funeral, she'd pressed the snooze button of life too many times. The meeting with Gavin last night had been her wake-up call. Now she was getting someone else involved, asking for their help.

Pouring a cup of coffee, she grabbed the bundle of mail and went into her office. The green light on the Internet modem flashed, reminding her that her system had come under attack. Last night, she'd turned off her main computer, stopping any potential hacker from reaching her files.

As the machine hummed, rattled, and beeped to life, she dropped the mail onto the desk and checked her day's schedule. She had only one appointment at ten this morning. Benita Gomez, a reporter for the *Westbury Times*. The woman stopped by a couple of weeks ago and made an appointment with Amy to talk to Lacey. She was doing a column each week on new businesses in town.

Lacey had checked out some of the write-ups and decided she couldn't buy this kind of publicity. She'd agreed to the interview.

There was a sharp tap on the front door and, for an insane moment, Lacey's heart leapt into her throat. She glanced at the clock of the computer. It was only six twenty-two.

Going to the front hall, she peeked through one of the

beveled glass panels next to the door. Donna Covington, dressed in a sleek teal running outfit, was standing on the front porch. She seemed tense and was staring hard into the fog at the garage across the driveway.

Lacey opened the door. "Hi, Donna. Is everything okay?"

"Oh, yes. I'm fine."

Her pale expression contradicted her calm words, though. Amy *had* mentioned that Donna had been sick this past week.

"I hope you don't mind me stopping by so early, but I saw you working through the window."

"You could see me inside my office from the road?"

"Oh." Donna shook her head. "No, I was trespassing like I do most mornings. I take a shortcut to the cemetery through your yard. Nice easy uphill start and I don't have to run on the road."

Lacey knew all about the dangers of jogging on the road.

"You don't mind that I cut through, do you?"

"No, of course not," Lacey replied, guessing this wasn't the reason for the early morning visit.

"I sent you an email yesterday about a job. I know it was a last-minute thing, but I was out sick and everything backed up."

"I know all about running behind. I haven't checked my email for a couple of days." Lacey was behind a lot more than that, but there was no point in mentioning it. "What do you need?"

"Well, we're doing new flyers for the health club. So, if you have the time, I'd love to get a price for new pictures of the facilities, inside and out. Some with clients exercising with trainers. You could either put together the flyer or just give me a price for doing the photos. How does that sound?"

"I can do that," Lacey said, trying to wrap her head around the business side of her life. She needed jobs like this to pay the bills. "Do you want the photos from the Westbury location?"

"We're actually going to use the same flyer for all the clubs in the state. But most of the pictures could definitely be from the facility here in town."

Travel time and the number of locations made it a little more complicated.

"You said you emailed me the information?"

"Yeah. Some of it. Most of it." Donna rubbed her arms as if she was cold. "I'll take you wherever I want to have the pictures taken. Why don't you give me a quote for one day of your time and equipment? Say, nine to five."

"And the flyer?"

"Actually, never mind about the flyer. We can put that together at our main office and send it to the printers. I really need good photos."

"When do you need the price quote?" Lacey asked.

"Is today too soon? That's why I stopped by this early," Donna said in an apologetic tone. "I have to get the money okayed by my boss tomorrow and we only meet once a week. Saturday mornings at the district office."

"I'll email you an estimate by five o'clock then. Okay?"

"Perfect."

Actually, translating what Donna wanted into hours made it really simple. She'd have to tack on a little extra since she was handing over the copyright on the shots, but that wasn't a big deal.

Lacey remained in the doorway for a few minutes after Donna left with a wave, and watched the dense early morning fog swallow up the other woman. All around her, the low branches of the trees hid whatever lay beyond the clearing immediately around the house.

Back in the office, she opened her email. She knew why someone like Donna would approach her about this job: she was a very little fish among the talented and well-known photography studios in western Connecticut. Which meant that she'd work dirt cheap to build a client list. These days, with the ease of digital cameras and smart phones, more people took their own pictures. And with the exception of an occasional wedding, there weren't too many well-paid assignments.

Lacey stared with disbelief at her email inbox. Not even three days and she had four hundred and eighty-four unread emails.

She skimmed through the various spam emails to find Donna's. Thankfully, Donna had put the name of the health club in the subject line.

Before opening it, Lacey noticed the subject line of an email about a dozen lines above Donna's.

Road Kill.

She stared at the address. A totally meaningless series of letters and numbers. There was no attachment to the email, but she couldn't bring herself to open it. Her finger hovered over the delete button.

Her mind shifted to the vulnerability of her system. Lacey opened the My Documents directory on her hard drive and sorted the folders by date. *Road Kill* had a new sub folder, inserted last night at ten fifty-five. She'd turned off her computer at midnight.

Opening the file, she stared at the single photo.

A woman. Clearly dead. The cord still around her neck.

CHAPTER FOURTEEN

IT WAS ALMOST happy hour and the string of bars and clubs and restaurants lining the beach road in Misquamicutt was humming with people.

Gavin had his arm draped around Lacey's shoulder. She had hers wrapped around his waist as they walked down the stretch of road beneath the late afternoon sun. There was a crowd gathered in the sandy parking lot. They stopped to see what was going on. Music was blaring, and on the flat roof, a half-dozen women in sparkling bikinis were calling out to the onlookers, dancing and tossing bead necklaces down. Lacey laughed. Gavin realized he'd never heard her laugh before.

He was just about to kiss her lips when blue, twelve-foot curtains suddenly rose up around the parking lot, cutting the crowd off from the road as attendants ran out with mats for everyone. Lacey took his hand and they sat down. The summer sun was golden, and the sandy pavement was warm. Immediately, the sex-advice columnist Dr. Ruth and a dozen assistants in lab coats were circulating among the couples on the mats. She had a microphone and was giving everyone directions.

It was a sex therapy clinic.

They'd already gone through exercises in spanking and in the joys of body-painting and were just about to start on oral sex.

A phone ringing in the distance brought everything to a sudden stop.

Gavin opened his eyes and stared up at the white popcorn ceiling of his bedroom.

Shit. Just when we were getting to good part. He picked up the cell phone, checking the number. Lacey. Talk about irony.

Taking a deep breath—which didn't do much for him—he answered the call. "Hello."

"I'm so sorry to call you this early."

Gavin drew a hand down his face, making sure he was awake. The sheet was tented over his middle. He adjusted his genitals and pushed himself up onto one elbow. He looked at the clock radio. Two minutes to seven.

"No problem. The alarm was about to go off. What's up?"

"I just found something else on my computer. Another file."

He pushed the covers off and swung his feet around to the floor. "More pictures of Terri?"

"No." Her voice trembled. "It's someone I don't know. A murder scene. Someone put the file in my system last night. It wasn't there before. I'm sure of it."

"Send it to me. Right now. Email it to me." He shut off the alarm radio as it was about to buzz. "Stay on the line."

Gavin gave her his email address as he walked to the next bedroom where he'd set up a home office. He opened the laptop. Last night, he'd wrangled a favor off Marg Botto who worked in the State Police Photography and Identification unit. Marg didn't ask why when Gavin called to see the crime scene photos from Terri's hit-and-run. She just gave him the access code, and Gavin spent time going over them. As he'd guessed, the pictures on Lacey's computer weren't from the batch taken by the cops.

"I just sent it," Lacey said quietly.

He sat behind the desk and retrieved the email. What opened

as the attachment on the screen was a close-up of a homicide. "Got it."

Gavin frowned, studying the photo. The murder weapon was clearly evident. The ends of a white cord lay haphazardly on the victim's collar and coat, and the Black woman's head was angled back, revealing the line cut into her throat during the strangulation. The photo was a close-up, showing only the chin and mouth —with the distended tongue—and the pink neckline of a shirt inside the lapel of her coat. Nothing in the picture gave away anything definitive as to the identity of the victim. The angle of the head and the blurred background to the body made him think she'd been sitting on the front seat of a vehicle when she was attacked.

"Could this be someone you know?"

"I don't know. I don't think so," Lacey said thickly. "There was an email sent too, nudging me to look for it. The file and the email subject line said the same thing. *Road Kill*. Same name as Terri's folder."

She talked faster. He could hear the panic in her voice. He didn't blame her.

"This other picture...of the strangled woman," he spoke softly, surely, hoping it'd help her calm down. "Have you called the police yet?"

"No. I just found it a few minutes ago."

"Good. Just wait a bit. Let me run this by one of my contacts. It shouldn't be more than a couple of hours," he told her.

He started drafting an email to Marg. She'd worked third shift last night and would, therefore, be at work for another hour. He sent her the photo. Two favors in one shift. He was pushing his luck.

"I don't know who this person is or why someone would send me the photo. If this picture is real, I'm terrified to think she was killed because of some connection to me. And the same caption." Her voice shook. "I didn't talk about it last night, but I'm responsible for my sister's death. It's my fault."

She broke down and the phone went silent.

"Lacey? Lacey?" he called louder, wishing he could reach through the line and just hold her.

A lengthy pause went by before she came back on. "I'm here."

He had no doubt that she was crying. "Let's think about what's going on here. The most important thing right now is the identity of the victim," Gavin said, keeping his voice steady. "This photo could be from last night or from a homicide twenty years ago. There's no telling."

"*Road Kill*," she said in a low voice. "Don't you think this creep is trying to tell me something?"

He couldn't disagree. "What we have going for us is that he likes to boast about the kill. This is a record of a trophy for him. And he's communicating. This is exactly what leads police to killers. This should help us find him."

There was an incoming call on his cell phone. He looked at the number. It was from the State Police.

"Lacey, I'm going to call you right back. Keep your phone handy."

He ended one call and answered the other. It was Marg.

"Where did you get this picture, Gavin?" Her tone was sharp.

"Who is it? Where is it?" he asked instead.

"Don't fuck with me. Where did you get it?" she demanded.

"I don't know who took this. It came through on the Internet this morning. That's why I sent it to you, to figure out what it is." He was not willing to throw Lacey into the wolf den until he could figure a way to drag her out.

Marg cursed profusely first. "It's a homicide. They discovered the body and the car last night in the parking lot of a tenement building in New Milford. Some guy coming home from second shift reported it."

"Maybe he took the picture," Gavin offered. "Is she identified?"

"Fay Stone. A state probation officer. An old timer. The badge and wallet and money were still in the car. This was no robbery."

The killer had emailed the picture the same night as committing the crime. Lacey's fear was totally justified.

"The next of kin hasn't been notified yet, so a word out of you and I'll drag your ass—"

"Not a word, Marg," he told her.

"Our crew is still at the site, taking statements and collecting evidence."

"Okay."

"I want you to do paperwork on this, Gavin," she ordered. "And you leave my name out of it. I don't want anyone knowing I'm doing you favors."

"Got it."

As soon as Marg let him go, he got Lacey back on line again. "I'll try to get there sometime before noon. Can you clear your schedule?"

"I'm in trouble?" she asked.

"We'll talk more when I get there."

"Okay," she said in a defeated tone.

"And Lacey," he added. "I want you to lock your door. Don't let any strangers in."

CHAPTER FIFTEEN

THE FIVE-HUNDRED-DOLLAR-A-PLATE CAMPAIGN breakfast for Katherine Green, the candidate for Connecticut's U.S. Senate seat, had over eight hundred people crowded into the Aqua Turf Club.

A retired Republican senator and a couple of the conservative, older Hollywood actors living in Roxbury and Washington Depot were attending to show their support for the challenger, and the polls were showing that Kathy—as she liked to be called—was neck-and- neck with her Democratic opponent. The purpose of this event was to beef up her coffers for the final media push.

Benita Gomez's press badge guaranteed her a free seat, but she wasn't there to listen to the political rhetoric. Most of the media understood that Kathy Green's success was inextricably tied to her family's tragedy and her willingness to display the past like an open book before the public. Before their official interview next Monday, however, Benita wanted to witness the woman's showmanship in person.

Benita interrupted the cozy chat she was having with the gray-haired woman sitting next to her as a text from her boss *dinged* on her phone. She scanned it quickly and wrote back: *I'm going anyway*.

A couple minutes later, Kathy Green took her place at the podium. Taking out a pad of paper, Benita jotted down some notes to bring up during her personal interview later.

With Green's gratitude part of the speech done, the crowd hushed for the feature presentation.

"No parent should ever have to lose a child." The very tall, immaculately dressed, and strikingly beautiful woman paused, making eye contact with a few people in the audience.

"It was a beautiful, warm and sunny Sunday morning in April. I called upstairs and begged and cursed, and finally went up myself to drag my daughter Stephanie out of bed. My husband, Claude, was making his world-famous blueberry pancakes downstairs."

Benita gauged the audience's reaction. They could identify with Kathy Green, with the routine. She was like them. She was one of them. A positive checkmark for any politician.

"Most of you in this room never met Stephanie," Kathy said, clearly struggling with her emotions. "She was a beautiful sixteen-year-old, academically near the top of her class. She ran cross country and was co-captain in basketball and crew. She volunteered at the soup kitchen one afternoon a week, and from the time she was fourteen, she was fascinated with my husband's work as US District Court Judge in Waterbury."

Benita wrote Judge Green's name on her pad. She'd left a couple of messages on his answering machine, but he hadn't returned her calls. She wasn't giving up.

"After breakfast, we went to church. Visited my mother at Heritage Village in Southbury. Watched a game together that after-noon on TV and had barbecued ribs for supper. I went to bed early that night to read one of my cozy mysteries. Stephanie was going out, as she often did on Sunday nights, and I remember feeling so proud of my daughter as she went out that door. As was her nature, she was spending the evening tutoring a troubled teenager down the street."

Benita circled a name on the open page of her notebook.

"You know what happened. That same night, my daughter Stephanie was gang raped and murdered not too far from our house. There were six of them. All of them, the spawn of Satan. Not one responded to her cries. Not one reached out a hand to help her. Not one felt a pang of conscience or showed one shred of humanity for my beautiful, loving girl."

No sound of clinking glass could be heard. No scrape of silverware. The servers stood, still as statues, staring at the podium. She held everyone and everything in her power, transfixed and silent.

"The impact of this crime against my daughter, against my family, was like a bomb exploding in my kitchen. It shattered our very existence," Kathy Green said, her voice quavering. "The phone call, the police at the door, the mad rush to the hospital while we were yet to be told that it was too late."

Benita studied her carefully. Kathy was looking searchingly into the faces of the audience.

"On the drive to the emergency room, I kept thinking that I'd forgotten to take Stephanie's crew sweatshirt out of the dryer and she'd want it for the next day. I was worried about her dentist appointment that Friday being too close to her after-school practice time. I was totally unaware that in a few minutes my heart would smash into a million little pieces."

Benita took more notes on the page. Kathy Green was very good at this. It didn't matter that the people who filled this hall agreed or not with her fiscal conservativeness or her support of reinstating the death penalty in Connecticut. She was a mother who'd suffered. A mother who had pulled herself up out of the abyss of despair. She had their vote.

"Weeks, months, years later, I was still living in a nightmare that I'd hoped I could awaken from. The trials. The lies. The painful testimony I had to make and listen to at each of the trials. The wait...and then the disappointment as the sentences didn't match my loss, didn't heal my pain."

Benita drew an arrow next to the name of all those serving time who had requested an appeal.

"And if my life wasn't shattered enough, my husband's nervous breakdown and then our divorce left me even more crushed. And then something happened. Something changed."

Benita put the napkin next to her plate and gathered her things, mouthing an apology to people at her table and backing toward the door.

The candidate was still speaking, but Benita had heard this part of Kathy Green's speech before. She was giving the credit for her transformation to God and to the people around her. Not to the grief experts or the therapists. But to the ordinary people around her. To the citizens of this state.

To be sure, Kathy Green had been through hell, Benita thought, but she also had a great speech writer.

Benita was almost ready for the interview next Monday.

CHAPTER SIXTEEN

"DOES your client have anything to hide? Are there going to be any surprises on her computer system that she would prefer the police not know about?"

Gavin had decided to call Farah Aziz before he arrived at Lacey's house. She was one of the top criminal defense lawyers in state. He knew her from her days as a prosecutor in New Haven. Smart and shrewd with the instincts of a pit bull, she'd worked enough cases in her early years in the juvenile courts to know the kind of baggage Lacey would be carrying for the rest of her life.

"You mean, other than two separate sets of crime scene photographs?" Gavin asked.

"Forget I asked. I'll ask her directly if she decides to hire me. Attorney/client privilege. Don't give me any more details."

Through Terri, Gavin knew most of the skeletons in Lacey's closet.

"Tell her she shouldn't call the police. She should call me first," Farah told him. "But you're assuming she doesn't have a lawyer on retainer already."

"I doubt she does. But I'll be there in under an hour, so I'll let you know."

Gavin recalled something Terri had mentioned about the

attorney who had represented Lacey sixteen years ago. The guy's name was Calkey or something like that. An old timer who'd long since retired. He'd convinced Lacey and their family to take a plea bargain instead of going to trial. Terri had always felt guilty about that. Three years in prison for a fifteen-year-old for being stoned and in the wrong place at the wrong time.

"Gavin, are you there?"

"I'm here," he said. "I was just thinking that law enforcement knows I've seen this second photo. I can't sit on it too long."

"Don't worry about it," Farah assured him. "Instead of Lacey reporting this new file, I'm going to do it for her. First, I have a certified forensic computer examiner who will check it out. She'll be able to get whatever clues might be in the system."

"How long is that going to take?"

"If Lacey calls me this morning, I can get her computer to my expert this afternoon. Then I'll call in the law. Of course, good luck to them in getting that computer without a court order anytime soon. And being Friday afternoon, that gives us enough time to dig into things."

"The locals won't be happy."

"That's between me and them. You're out of it. And you know Lacey's rights. She shouldn't speak to them without her attorney present anyway."

"Got it." Gavin decided this was the best time to bring up the topic of money. Farah was also one of the highest paid attorneys in the state. He didn't want Lacey to get sticker shock and shy away from the best. "And Farah, can you bill me instead of her? For most of your retainer and then your fee? And I don't want her to know."

There was a long pause on the line.

"Lacey hasn't settled any of her sister's estate," he explained. "She's going to have the life insurance and retirement funds soon enough, along with whatever else Terri had been saving up. But for right now, I'm guessing she's running close to empty."

"I'll work up some numbers that won't break the bank," Farah said good-naturedly, not pushing him on his motivations.

Ending the call, Gavin regretted not correcting Farah about her assumption that Lacey was his client. When it came to his work, if it was with NHPD or as a private investigator, he followed strict ethical rules.

Gavin turned on the radio to stop himself from overthinking the situation.

"...third time this month, a mutilated body has washed up on a Connecticut beach. State Police are reporting the discovery of a headless torso of an unidentified male in Mystic. Authorities are not saying if they have any clues about who is responsible for these brutal murders..."

"Fucking Bratva," Gavin cursed under his breath, knowing full well the butcher who was responsible.

CHAPTER SEVENTEEN

THE LACK OF SLEEP, the photos on her computer, the three cups of coffee she'd gulped down this morning, had put Lacey into a near manic state. Her heart was racing. Her hand shook. She jumped at the normal old-house creaks as she paced from room to room. She couldn't sit long enough to concentrate on any of her work. She was afraid to check her email. She felt sick to her stomach.

Eighteen cities and towns in thirteen years. In the past, she had a perfect solution for dealing with stress, with any kind of stress. She'd move. New apartment. New low wage job. New people who had no idea about her screwed up past. But coming back here was supposed to be the end of that, the end of a very painful trail. There was nowhere else left for her to go.

Lacey was drinking her fourth cup of coffee and staring blankly at the deep grooves on the old wooden kitchen table when the doorbell chimed. *Gavin.* Her heart thumped. Leaving the coffee mug in the sink, she took her time walking to the front door. She was totally surprised to look through the glass and find a short, thin young woman standing outside. The two black bags she had hanging from her shoulder gave away her identity.

Lacey unlatched and opened the door. "You're the reporter. I'm sorry you're here, but I left a message at —."

"Hi. Benita Gomez." The young woman smiled, her hand outstretched, interrupting Lacey. "Ten o'clock. I did mention to you that I'd be prompt."

The jacket of the navy blue business suit was askew because of the weight of the bags. Lacey shook her hand. Strong, confident fingers wrapped around hers. The skin was cool. "I called your office and left a message. They told me they'd get hold of you."

"I've been on the road. They didn't," she replied in a stressed tone. "I'm coming directly from another event. Something wrong?"

"I'm sorry, Benita. Some urgent business has come up," Lacey explained. "I have to postpone our interview."

Dark lines immediately creased the young woman's forehead. "But you're home and I'm already here. I promise this won't take more than ten minutes of your time," Benita said in a persuasive tone. "This interview is for an article we're running next week and I'm up against a deadline."

Lacey didn't know if she could keep up the appearance of a relaxed attitude for *any* amount of time. Gavin had sent her a text when he'd left New Haven. He should have been here by now.

"I already took a lot of the information I need from your website," the reporter persisted. "We could do it in five minutes. Please."

Lacey didn't want to do this, not for five *seconds*. But what else she could do now, other than keep pacing and feeling sick to her stomach until he got here? She opened the door reluctantly. "Five minutes."

"Thank you. You don't know how much I appreciate this."

Lacey left the front door unlocked and led Benita Gomez to the living room. She was surprised when the reporter pulled a camera out of one of the bags as the two of them sat down.

"No," Lacey objected immediately. "No photos."

"I was hoping to take some pictures of you for the article."

"You can use the headshot from the webpage. I'll send you a high-resolution copy."

It was obvious Benita was displeased, but she kept her tone friendly. "Action photos of you, looking like you're working, would really look great in the paper. A picture's worth a thousand words."

"I know. That's my business," Lacey said curtly. "For today, the headshot will have to do."

"Is a tape recorder okay?" she asked next.

Lacey's impulse was to object to that too. In fact, she just wanted the woman to go.

"Five minutes," Gomez repeated, placing the tape recorder on her bag. "Just to start, briefly tell me about your business."

Lacey realized her hands were shaking. She tucked them under her legs and tried to calm her agitation with a couple of deep breaths. "Watkins's Photography. I—"

Benita interrupted right away. "And you bought your business from...?"

"Brett Orr. Two...two and a half months ago," Lacey replied. The client list and equipment had changed hands, but Terri was the one who'd convinced her to branding their last name at the same time.

"Certainly, a well-established business in town," Gomez smiled. "So how is it going?"

"Great," Lacey lied. To save face, she started reciting lines from her brochure regarding the kinds of services she offered. She sounded as enthusiastic as a wind-up doll. She went on to say how she was hoping to expand into media and video production.

The reporter held up a pen, interrupting her. "Why Westbury? You're originally from Sherman. Why not start your business there?"

Lacey stared at her a moment, fighting back a pang of annoyance. Her past was public record. Anyone could know what happened sixteen years ago. She decided not to correct the woman, even though she was *not* originally from Sherman and had only lived there for four months.

"My grandfather's house was here in Westbury," she said instead. "I live here now."

The reporter took some notes.

"You've had a tragic life, your sister dying in a hit-and-run last month." She made eye contact, pausing, acting like she cared.

Lacey looked away. The string of intelligent responses she'd put together and memorized for this interview blurred and faded into a mass of pointless sounds.

"But it *is* true that your parents died in a murder-suicide when you were in jail here in Connecticut."

Lacey fixed her eyes on the woman's face, her hands fisting involuntarily. Pain exploded in the back of her brain, threatening to split her head in two. "I don't want to talk about my family."

"Okay. Then what do you think of the sentence reduction appeals that have been filed by the lawyers of your friends who are still in prison for Stephanie Green's murder?"

"I *don't* think about them. I don't know anything about it. Those are not my...I do *not* follow any of that. Look, you're here to interview me about my business. Let's stick to—"

"Since you've been back, have you been in contact with Stephanie Green's parents?"

Lacey stood up. "This interview is over."

The reporter didn't move from her chair. "What's your opinion of Kathy Green's run for office? Will she have your vote?"

Lacey moved toward the door. "I'm asking you to leave *now*."

"I'm giving you a chance to tell your side of the story, Lacey." Benita Gomez was not moving. "Did you know that Kathy Green speaks of you in the same breath with all the others? I was at one of her campaign events today. She referred to you as a cold-blooded—"

"*Out!*" Lacey said, boiling over.

"Is everything okay?"

Gavin was standing in the open doorway behind her, his coat

still on. Lacey glanced up at him, fighting back tears of fury. She'd been completely blindsided here.

"Would you *please* show Ms. Gomez to the door? We're done with our interview."

Lacey slipped past him and stormed off toward the kitchen.

CHAPTER EIGHTEEN

"THIS IS MY CELL PHONE NUMBER." The reporter handed Gavin a business card. "I'm doing a feature story on the Green case, with or without Miss Watkins's cooperation. It's up to her how she wants to come across in the article."

Forceful, ambitious, and intentionally blind to the consequences of her stories, Benita Gomez belonged to that breed of journalists that Gavin had run into occasionally during his career. The ones with serious aspirations of greatness. Those who would step on anyone on their way to the top. Collateral damage was not their problem.

He closed the door on her and tossed the card onto a table in the hall. He hung his jacket on the pegboard then went in search of Lacey.

She was in the kitchen.

"She *lied* to me," Lacey exploded as soon as he walked in.

Gavin's attention was drawn to the counters. It appeared that she had taken every box, bag, and spice bottle out of the cabinets. She'd done a half decent job of emptying the fridge too. An extra-large metal mixing bowl was on the kitchen table. She was throwing things into the bowl without pausing to measure anything.

"A lying *bitch*. She said she was doing an article on my business. *Liar!*"

Crossing his arms and leaning one shoulder against the door-jamb, he watched her. This was so much better than the vulnerable, defeated Lacey of just a few minutes ago. Her older sister used to have a wicked temper. Everyone at the department had given Terri a wide berth whenever she'd unleashed it. And Gavin was currently watching some shared family genes in action.

"No sense of principle. No respect. *Asshole!*"

An egg crashed against the side of the bowl and a chunk of the shell disappeared into a cloud of dry ingredients. She poured enough oil over the top to drown everything beneath it. He was starting to enjoy the show.

"How can she live with herself? What does she see when she looks in the mirror? *Such* a liar."

Diving elbow deep into the concoction, she started kneading like a madwoman. Liquid, flour, and egg sloshed over the sides, and lumps of gooey unrecognizable glop soon speckled her face and shirt.

"What, uh, exactly are you making?"

Her cheeks were bright red. The green eyes were spitting fire when they looked up to him. "Bread."

Gavin knew better than to smile when she reached up to push a strand of hair out of her face and left a streak of dough on her forehead.

"What kind of bread?"

"Let-me-beat-the-crap-out-of-lying-reporters   bread." She punched the mixture in the bowl, sending more of the mess flying.

"A good one."

"It's a variety of burn-out-my-frustration bread."

"Can't wait to taste it."

"The bread will be crap, but when I'm done, I'll be cool and collected."

His mind flashed back to the dream. For a split second, all he could think of what she'd be like having sex. Cool and collected? Or a fireball?

"You should start giving a class on this."

"Nothing here will be edible."

He disagreed, his gaze moving down the lines of buttons on the front of her shirt. They'd been about to have oral sex on the beach. Five more minutes of sleep this morning would have done it. He forced his thoughts out of the gutter. "I was thinking more like an anger management class."

"No one will call me when that woman is done exposing me. There will be no school pictures or family Christmas cards or wedding books or children's portraits or brochures for fancy health clubs. There will be no business left at all. She is going to take away the last shred of *me*." Each word was accentuated by a punch of the dough. "There will be *nothing* left."

Lacey stopped, looking at her hands, the counter, and the mess she'd created around her. She looked drained.

Gavin's gaze remained on her face as she struggled to pull a blanket of calm around herself. Her long lashes were blinking back tears and her skin was flushed.

Without looking at him, she eventually yanked the trash can out from under the sink and emptied the bowl of dough into it.

"I'm sorry. I lost it for a few minutes."

He stood quietly, giving her time and space to rein in her emotions.

"The picture that showed up on my computer. You were coming over to tell me what I should do about it."

Anyone else watching her might have thought that she *was* back in control, that her bread-making routine had worked. But it'd be a lie. She washed her hands in the sink and then picked up a sponge, starting to wipe down the mess on the counters and the table. She was trying so hard to keep her composure intact, but she was teetering on the edge.

He knew Lacey had no other family in Connecticut. He doubted if she had any close friends, either. There'd been no one with her at the funeral. It didn't take skilled insight to know she was alone and feeling it right now.

Everyone needed consoling sometimes. Everyone needed to know that there was someone else out there who cared. But Gavin didn't trust himself to walk over to Lacey and just hold her in his arms. Besides, Farah Aziz was waiting for Lacey's call.

He had to tell her. He had to stick to business. "Do you know a person named Fay Stone?"

Lacey straightened up beside the counter. The green eyes tried to focus on his face.

"Fay Stone? Probation Officer Fay Stone?" Her words were barely a whisper.

The sponge slipped through her fingers and dropped to the floor. She wobbled. For an instant, he thought she was going to pass out. He was at her side in two quick steps, taking her arm. Beads of sweat ran down her face, but her skin was freezing cold.

"Sit here." He pulled out a chair and sat her in it. "Put your head down and take deep breaths. I'll get you something to drink."

Gavin searched the cabinets and found a glass. He filled it with tap water. She was sitting where he'd left her, motionless, her eyes closed. He wasn't sure she was breathing. He pressed the glass against her fingers.

"Here you go."

She opened her eyes, and he saw tears drop before she was able to blink them away. Her hands closed around the glass.

"Drink it."

She took a long sip.

Gavin was afraid she would sink to the floor if he stepped away. He pulled up another chair and sat down, facing her. His knees trapped hers. His hands cupped her elbows. He was close enough that she could lean into him if she wanted.

"Drink all of it."

This close, he realized that her eyes were a dark crystalline green. More beautiful than he'd thought. Her lips were full and soft. He reached up and wiped a patch of dough from her silky skin. The red mark left behind was more than a hint of the fragility that existed beneath her thin outer shell.

She put the glass on the table.

"Fay." She folded her hands and stared at them. "After I got out of jail, Fay Stone was my probation officer for the six months that I was still in Connecticut."

He took her hands in his. They were ice cold. He was relieved when she didn't pull away. "The picture on your computer?"

"It could be Fay. Now I can see it. It could be her. It *is* her."

"When was the last time you saw her or spoke to her?" Gavin asked.

"I ran into her a couple of months ago, coming out of the library in New Milford. She recognized me. We chatted for a while, catching up on my news. Then I saw her again last week. She'd heard about Terri and called me. We went out for coffee here in town. She wanted to bring her niece over for a sitting. Christmas pictures."

"Was there ever any problem between you two?"

"Problem?" She met his gaze. "No. She was one of the only good things I recall about my supposed rehabilitation. She made it easier for me to leave Connecticut, pushed to have my probation period reduced. She wrote glowing reports about me. She... she was kind to me. Happy for me that I was back in Connecticut and trying to make my business work."

The tension was easing in her. He could feel it. He let go of her hands, and she pushed her chair back, getting up and giving herself distance. She wasn't ready to be this close.

"When was that picture taken?" she asked, her voice trembling slightly as she turned around by the sink to face him.

"Last night."

A hand went to her mouth. It took a few long moments before any words escaped her. "The photo was downloaded to my computer last night. It's me. Terri is dead. Now Fay. Someone is killing innocent people to get at me."

"Do you have an attorney, Lacey? A person you can trust?"

Realization locked her gaze on him. There was the slightest shake of her head.

"I have a name and a phone number." He opened the contact information on his phone. He told her about the conversation he'd already had with Farah Aziz. "I think it's really important that you speak to her before calling the police again."

He went on to explain how investigations worked. It would be in her best interest to already have representation, as it was obvious someone was targeting her for whatever purpose.

Lacey stood there, listening. She reminded him of a narrow sea wall with hurricane force winds and waves bashing away at her, washing over her.

"Farah wants you to call her right away."

Lacey picked up the cell phone off the counter and walked over to him. Looking at his phone, she dialed the number. Farah must have answered right away; Lacey left the kitchen, her voice low, her spirit clearly crushed.

Gavin ran a hand down the back of his neck. Her desperation was cutting more deeply into him than he would have imagined. He'd be a fool to try to analyze it. Loyalty, debt, guilt, attraction. Whatever the motivation was, it didn't matter. He was *going* to help Lacey get through this.

He stood. The supplies for her bake-and-box workout were still scattered around the kitchen. Even as he started putting things away, his mind was already organizing the *who* and the *why* possibilities behind the photos and the killings.

There was one obvious answer. Stephanie Green's murder. He had to get his hands on those case files.

CHAPTER NINETEEN

"WHAT DO you think they're doing in there?"

Amy pulled out the ear buds, closed her laptop, and spun the receptionist's chair around. She batted at empty air. "You're not supposed to be back here, Nick."

"Who's going to kick me out?"

"Me." Her hands were trapped against her chest as Nick kissed her firmly on the lips. He groped her breast before pulling back.

"Let's have sex right here."

Amy tried to push him away. "You are going to get me fired. People can see us from the weight room."

Nick had been replacing ceiling tiles in there this afternoon because of some water damage.

"There's no one in the weight room."

"Donna is here today. She's going to come around and—"

"I'd say she's otherwise engaged," Nick whispered into her ear. "Let's see. Donna and Ron Marteka locked up in her office with the blinds down." Donna's was the first of four glass-fronted offices behind the reception area. "It's been at least half an hour. What do you think they're doing?"

"Come on," she asked. "You think Ron and Donna are an item?"

"I wouldn't go that far," Nick corrected. "But they definitely are having sex. Lots of it. Or at least, they used to."

"But Ron is married," Amy told him. "I was introduced to his wife Veronica my first day on this job."

"Yep. And I'll tell you something not everyone knows. She's the daughter of Boss Man Bratva. Ron married her right out of high school," Nick told her. "So, getting a little on the side with Donna is not too swift, considering his father-in-law's reputation. They'll find him floating in New Haven harbor if he doesn't smarten up."

"Seriously? Veronica's father is a criminal?"

"Uh, yeah. Totally connected. They say he's the top mob boss along the shoreline."

"Scary."

"To you. But I guess not so much to Ron. He's stupid and a player at the same time. Act straight. The blinds are going up. I'm getting back to my job."

Amy tried to look nonchalant, and a moment later she heard the door to Donna's office open.

"We'll talk later," Donna said in a hushed tone from the office.

"What are you? Stupid? I'm done talking." Ron's voice was harsh. "Finished. Push me and I'll..."

He marched off without finishing the sentence. Amy recognized Donna's light step behind her.

"How is it going?" she asked in a tense tone. "Any phone calls?"

"No, it's been really quiet. But I'm getting ready for the after work rush," she said.

On the other side of the counter, Ron moved toward the door.

"Hey, Ron." Nick's voice came from the direction of the weight room. "How's it going?"

"Good. You?"

"Okay. How's my truck coming?"

"It's coming."

"Glad to hear it," Nick said good-naturedly, stopping in front of the counter. "But I've been waiting forever to get that baby out of your body shop. When are you looking at finishing it up?"

"I'm still waiting for the front fender. It should come in next week."

"That's what you said two weeks ago."

"Look, pal, if you're unhappy with the service, take it somewhere else. That's the best I can do."

CHAPTER TWENTY

BY FIVE O'CLOCK THAT AFTERNOON, Lacey had no doubt that she was in trouble. But at least now she had a team around her and a game plan.

Farah Aziz was one of those attorneys that Lacey could only imagine on some TV lawyer show—calm, confident, and reassuring. They had spoken a number of times on the phone today. Her fees were steep. But surprisingly, all Farah asked for to get started was a small credit card transaction. By early afternoon, she had a technical assistant at Lacey's house. The young woman had collected her computer, and at the same time, she had done an overhaul of the system security and set up an old laptop that she could use to communicate with clients.

Now she had to use a twenty-four-character password in order to get online. Also, a separate guest log-in had been set up for Amy. And the firewall prevented anyone from getting access without her permission.

Feeling a bit more in control, she had to figure out all the costs and how she would be able to afford all this help. But that was a headache for another sleepless night.

Gavin spent the day at the house, taking over the living room and conducting his own business. For Lacey, it was a relief to be able to walk in and ask the questions that kept popping into her head. She was walking a tightrope and it was essential not to miss a step.

Spending a couple of hours in her office after Farah's assistant left, Lacey finally caught up with the email and phone messages from her existing clients. There were no new queries except Donna's, and that only took a couple of minutes to put together.

By six o'clock her stomach was growling, but she called Amy first and gave her a watered-down version of what was going on. She also told her the new information on the Internet connection.

"I already have a call in to an alarm company. They're supposed to let me know how soon they can come over and install a system. There'll be one installed in your apartment too."

"That sounds great."

"I don't mean to scare you, but is there anyone staying with you for the weekend? I'd hate to have you all alone back there."

"You sound like my mother," Amy quipped.

"I have serious reason to be worried," Lacey said. "You can come stay in the guest room at the house. Please, Amy."

"I'll call Nick right now. He won't refuse if I tell him you're worried."

Lacey liked Nick, though she worried that Amy was setting herself up for heartbreak once the good-looking carpenter decided to move on. "Starting tonight?"

"He was planning to come over anyway."

"Good."

Relieved, she closed the laptop and swung her chair around. Gavin was leaning against the doorway watching her. The twist of a knot deep in her stomach had been a common occurrence today. She couldn't look at him without going a little soft in the knees. It was crazy.

"You've given me no lunch or dinner. I'm starving. Do you have anything good to eat or drink in this house?"

"I don't think so. But I can check." Pushing to her feet, she started for the door. "What qualifies as good?"

His dark gaze followed her. Lacey was insecure about her limp, but he somehow managed to make her feel like she was some Victoria's Secret model working the catwalk.

"Your coffee doesn't."

She backhanded him in the stomach. She might as well have hit a rock. "I didn't hear you complain when you were chugging down the last pot I made."

"I couldn't keep my eyes open."

Lacey slipped past him into the hall and glanced into the living room. His laptop sat open and loose pages of paper were scattered around the coffee table. The imprint of his body on the sofa told her he'd been lying down.

"It was way too comfortable in there." He moved behind her. The brush of his breath tickled her ear. "Now I have enough caffeine in my system to stay up all night."

The words made the knot move deeper in her belly. She had no doubt what he meant. Her body tingled all over.

"You get back to work. I'll check the fridge."

"I'm done for today."

He followed her into the kitchen. Lacey had to switch gears and get her mind off Gavin's charms. She didn't know how long she could resist him. She didn't know how long she'd want to. And this wasn't like her.

"Do you think they're going to come after me with sirens blasting?" she asked, opening the fridge door, putting it in between them.

"I don't think they're going to come here, at all," he said. "This is what will happen. Farah calls the police and reports the picture. They already have your fingerprints on file from before. But they might try to ask for a DNA sample if they don't already have a suspect in custody. That's when your attorney reads them the riot act that they're violating your rights."

"You make it sound so non-threatening."

"Farah knows what she's doing." He picked up the empty mugs from the kitchen table, and set them in the sink. "Don't worry about the cops. You're a victim here. Try to remember that."

She felt chilled deep in her bones and wished she could stop worrying, even for a short time. First Terri. Then Fay Stone. Who would be next? She worried about everyone around her. And right now, Amy topped her list.

"You're standing before an open fridge and shivering." He smiled at her. "Come here and I'll warm you up."

"Food." She hurriedly leaned into the fridge. A six-pack of beer and half a bottle of white wine—leftovers from Terri's last visit—were the only things in there. "I'm about a century overdue for major grocery shopping."

She closed the door and leaned against it. "I'm sorry, but I guess we should call it a night."

"My offer for dinner still stands." Gavin walked toward her. "How about us going out and having a sit-down dinner someplace nice? My treat."

Lacey tried to think of an excuse. "I don't know."

Was it the invitation or his approach that made her hesitate? She took a step toward the kitchen door, but her hip came up against the cabinets. There was nowhere to go.

"It's only dinner. I don't bite."

She had to tilt her head back to look up into his face. That was a mistake. She wasn't accustomed to men with his type of high-voltage attractiveness. "I got no sleep last night. I'll be dozing off at dinner and embarrass you in public."

"You can take a nap on our way there. I'll drive." He put a hand on the small of her back, pushing her toward the door. She felt the heat of his fingers through her cotton shirt.

"Where are we going?" she asked, moving despite her common sense.

He mentioned a steak house in Litchfield.

She looked down at her clothes. Old jeans and a plaid oxford shirt. "Can I at least go change?"

"So long as you don't fall asleep upstairs. I'm not beyond coming up after you. And then I *might* just bite."

His voice poured over her with suggestiveness. The ex-detective, private investigator, Gavin MacFadyen was going for the kill and she was playing along with it.

The prospect was thrilling and terrifying. Lacey didn't know if she should jump with joy or go dig a hole six-feet deep to hide in until he gave up on her. "I'll be down in ten minutes."

"I'll wait in the car. Keep your bedroom shade open."

CHAPTER TWENTY-ONE

THE SUN SINKING in the west burst like flames through the brilliantly colored trees. Beyond them, the light shimmered across the surface of the blood red lake. Instead of heat, a chill rose from the glassy surface on every breeze, brushing across skin and scalp, cutting through to the bone, a reminder that winter and death lay ahead.

Following a well-trodden path along the shoreline, the lines of a Poe story ran through Judge Green's head, as they had a thousand times before.

I vowed revenge. I must punish...

An enemy lured into a wine cellar during Carnival. Revenge. Brick by brick, walling in a fool. Revenge.

The deep lines on the weathered face. The hollow eyes of a lost soul. The stooped shoulders of a broken man. This wandering phantom had little in common with the confident, powerful man who once presided from the bench of the state's courts.

He cared about none of that now. He wanted only one thing.

Judge Green stopped. A black stream lay just ahead, descending from the wooded hills. Rushing through a smoothed rock channel, dropping to a pool, and then flowing quickly through a jumble of boulders, the sound of the gurgling water blocked out any other noise. It was the sound of a girl's blood pumping from a severed vein.

He looked out at the lake as the sun cast one final ray of light across the water before dropping below the line of distant hills. And then shadow enveloped it all.

I vowed revenge. I vowed revenge.

CHAPTER TWENTY-TWO

GAVIN LOOKED from the white-knuckled hands twisted in Lacey's lap to her silhouette as she gazed out the window of the car. She was afraid and he didn't blame her. He'd tried to lighten the mood any chance he got, but her worry was legit. Lacey's past had been well south of normal or safe, a far cry from anything he would wish on his worst enemy. And now—lonely, aching with grief, and afraid—she was trying to hold herself together.

His attraction to her was growing. He'd already decided he wanted more than sex. He knew in some ways it was his stupid male need to protect, the hardwired desire to give her a shoulder to cry on and to fill the obvious void she had in her life, but there was something else going on in him as well. He could feel it.

But he had to be patient. She was a runner. And he knew all about being a runner. His sister, Elsie, had been one.

"We're here," he said quietly, pulling into a parking space on the street in front of the restaurant.

She unclipped the seatbelt and pulled the visor down, taking a quick peek at her face before pushing it back up.

"Are you okay?"

She nodded and got out of the car before he could come around to help her.

Gavin had called before they left her house and, since it was Friday night, the only available seating was in the bar. He'd eaten here a number of times before. The food was decent and the menu was the same, regardless of where they served you.

Lacey stayed in his shadow as they were ushered through the crowded restaurant. When they reached one of the tables lining the wall, she chose the seat facing the wall, giving him the view of the restaurant.

"Is this okay?" he asked her.

"It's great."

He helped her shed the fleece jacket she was wearing, thoroughly appreciating the red, low-neck sweater she wore over jeans. Too bad he hadn't talked her into ordering take-out. There was plenty of the room on the sofa in the living room for the two of them.

"I can't remember the last time I went out for dinner."

Before taking his own seat, Gavin shot an annoyed glare at a loud foursome of men standing by the bar a few feet away. The two facing them were eying Lacey with too much interest.

"You and Terri spent every weekend together after you came back to Connecticut. Don't tell me that cheapskate wouldn't go out to eat."

"You can't be talking this way about my sister."

"Oh, yeah." He nodded as a busboy brought glasses of water for them. "She always packed her lunch. Brought coffee from home. She wouldn't go out for lunch or for drinks after work for anything unless she was sure someone else was picking up the tab."

"She must have had her reasons because she was very generous when it came to me."

"Cheapskate," he repeated.

A hint of a smile touched her lips. "We didn't go out because we had a lot of work to do on the house. Redoing the bathroom, the kitchen. Painting inside and out. So we ordered in a lot. But I also like to cook. I did a lot of it for the two of us."

"Seriously?" He deadpanned. "I've seen you in action in the kitchen."

"Hey," she drawled, her smile widening. "I was angry this morning. That was therapy."

"Yeah. I heard you."

"I'm actually a decent cook when I set my mind to it. Sometime maybe I'll cook for you so you can judge for yourself."

Gavin found himself staring. He loved it when she let her guard down. His gaze moved down the stretch of her neck to the neckline of the sweater and a small patch of black lace peeking above. She had perfect breasts. *Easy, champ*, he told himself, glancing around.

The waitress glided up, ready to take their drink orders. Lacey was fine with the water. He ordered a beer.

"You don't drink?" he asked.

"I haven't for a long time. Not since...not since it's been legal for me to drink. No alcohol, no drugs." She shrugged, reaching for the water glass. "I don't miss them either."

"Do you mind that I ordered a beer?"

"Not at all. Terri drank. But she always brought her own to the house."

He watched her sip the water. A droplet clung to her lip. The flame of the candle burning in the hurricane lamp on their table danced a shadow between them. She had one of those faces that, the more you looked at it, the more you appreciated the symmetry, the exotic way it all fit together. Without even trying, she was a stunner.

"You stare at me a lot. Is that because I look like Terri?" she asked, her emerald gaze locking with his.

"You don't look like Terri."

"Sure we do. Everyone said so."

"Then they were being generous to your sister," he said frankly. "There are some similarities, but I thought I'd made it clear why I stare at you."

Lacey blushed, her gaze following the movement of her fingers as she reached for the glass of water again. "Terri told me you were divorced."

"So, she talked about my personal life with you," Gavin said. "And what dark secrets did she tell you?"

"None. I'm sorry. I shouldn't have brought it up. It's none of my business. It—"

"No. I'm glad you did," he said, interrupting her. "Yes, I was married and divorced in my late twenties. It lasted less than two years."

The arrival of the waitress with his drink curtailed that conversation. Neither of them had looked at the menu. Rather than sending her away, Lacey took a quick glance and placed her order. Gavin ordered what he always had.

"Where were we?" he asked, liking the fact that she was interested enough to bring up his personal life.

"I'm paying for dinner," she said instead. "Also, I'd appreciate it if you'd give me some kind of ballpark figure of your fee."

"I told you last night. You're not paying me."

"Last night it was not as complicated as it is now. You already spent the day with me. You found me an attorney."

"Stop." He reached for her hand across the table and took it firmly in his own. "This is not a business dinner. You aren't going to hire me to do what I'm already doing."

"But—"

"No billable hours. No talk of money. This is a friend helping a friend. That's what this is. I'd appreciate it if you'd just accept that."

"That arrangement might have worked with Terri since you two were partners. She would have somehow reciprocated. But with me, I don't know how I can repay you. So, no thanks."

"You really are stubborn, you know that?"

"I consider that a compliment." She smiled, freeing her hand and hiding it under the table.

"Well, it wasn't," he said in mock criticism. He studied her for a moment longer, forcing his mind to follow a professional track.

"Okay, I have an idea. All the jobs I've landed so far have been through word-of-mouth. We'll barter this deal. You can help me with a promotional package for my business. Something like flyers, advertising, what should go on the webpage. I haven't done anything like that. I could use something classy."

"So, no people in handcuffs."

"No. And no shots of gorgeous, naked women through their bedroom windows either."

She bit her bottom lip, a blush spreading on her cheeks. "That's good to know."

"Not as high-rent as a Pinkerton marketing campaign, but a little more professional than some college kid playing Sherlock Holmes."

"No Sherlock Holmes." She smiled. "You may lose some British royals from your client list."

"I'm willing to risk that." He got serious. "Right now, I'm doing event security to pay the rent. But the area I'd really like to get into is investigating missing persons." He wondered for a moment if Terri had told her about his little sister.

"That's sounds like a pretty dignified way of making money in your business. Will that pay the rent?"

"I don't know. We'll see how good your flyers are. Deal?"

She nodded. They both went silent when their waitress came back with a basket of bread.

"How about you?" he asked. "Do you see yourself continuing to build the photography business?"

She shrugged. "Buying Brett Orr's business was an excuse for my sister and me to get back together. But now, with Terri gone, I'm not sure what I'm doing back here in Connecticut. So, I don't know. And I might not have much of a choice once that reporter tells everyone who I am."

"You might be giving her too much credit. The people in Westbury might already know who you are. Maybe they don't care."

"There are a lot of new families in town. I'd put my money on the fact that most people *don't* know of my past. I guarantee that my life *will* be different after my past is exposed. It'll be miserable."

She took a piece of bread and made a production of buttering it, but then left it untouched on the plate.

"If you were going to move, where would you go? Back to the Midwest?" he asked.

"No. There's nothing for me there, either. Never was."

"I remember Terri mentioning you were going to school."

"Part time. Community college. And then later, state college," she told him, playing with the same piece of bread. "I got my degree, but there were no jobs, so I went back and took all these classes in photography. I never belonged out there. I never built a foundation. No career. No friends or community. Nothing even close to it. I'm not sure I want to go back to that."

She needed something permanent. A steady, healthy relationship. At one time, the circumstances of Lacey's life would have had him steering clear. But right now, it was having the opposite effect.

"You know, this is the difference between me and my sister. Terri always knew what she wanted to do. Who she wanted to be. Where to live. Today, tomorrow, five years down the road, or fifty. She was a planner and a doer. She had a good, reliable road map for everything she did. At the opposite end of the spectrum, there's me. I'm pretty good at acting on impulse, avoiding conflict, and not making decisions. Commitment really hasn't been my thing. It still isn't."

Gavin wondered if the last was intended as a warning. "Don't sell yourself short. You've been through a lot."

"You don't have to make excuses for me," she said in an earnest tone. "I'm thirty-one years old. There are no safety nets left. I have to live in the real world."

He wanted to tell her that, considering the circumstances of her teenage years, she'd done pretty well. But Gavin knew that wasn't what she needed right now. Still, she also didn't need to wallow in more gloom.

"Thirty-one. That's all?" he asked instead, snatching the bread she'd buttered off her plate and taking a bite of it before putting it on his own plate. "I didn't realize I was robbing the cradle by asking you out."

She watched him with some amusement. "How old are you? Sixty-five?"

Gavin almost choked on the bread. "You know how to hurt a guy."

She leaned her elbows on the table, smiling. "I was just kidding. You were at the minimum age when you opted for the twenty-year retirement plan. So how old are you now? Forty-two, forty-three?"

"Forty-three," he told her.

"That's safe enough. I doubt you'll croak on me at dinner."

The image of the two of them locked away in a bedroom flashed in his mind. His gaze moved down to the neckline of the sweater again.

"I won't croak on you anytime. Or doze off in my rocker, either. I'm Watkins coffee-fortified and ready to go all night."

She laughed and sipped her water. "You're bad."

"Thank you."

Their salads arrived. Lacey straightened the silverware on her placemat before looking up at him again. "I do have a question for you."

"Shoot."

"What's your impression of me?"

This was no sexual overture. She was serious. A lot of what Gavin knew of her had been shaped by what he'd learned from Terri. But last night and today had given him ideas of his own too.

"Do I answer that as a man or as a potential client?" he asked.

"Client, of course. Didn't you just ask me to help with your marketing?"

"Yes, I did," he replied, though he'd have preferred to go the other way.

"Being a business owner is still new to me," she pressed. "I need to know whether I come across as professional and confident. As someone people can trust to do a good job. And please forget how I treated that reporter this afternoon. I should have done a better job of controlling my temper."

"I already hired you, didn't I? So I'd say you are all of that."

She waved him off and took the rest of her bread back, this time nibbling on it. "You had an ulterior motive for hiring me."

She'd guessed.

Gavin didn't have a chance to say anything more as a white-haired couple led through the bar by a hostess came to a full stop at their table.

"Lacey! What a small world. I was just telling Barb this afternoon that we should swing by your house and see how you're doing these days."

Gavin was introduced to Brett Orr and his wife. Busybodies, for sure, but openly caring. They wanted to know everything that she'd been up to and what Gavin's connection was to her. Lacey was polite and personable. At the same time, she didn't make any mention of the problems she'd had this week.

"Can we sit here at this table?" Brett asked the hostess, motioning at the open table next to theirs.

Gavin didn't miss the disappointed glance Lacey sent him.

CHAPTER TWENTY-THREE

MORE THAN A DOZEN luxury cars lined the circular driveway of the stately waterfront house. The place belonged to Bratva, or rather to a paper corporation created by the crime boss's lawyers. Three valets stood together at the front steps, smoking and waiting for new arrivals. The house and drive were both invisible from the road, hidden by stone walls and a stretch of dense evergreens. The gated entrance of the property was blocked by an SUV with two armed men inside.

Select invitees paid premium prices to attend events held here. Tonight, promised high-stakes gambling, plenty of recreational drugs, and a nice selection of young women, girls, and boys to satisfy each guest's particular tastes.

It was early yet. Most of the people on tonight's guest list had yet to arrive. But as always, there were a few who'd stopped in before going on to other engagements.

Bonnie, one of the managers overseeing tonight's event, was in the butler's pantry off the kitchen when her walkie-talkie crackled to life. She was needed upstairs. As she started toward the mansion's back stairs, she knew right away the trouble had to be in the bedroom overlooking Long Island Sound.

It was always him.

The client, a gentleman in his sixties, was a bruiser who liked to play rough with the girls. His escort, just fourteen, had been brought up from Maryland this past week.

A second call advised that she should hurry.

The timing could not have been worse. People were arriving. A disturbance could have them bolting for their cars.

She ran upstairs.

"*SHUT THE FUCK UP!*" the heavyset man bellowed in the open doorway to the bedroom before turning around and spotting Bonnie hurrying down the hall.

Two of her assistants were standing across the hallway, looking helpless.

"What the hell is this?" he shouted. "Listen to this racket. She sounds like a wounded animal. And I can't shut her up."

Bonnie heard the sharp wail piercing the air. The cry of a child in pain.

"If you would just step into the room across the hall, sir," Bonnie suggested, noticing that the client was stark naked. "I'll get your clothes."

"Your boss is going to hear about this. Total bullshit. You supposed to screen these girls."

"I know, sir. I apologize. This will never happen again." She opened the door to the room for him. "If you'd be kind enough to wait here, we'll send you up a different girl."

"I don't want any old hag. No saggy titted—"

"No. No. No. Of course not. Please, if you'd just wait in here."

As the man stepped in, Bonnie closed the door and sent her assistant running.

The girl's howling cries had not lessened. Bonnie went in and closed the door behind her. Every light inside the spacious bedroom was lit. The girl was curled up in a ball at the bottom of the bed, sobbing, a sheet pulled up to cover herself.

"Hey, hey, what's all this noise??" she scolded in a soft tone, gathering up the client's clothing from the chair and floor. A used condom had been tossed by the foot of the bed. She opened the door and handed the clothes to the waiting attendant. She closed the door again.

"First time is the hardest, baby. But it will get better."

From experience, she knew that soft talk, the promise of a shopping trip, and some babying worked best. These girls either needed a *boyfriend* that they would work for or they needed someone to mother them. For now, this one needed Bonnie.

Young girls with baby faces and large firm breasts were hot. This girl—what was her name?—could be back on the job in a couple of hours if Bonnie could work her magic.

She pulled the sheet off the girl and saw the blood on the mattress. It had already soaked through. "It's okay, honey. They're never like him. Just let me take care of you."

With her knees drawn up to her chest in defense, the girl refused to look up.

"Let me see." Bonnie sat on the edge of the bed and took the girl's chin and lifted it. Fat fingers had left a large bruise across her mouth. Her lip was bleeding. And there were other marks too, on her side, her back, her bottom. She would not be working again tonight.

"Bastard. He beat you, didn't he?"

The howling had subsided to soft whimpers and tears leaking from closed eyes.

"Come on. Come with me. Let's clean you up." She took the girl's hand and physically pulled her off the bed and into the bathroom. Turning on the water in the spacious shower, she ushered her in.

They had few rules, but they were clear. A client paid more for a first-time girl. But no one marked the merchandise. She sailed into the hall and paged Sergei, one of the male house managers, to come up.

This type of thing happened more often than they liked. Often enough that protocol had been set on how to deal with it. The same manager wouldn't approach the client. They wanted the creep to know that everyone in the house knew what he'd done.

Pacing back and forth in the hall until Sergei came up, Bonnie explained what had happened. He would make sure the guest was charged appropriately for the loss.

Going back inside the room, she heard the shower still running. Bonnie had been doing this job long enough to recognize the look she'd seen in the girl's face. It was that wretched *I'm going to do something stupid like cut my wrist or overdose on pills* look. There was an investment in these girls—bringing them in, conditioning them, feeding, housing, and clothing them. Each girl had to produce a return on that investment or it came out of Bonnie's percentage. This girl would not be allowed to hurt or snuff herself. That definitely wasn't going to happen. Corpses made Bonnie's job very difficult...because corpses didn't earn.

Walking around the bed, she started pulling off the bedding. The mattress was stained with blood too. She'd have to get one of the boys to flip it.

Bonnie was about to go into the bathroom and check on the girl when her walkie-talkie crackled again.

"We got uniforms at the gate."

"What do they want?" Bonnie went to the window and peered out. She couldn't see anything from here.

"They say they got a 911 call from the house."

Bonnie looked sharply at the open bathroom door. The shower was still running. Right from where she was standing, she could see a wall phone next to the mirror. Under it, there was a puddle of water on the granite floor.

"Stall them."

Bonnie took out her cell phone and dialed the number of her contact in the police department. He answered.

"Call off your dogs. They're at the house."

"What did you do now? Who the hell called them?"

"That's none of your goddamn business," she responded sharply. "Get them out of our hair."

"Hey, don't forget, I work for Bratva too. You could show some—"

"Save it, pig boy. I hear you're in a shitload of trouble," Bonnie threatened. "Alisha didn't have the list on her that she stole. Your job was to get it back."

"Look, I'm not the one who fucking lost it."

"But you'd better get it back. And soon."

"I'm working on it."

"Yeah, do that. But for right now, get that goddamn police car away from this property."

CHAPTER TWENTY-FOUR

"I BET you never had any idea that I'm the proud owner of three umbrella lighting kits, all different sizes, thanks to Brett Orr," Lacey said, breaking the silence in the car.

"That's true. I'm impressed."

All during their dinner, she had been very aware of Gavin. He had constantly watched her through those thick, dark lashes. He was attentive, thoughtful, and making moves on her while being funny. His demeanor didn't overtly change, even after Brett and his wife had been seated, for all intents and purposes, at their table. The brush of his fingers or the bump of his knee. His hand on her back when they were leaving the restaurant. Later, a whisper in her ear, his lips touching the sensitive skin of her neck as he opened the door of his SUV for her.

Heat had rushed through her body. And now, this silence that spoke volumes about the current that was running between them. Her fingers were shards of ice, but her face was on fire. And there was the extra *thump* in her heart every time his dark eyes drifted off the road and glanced in her direction.

"And there are two more busted umbrellas that he gave me at no charge."

"Fascinating," Gavin replied.

"Yes, they're sitting in the basement."

"Wow. Actually, it was pretty impressive that he could recite the entire list of equipment he sold you. The burning question is, what will you do with those nine electronic timers?"

"Only one of them works," she admitted, more at ease not thinking about what would happen once they got back to her house. Would he expect her to invite him in? Could she resist his pull or the reaction of her own body? "I didn't want to ruin Brett's night by saying so."

"Actually, I'm most impressed with what I learned about backlit portraits," he added. "I'd say, after that dinner, I'm now qualified to start my own photography business."

"I'll sell you mine." She couldn't let this go in the direction she knew they were going; she couldn't afford to let things go too far. Lacey knew how her mind worked. Before the two of them got anywhere near first base, she'd be planning an escape route aimed at never seeing him again. No, she needed him to do what he was already doing for her because she had no idea what she'd do if it weren't for his help.

"Sell me yours? Hell, no. What, can't handle a little bit of competition? Scared?"

Less thinking and more talking. She repeated the words in her mind.

"Yes, I'm scared."

The words tumbled out of her mouth as the conversation they were having merged with the high-speed chase going on in her head.

He was looking at her. His tone had downshifted to a more serious gear when he spoke again. "You shouldn't be scared. There's nothing scary about me."

"I know. But I like to keep you as a friend. Nothing more."

"We can keep it at that." The dark eyes lingered on her face for an extra beat.

"Okay. Good."

"Could you give me a reason?"

"Because it's safer that way. It doesn't complicate things. That's all...that's the most I can handle right now."

The car passed the road sign for Westbury. They were a couple of miles away from her house. She stuffed her fingers under her legs, trying to warm them before she'd have to leave the car. A handshake. That was all.

He didn't press her or try to change her mind. If he was disappointed, he didn't show it. She should have been relieved. She *was* relieved. But she was also sad too. Sad for herself. To live like this left no room for daydreaming, no chance for romance. She never would allow herself to get close enough to any man to even dream of falling in love. Perhaps, if she were constructed more like her sister, she could find comfort and affection in another woman's embrace. On the surface that seemed so much less threatening. But even for Terri, there had been no happily ever after. No soul mate. The two of them were screwed up for life because of their childhood.

Lacey pushed the power button, lowering the window. She hoped the cold autumn air would stop the sudden rush of emotions bringing tears to her eyes. When did she allow herself to get so soft?

She needed to change the subject. "I was thinking that tomorrow I'd go down to New Haven...to Terri's apartment. The rent is paid until the end of this month. But I think it's time to sort through her things and make arrangements."

He slowed the car and turned onto her road. "Didn't you tell me before that you haven't been back there since the funeral?"

"That's right. I spoke to the building manager on the phone after things calmed down. And I filled out the form at the post office, so her mail is being forwarded here. She never had a dog or a cat, not even a goldfish. And when it came to houseplants, she boasted her specialty was killing them, so I didn't worry about going back."

"The first time in there will be the hardest," he told her as the car crawled slowly into her gravel driveway. "Give me a call in the morning and I'll meet you there if you like."

Lacey could use the help. In some ways Gavin knew Terri better than she did. He'd spent more time with her in recent years. But Lacey was terrified of her own reaction. What would happen if she fell apart?

"Thank you for the offer," Lacey said quietly. "I think I'll be okay. I'll call you if something comes up."

The SUV rolled up next to Lacey's parked car.

Before they even stopped, a rank smell wafted in through the open window. It wasn't a skunk. It was something dead. She glanced toward the front porch. The lights were off.

"You left those lights on when we went out," Gavin said, reading her mind.

She heard the click of the door, double testing the lock. Her window went up from his side panel, and he immediately backed the car up and inched forward, cutting the wheel until the high beam of the headlights shone on the front porch.

A decomposing animal had clearly been left on her welcome mat, the size of a raccoon or maybe a cat. From this distance, there was no identifying it.

"You must have had a visitor while we were gone."

"This is not the first time. I've found two other dead animals before." Lacey watched him as he pulled a gun out from under his seat and loaded a clip into it. He seemed calm, all concentration as his gaze swept across the house and the woods.

"On your doorstep?"

"No, but on the property. One was on the driveway. Another was on the path Amy takes to walk to the house."

"Your admirer is getting bold. He even knocked out the lights on the porch." The dark eyes turned at her direction. "Where's your phone?"

She scrambled for her purse and took out the cell phone. "Right here."

"Your house key?"

She reached in again and came out with the keychain. Lacey realized her hand was trembling when she singled out the specific key that opened the front door. She handed it to him. "This one."

"Good. Move behind the wheel and lock the door when I get out. You see or hear *anything* unusual, and you gun the car out of the driveway. Hear me?"

"Leaving you here?" Lacey looked around them at the dark woods surrounding the house. The light she'd left on inside in her kitchen was still on. "I don't think you should get out."

"Lacey." His sharp tone snapped her attention to him. "This is what I do. Now do as I told you."

Gavin called 911 first and, in a clipped tone, reported the incident. She scrambled over the console and got behind the wheel when he got out. He'd left the car running. He knocked sharply on the window and Lacey locked the door.

She watched him move across the drive, his flashlight fixed on the carcass on the porch. The temperature in the car must have fallen by a hundred degrees because she could hear her teeth chattering. She felt sick to her stomach. She couldn't drive away. She wouldn't. Already, two people were dead because of her.

Gavin cast a cursory glance at the animal before checking the lights. They stayed out.

Her phone buzzed and Lacey's stomach jumped into her throat. She glanced at the display. It was Farah Aziz. She looked up as Gavin left the porch and walked along the front of the house, looking in windows as he went. She decided to answer the phone. Before the attorney could explain the reason for the call, Lacey told her what was going on.

"Did you call the police?" Farah asked.

Her voice wouldn't come out. Lacey realized she couldn't see Gavin anymore. He was going around to the back. But what would happen if someone was waiting for him there?

"Talk to me, Lacey," the attorney demanded.

"I'm here."

"Where is Gavin?" Farah asked.

She explained.

"Can you see him?"

Lacey held her breath for the longest moment. And then let it out with relief when she saw him appear around the other corner of the house. He stepped back to the porch again and opened her front door.

"He's back. He just went inside the house." She turned on the heat to high. "And yes, he called the police before getting out of the car. But there's still no sign of them."

"I'm glad he called. I want one of those Westbury uniforms to log this into their books. Someone is harassing you. Someone wants you to be scared."

And they were succeeding. Those words that had started it all wouldn't leave her mind. *Road Kill.* From where she was sitting, she could track Gavin's movement through the house by the lights turning on and off.

"The reason I called," the attorney continued. "I reported the photograph of Fay Stone that showed up on your computer. And tonight, I've already had some back-and-forth conversations with the New Milford PD and the State Police."

Lacey's gaze was drawn to the upstairs window when her bedroom light went on. As she saw Gavin's silhouette pass by, she felt a fleeting moment of embarrassment, recalling this was the view he had when she'd been parading around after her shower last night.

"...they knew they were walking a slippery slope when they asked for your DNA sample."

"DNA?" Lacey asked, her attention returning to the phone. An additional worry pitted in her stomach now.

"They're not getting any. Don't worry."

"Am I a suspect in Fay's murder?"

"They have no suspect, so as a result, everyone is a suspect," Farah told her. "The New Milford police want to talk to you, probably just to ask some standard questions such as when you saw the deceased last and that kind of stuff."

"I'd prefer that they not come to the house," Lacey said quietly. "This is my place of business. Even though I'd love to see a police car right this second, I feel like I've had my quota of visits from them."

"That's no problem. I'll call them and say we'll go to the station. They prefer that, anyway."

"*We?* You're coming with me?" she said, relieved. Sixteen years ago, Lacey had been dragged from the police station to the State Police barracks to court and back to the police station until her initial confusion and terror gave way to bleary-eyed exhaustion. She never wanted to go back. Ever.

"It'll be good to get it out of the way."

"Could we do it tomorrow? I know it's a Saturday, but maybe they could meet with me anyway." Lacey didn't want another thing hanging over her head. She had nothing to hide. She'd answer their questions. She would even give them a DNA sample if Farah let her.

"I'll try to set up a meeting there in the morning, say, nine o'clock."

"Thank you."

The attorney continued giving her directions as Lacey watched Gavin open the front door and step over the dead animal and onto the porch.

No sirens, but the lights of a police car preceded the vehicle as it turned into her driveway.

"The police are here," she told Farah.

"Good. But one last thing," Farah replied. "A preliminary report from my computer expert says that whoever planted those files on your hard drive didn't need to be a genius."

"What do you mean?"

"The files were transferred through your network. Nothing tricky about it. You had no security, so anyone could have set up shop within the router's radius, tapped into your system, and dropped the files. She's checking the IPs to see what she can find out."

Gavin was speaking with the two cops who'd just climbed out of the police car. Lacey's mind raced. Amy's computer was linked to her network. But there was no way she could have done it. How about Nick? What did she really know about him?

Damn. It could have been anyone.

CHAPTER TWENTY-FIVE

South Norwalk, Connecticut

A SIX-PACK of rolls from the young Portuguese woman locking up the bakery, half a pizza from the couple heading back to their car after dinner, a pre-licked lollipop from the little boy walking a dozen steps behind his mother out of the grocery store, and ten dollars and seventeen cents in donations, all in change.

"Tonight is a good night, Lord. Hallelujah!"

Holy Joe, as everyone called him downtown, was a part of the old downtown establishment in the revitalized shoreline town. He carried his life's possessions in a grocery cart that he swapped every now and then when this one got rusty from the bad weather. Missing one eye, Joe had a stump for a left arm. People thought he was a homeless veteran. Maybe he was. Maybe he wasn't.

Joe's mind didn't work like most people's. He couldn't remember everything. Couldn't even remember if he ever *could* remember everything. When he thought about it, he thanked the Lord for it. No doubt, Jesus was kind enough to keep things best forgotten about his life in the dark for him.

Holy Joe was polite, said his prayers out loud, and people

made few complaints when they found him sleeping in odd places. The local police knew him and only scooped him up off the street on the coldest nights.

"Our Father, who art in heaven, hallowed be Thy Name."

This time of year, on the nights when it wasn't raining, Joe's favorite place to camp was behind the two clothes dumpsters they'd put at the far end of the private commuter lot not far from the train station.

"Thy kingdom come. Thy will be done, on earth, as it is in Heaven."

The good thing was that folks' donations weren't always stuffed inside the metal boxes. Every night, Joe found something good that had been left out. Often, it made for extra layers as the weather got colder.

"Give us this day our daily bread. You've done that, Jesus," Joe sang out loudly, looking down at his Portuguese rolls. "And forgive us our trespasses, as we forgive those who have trespassed against us."

Pushing the cart across the broken pavement of the empty parking lot, he could already see the moonlight reflecting off a large trash bag next to the white dumpsters.

"And lead us not into temptation," Joe said happily.

He poked the bag with one foot. There was something heavy inside. He leaned down and tore open the bag. Even in the darkness, he could make out the bloody face and open eyes of a young Black girl staring blankly at the moon.

"But deliver us from evil."

CHAPTER TWENTY-SIX

"They think it was a Halloween prank."

"They're morons," Gavin said into the phone.

He was sorry that he had to leave Lacey with those cops. But five minutes after the locals had arrived at her house, a phone call had come in from a security job he had going in New Haven. He had to run.

"One good thing," she told him. "They took the carcass away."

"I'm sure they're down at the Westbury crime lab right now, checking it for fingerprints of international pranksters."

"Round up the usual suspects," she responded.

Gavin had checked the house and the property himself. He doubted whoever had done this was hanging around, waiting for Lacey to get back home. Still, she was too vulnerable in that house. And it was ridiculous that no one was putting two and two together.

"Actually, it's probably a good thing that you left," she said, her voice suddenly sounding very tired.

He envisioned her in that bedroom, talking to him on the phone as she got ready for bed. Gavin could imagine her tucked in, surrounded by the pillows she had piled up there. Once he knew the house was empty, the intimacy of going into her private space had really hit home. Not that it made any difference. She was already in his head. "And why is that?"

"I think the local law enforcement has already decided that what's going on is out of their jurisdiction, even though it's right here in Westbury. None of the things I've reported seem to register on their radar as important to them. With you here, though, I'd probably have to deal with macho pissing contests between a big-city detective and small-town cops. That would not be good at all."

"I wouldn't let it get down to that. Trust me. I'd just tell them what they needed to do and then they would do their job."

"There. My point exactly." There was the sound of a stifled yawn. "I'm sorry, that was rude."

"What are you doing?" He already knew what she was doing.

"Trying to get some sleep. I was up all night last night."

"What time are you planning to go to Terri's apartment tomorrow?"

"I don't know. I'll get there after they're done questioning me in New Milford." Lacey had already told him about the conversation she'd had with Farah Aziz.

Gavin had expected it. This was the very reason why he'd wanted her to have an attorney present when the time came for this questioning.

"I liked Fay," Lacey said. "Even though our relationship was professional, we were sort of friends. But who's going to believe that? And I have no alibi for the night she was killed. Nothing. I mean, nothing after you left. It's terrifying that they consider me a suspect."

"I doubt that they consider you a serious suspect. This is just procedure," Gavin said calmly, stretching the truth. Lacey's felony was a strike against her. And the photograph of Fay Stone's corpse on her computer, although she'd voluntarily offered it to the authorities, was another strike.

"What time are you meeting Farah?" Gavin asked.

"Nine o'clock, at the station," she whispered. "I can't believe how scared I feel."

"You'll be okay," he said gently. "She's a great attorney. Remember to trust her."

"Yeah. That falls into the Nearly Impossible category. I have a lot of work to do in the trusting department."

CHAPTER TWENTY-SEVEN

FOR MANY PEOPLE in her age group, Friday night was date night, or at least movie night or drinks-with-friends-night. But there would be plenty of time down the road for those things.

Right now, Benita Gomez needed to dig up as much as she could for the Green feature story. Her boss had already okayed a three-part article. And Benita had called the editors at the Hartford and New Haven papers and they were interested in having her do individual freelance stand-alone pieces. The three angles made it brilliant. *The Victims. The Guilty. What Tomorrow Brings.*

For the initial article, the Green family was the focus. As a candidate for the senatorial race, Kathy Green's participation would definitely make the article. Judge Green was another story. He was a recluse. Still, there were enough accounts out there about him to make the man a seriously tragic figure. Days before Stephanie's murder, he'd launched a State Police investigation into drug trafficking in the Sherman area, focusing especially on distribution in the crowded high school. There had been loud speculation at the time that his daughter's death had been an act of retaliation. After Stephanie's murder, he suffered a nervous breakdown and was never the same man.

Benita knew where Judge Green lived and what his daily routine consisted of. He wasn't one to answer phone calls or take appointments for interviews. She planned to pay him a visit. Perhaps she'd even run into him 'accidentally' this weekend by Black Rock Lake where he had his cottage. Even a line or two, whatever she could use from him, would be a bonus.

The "Guilty" segment of the series was turning out to be the most interesting piece and the one that Benita was having unrivaled success collecting information for. Timing was everything in journalism. During the past couple of weeks, she'd started making visits to the gang members who were in prison for the murder.

Four of the five had already met with her. They had obvious remorse, but the prospect of spending forty years or so in prison could do that to a person.

All of them had sentence reduction hearings scheduled over the next couple of months. Michael Phoenix, the man whom the judge and juries had been the hardest on, was serving a hundred and twelve-year sentence. He was the leader, by all accounts. He was the only one who still refused to meet with her. She knew Michael had one regular visitor.

Benita was not about to give up. And she'd spread around enough cash to finally get the name and address of his visitor.

She stared at the piece of paper pinned to the cork board. Her phone messages had not been returned. It was time for a personal visit.

Benita envisioned dedicating a chunk of this second part to Lacey Watkins. Compared to what the rest of the crew received, Lacey had ended up with a pretty short sentence. A walk in the park, according to Kathy Green.

The third article would be about the hearings for sentence reductions and Katherine Green's political career—one being dependent on the other.

Benita stared at all the sticky notes and printed articles and pages of information and reports she'd collected on this case.

There was enough here that she could write a book. And she would definitely consider that, especially if Katherine Green won her seat in the Senate. Either way, she was certain these articles would bring an impressive string of journalism awards.

Then she'd have her nights out with friends.

A noise outside the front window of the office snapped Benita out of her daydream. She was the only one working this late. Swinging her chair around, she stared at the wall of glass that cut off the dark street. She couldn't see anyone outside. The door was locked at five when their receptionist left. Most of the lights in the office were off. Her bright desk lamp put a spotlight on her. And for the first time ever, she felt vulnerable.

There was that sound again, like a pebble hitting the glass. She turned off the light and stood up. She was getting totally freaked out.

Her cell phone rang.

"Benita Gomez," she said, her eyes riveted to the window. The lights outside showed no movement on the street.

"Are you still good for your word?"

She recognized the voice. "Absolutely. You know I am."

To become the queen bee, you needed an army of worker bees. Benita was becoming a master at building troops.

"Cash?"

"Got it."

"Write this down."

Benita grabbed a pen. "Go ahead."

"Tomorrow, nine o'clock. The New Milford police are bringing in Lacey Watkins for questioning about the murder of her probation officer, Fay Stone."

Benita's heart raced with excitement. "Got it."

Ending the call, she stared at the information. This was good stuff. She turned around and looked at the wall of windows again. There was no one on the street. It had been her imagination. She had nothing to be afraid of, at all. She was on her way up.

Now, how could she best use this to her advantage?

A quote pinned above her desk caught her attention.

To do anything in this world worth doing, we must not stand back shivering and thinking of the cold and danger, but jump in and scramble through as well as we can. —Sydney Smith

And Benita knew exactly where to jump in.

CHAPTER TWENTY-EIGHT

THE QUESTIONS LACEY was asked at the New Milford police station were filtered through Farah Aziz. Nothing hypothetical was allowed. No fishing. Everything needed to be related directly to the meetings she'd had with Fay Stone. The attorney had reminded the two detectives at the very beginning that her client was there of her own free will to help them solve a homicide. They were not welcome to ask any unwarranted personal questions.

It was a pleasant change for Lacey to see cops squirm and try to do the right thing in her lawyer's presence. At five feet tall, a hundred pounds, and perhaps in her early forties, Farah might as well have been a giant looking down at them. There was no doubt that these men had done their homework. They knew enough about Aziz not to mess with her.

Summarizing every meeting she'd had with the probation officer since being back in Connecticut, Lacey finished up in under an hour.

"You did well," Farah told her afterwards. They followed an escort through the building back to the front doors of the police station.

"Thank you." Lacey felt tension cramping every muscle in her neck and back. The feeling wouldn't go away until she was miles away from this building. "Why didn't they say anything about confiscating my computer?"

"I settled that with them on the phone," Farah explained. "My forensics person is on their approved expert list. Once a report gets generated, it'll be shared. But even with that, I have some discretion because of my responsibilities as your attorney."

"You really trust me," she said with some amazement.

Farah's nod was barely visible, but it was enough for Lacey.

Suddenly, emotions welled up in her. Last night, she'd been exhausted. Still, she'd only slept for an hour, staring at the ceiling and thinking of what lay ahead. The police inquiry today. Guessing what the crazy person who'd been sending her the pictures through the Internet was planning next. Who'd left the dead animal and why.

On top of all of this, she felt incredibly lonely. She had no friends. No family. Not a single person who knew enough about Lacey and her past that she could talk to about what was happening in her life. There was Gavin. But she was attracted to him and terrified about leading him on when she wouldn't do anything about it.

They reached the double doors that opened up into the lobby. This was as far as their escort came.

"Are you going back to Westbury?" Farah asked as they were buzzed out.

"No, to New Haven. I have to start the process of clearing out my sister's..."

The words died on her tongue. Lacey stared through the glass exit doors at the news vans and reporters gathered in front. The center of attention was a tall woman with her back to them. Lacey would recognize her anywhere. Kathy Green.

The candidate was speaking into a portable PA system, and she was loud enough to be heard inside. "...and now she's being investigated for yet another murder. Here is another case of a repeat offender. When are we..."

"She's talking about me," Lacey turned to Farah. "How could she know I'd be here? Or that I have any connection with Fay Stone?"

The attorney was already speaking to the officer at the reception window, demanding that they be allowed back in.

Lacey took a step back. The tinted plate glass protected her from the mob outside, for now, but she could see the hungry looks. She could hear the harsh personal attack from Kathy Green.

Her attention shifted to another familiar face. Watching the spectacle at a distance from the visitor's parking lot, Benita Gomez was leaning against Lacey's car, a photographer at her side.

The reporter's gaze was fixed on the plate glass, and Lacey felt as if she were looking directly at her.

And the look said, *I warned you.*

CHAPTER TWENTY-NINE

THE FOUR MEN convicted of Stephanie Green's murder were serving their sentences at the Northern Correctional Institution in Somers, a maximum-security prison housing inmates doing time for violent crimes. Regardless of the walls and bars and segregated cell blocks, news inside the razor-wire topped fences traveled at the speed of light. Any kind of fight, accident, or murder was known to every inmate hours, sometimes days, before anyone on the outside world—including family—would hear about it.

Peter Sclar was the driver of the van who'd taken the group of teenagers to the lake the night of the Stephanie Green's murder. Since coming here, he'd picked up the nickname of Purdy, and everyone now called him that, even the guards. Serving a forty-seven-year sentence, he took every minute of the time he was allowed on family visit days. His brother, two sisters, his mother. They had set up a schedule and one of them always showed up.

Purdy loved to listen to everything they had to say. From news of the new dog his mother had rescued to his nephew's soccer games to how the new mailman on their street seemed to only deliver every other day. Nothing was too dull. This was the only way Purdy could survive this place, living life through their stories.

Today, though, Purdy was the one with news.

"Michael did it. They caught him hanging himself in his cell this morning."

"Is he dead?" Purdy's younger sister asked in dismay from behind the glass divider.

"Might as well be. Word is he still had a pulse when they took him to the infirmary. But they say he was hanging there long enough to do the job. He's in a coma, but it doesn't look good."

Silence fell between the siblings. Their gazes connected. Her question was understood without having to be asked.

"You should make the call," Purdy said.

"The shit will hit the fan."

"It doesn't matter," Purdy told his sister. "Michael might have just hours left, if he makes it at all. Make the phone call."

CHAPTER THIRTY

BY THE TIME Gavin arrived at the New Milford police station, the press conference had ended, and Kathy Green was gone. But a news van and a handful of reporters were still lurking in the parking lot. He drove to the back of the building, to a door that was reserved strictly for police personnel.

Calling Lacey, he parked at the curb and got out of the car. A minute later, she was escorted out by a uniformed officer. She looked tense, scared, glancing around the parking lot like she was ready to run. He could imagine the chaos the police questioning alone would have wrought in her. To realize that she couldn't just walk out of there—with the wolf pack of reporters waiting outside—had to be the tipping point. Gavin had heard the note of panic in her voice when she'd called him.

He wanted to pull her into his arms and tell her that she was safe. Instead, he helped her quickly into the car.

"Thank you for doing this," she told him as soon as he got behind the wheel. "Thank you for getting here so fast. I didn't see it coming. This is two days in a row she's done this to me. I was so rattled."

"It's okay." He watched her struggle with the seatbelt. She was still worked up.

"Farah was on her way to New York City, but she offered to get my car from the parking lot and bring it to the back. But that lying bitch has been perched right there next to it. Waiting for me. She knew which car was mine. I was afraid she'd follow me. I can't believe I'm letting her do this to me."

"The same reporter that showed up at your house? Gomez?"

She nodded. "I hate people like that. She thinks she can bully me, harass me into talking to her. I don't know how she found out that I was here. How could any of them know?"

Frustrated, she let go of the belt, but Gavin caught it. He clicked it into place.

"What is she going to do now, camp out on my front lawn? What can I do about it?"

"You just have to wait her out. Reporters work to deadlines. She probably has a story that has to be submitted today. She'll move on to something else before the day is out."

"With her, it's more than that. She *wants* more. I don't feel safe. Everything is closing in on me. First Terri. Then Fay. Whoever is behind the killings is taunting me. I keep worrying about who might be next. Then Kathy Green, the reporters, the police. They all think I've done it. I'm guilty. What am I doing here? Why am I dragging you into this?"

She reached over to undo the seatbelt. She was going to bolt, but he caught her hand, stopping her. Her hand was ice cold.

"Lacey."

She tried to pull away.

"Lacey, look at me."

Storms were raging in her green eyes when she finally met his gaze. She was a doe, and she'd scented the hunters tracking her. But if she ran, he couldn't protect her. History would repeat itself.

"You're not alone."

"But I am. And I'm also a target when I sit around waiting for him to strike."

"You won't. I won't let you be. Not anymore." He held her chin when she tried to protest, bringing her face closer to him.

She didn't struggle, just froze. "You have a great attorney who will take care of legal side of things. Then you have me, a tough son of a bitch who promises to plan for twenty-four/seven protection. I will not allow anything to happen to you."

"I can't ask you to do that."

"You're not asking. I'm going to make it happen."

"Gavin—"

Her complaints were silenced when he pressed a finger to her lips. His thumb brushed the soft texture. Lacey's eyes darkened. Her gaze moved down to his mouth and for a long moment stayed there. She sat back, breaking the touch, just as he was contemplating kissing her. She looked away, but he saw the blush climbing into her cheek.

"Actually, I was thinking of maybe staying at Terri's apartment in New Haven. At least for the weekend. That would give me a chance to go through her things and start sorting them out."

"That's a good idea," he said, starting the car. Driving out of the parking lot, he could see the news crews still hanging around in the front.

"What should I do about my car?"

Gavin could see Benita Gomez and a taller man in deep conversation next to it. "I'll bring you back this afternoon. They're not going to hang around here all day."

Leaving the police station and the reporters behind, Gavin decided to bring her up to date on what he'd been doing most of this morning.

"I've started to pull together whatever information is available on Stephanie Green's murder case and trial."

He felt her eyes fix on him. "Then you believe me. You think that Terri's and Fay's murders could be related to it."

"I think whoever is taunting you, whoever is sending you those pictures, could have a connection to that case. But you have to remember that your sister and Fay both worked at jobs where you make enemies. But for right now, I'm focusing on one end of the string."

She didn't argue with his logic.

"I need some background on the case. Things that don't show up in the reports." He looked over when she didn't say anything.

She was rubbing a spot by her temple. "Can we stop at a drive-thru somewhere? I could use a cup of coffee."

"Definitely. Actually, I could eat something. Have you had breakfast?"

She shook her head. "You aren't in charge of feeding me three times a day."

"This will only make two meals."

"If we stop for food, I'm buying."

Gavin nodded, letting her have her way. This would be her first time at Terri's apartment since the funeral, and he had no doubt that Lacey would be upset when they got there. He wanted to talk about the Green case before that.

The diner on Route 7 had just enough cars in the parking lot to promise decent food and still give them some privacy. Inside, they chose a booth in the corner, away from other people. They both ordered, but it wasn't until Lacey had a cup and a large pot of coffee in front of her before she looked at him.

"Ask away."

The files Gavin had gone over made it look like a standard open-and-shut case. The group had been arrested at the scene of the crime and Lacey was an eyewitness. No serious investigative work was required. They were the kind of court cases prosecutors loved. He opened the notepad on his cell phone where he'd already jotted down some questions.

"What can you tell me about Stephanie Green? What did you know about her before the night of the murder? How well did you know her?"

"I only went to school with her for about four months. We were both sophomores. I knew her face and her name, but that was it. She was popular. I wasn't. She was a varsity athlete. I could barely walk because of my hip fracture and surgeries. She liked older boys. I had just gotten into drinking and drugs. She was beautiful and smart. I was a punk and a loner."

Gavin watched Lacey as she stared into her coffee cup. He also knew that Stephanie Green came from rich, doting parents, while Lacey's father had almost killed her in a beating before she'd left Cleveland. And that her mother had refused to cooperate with authorities.

"How about the other five people at Sherman Pond that night? How well did you know them?" he asked.

She shook her head. "They were all seniors. Some of them were older and should have already graduated. Michael Phoenix was the only one that I'd talked to before that night." She twisted a piece of her napkin into a thin spiral. "I'd bought weed and pills from him a few times after I started doing drugs."

Gavin already knew that. "So, he was a dealer."

She nodded, topping her mug with more coffee.

Michael had several minor possession charges prior to the night of the murder. The rest of the group had no priors. "How about the others. They sold drugs too?"

She shrugged. "I'm not really sure. Michael had a number of kids that hung out with him, but I didn't know them. The four with him that night at Sherman Pond were only some of his people."

The number of suspects just multiplied. The murder trial had only focused on the people present at the crime scene. They'd been found guilty of premeditated murder. If there had been any investigation into others, Gavin wondered who else might have been found to have foreknowledge of the crime.

"Do you remember the names of the kids at the lake?"

"Elizabeth Kinard. Peter Sclar. John Crowell. Drew Densky. Their names were burned into my brain during the trials."

"How about the names of other people in Michael's circle of friends?"

She shook her head. "I don't remember any of them. Like I said, I didn't know them. It's been a long time."

Their waitress came back with their orders. Gavin pushed his phone to the side and decided to wait on asking more questions until after she ate. But Lacey wasn't interested in food.

"You probably want to know how Stephanie was connected to this group," she said.

He nodded.

"She wanted Michael. That was obvious from the ride to the lake. But I found out during the trial that Stephanie had been talking to her father about all the drugs and the dealers at school. He was a judge."

"Yes, I read that. The DA used it as the motivating factor for the assault and murder. That made it first degree. Long sentences. The rest of it is history."

"Yeah, my history. Three years in jail...for being an idiot." She picked up the fork, played with her food, then put it back down. Her misty gaze met his. "I hope you believe me when I say that I knew *nothing* of what they were planning. I was messed up. I was stupid. I put myself in the middle. But I had *no* idea that they were planning to hurt her...to kill her that night. I thought...I know that she wanted to go out with them. I just figured that I was the little lie used to pacify over-protective parents."

Gavin took her hand. She didn't pull away. "I *do* believe you. And I know those prosecutors and whoever else was working the case back then believed you too."

"But I don't think her parents ever did. They blamed me. They still do. I was the face that they saw at their door that night."

His thumb gently caressed the back of her hand. He wished he could lie about how people get over a loss like that. But grief, anger, blame don't just go away. Healing doesn't follow any time schedule. He still felt responsible for what had happened to his sister.

"Have you ever asked yourself why you and not someone else?" he asked. "Why did Michael Phoenix ask *you* to get Stephanie? Why not someone else?"

"I've asked myself that a million times. The truth is, I was convenient, naïve, and willing. He knew me. I was a sophomore. As a user, I was already in his pocket." She pulled her hand away and put it in her lap. "But what would have happened if I hadn't been at that donut shop at that specific hour on that night? That wasn't a usual place for me to hang out."

"So, he didn't walk in there looking for you?"

She shook her head. "He came in looking, and then it was like...oh, you'll do."

Gavin looked out the window at the passing cars. How many times had he seen this happen, where circumstances and stupid choices and bad luck collided to create lives scarred with tragedy. Or not.

How did that old poem go? *Two roads diverged in a yellow wood...and that has made all the difference.*

The problem was, sometimes the difference was deadly.

CHAPTER THIRTY-ONE

THE SATURDAY MORNING meeting at the health club chain's district office always ran like clockwork. In and out in two hours with enough time for chit-chat and coffee. The three district managers were efficient, organized people that Jane Clark trusted fully.

Today, Jane was surprised when Donna Covington walked in fifteen minutes after they'd started the meeting. But being late wasn't so much what triggered the regional manager's concern, but the way Donna looked. Pale with dark circles under her eyes, smudged make up, carelessly brushed hair. She looked as if she hadn't bothered to look in the mirror. This was not the impeccably dressed woman they were accustomed to seeing.

"Everything okay?" Jane asked as the other woman sat at the far end of the conference table, close to the door.

"Ran into some traffic," Donna tossed off.

Jane motioned to the district manager who had been speaking to continue.

Making a practice of not wanting to know too much about the personal lives of her employees had many advantages, but it had some pitfalls too. What Jane knew was that Donna was in her early thirties, single, beautiful, fit. She drew in husbands who pretended to work out while they eyed her boobs and ass and the skin tight outfits she strutted around in. Just as important, the wives of those husbands came in and hired personal trainers to keep up with Donna. And the company made a lot of money on those skin tight outfits the wives bought in the club store, even if they didn't look quite as good in them.

Jane also knew Donna wasn't married. But that was it. While others chatted about boyfriends or first and last dates, or about a sick child or an aging parent, Donna kept her personal life private from the group inside this room.

"The flyers." The manager who was speaking stopped and looked at Donna. "You were supposed to get some pricing on that for us."

There was a pause with a deer in the headlights look on Donna's face.

"Yes, I am. I'll get a price," Donna said absently. "I'm looking for the right photographer."

Someone's cell phone buzzed. It was Donna's. In a rush, she answered it.

"Where?"

The metal chair she was sitting on flipped backward as she suddenly stood up. Donna struggled, trying to listen to whatever was being said by the caller while she reached back for the piece of furniture.

"Which hospital?"

Jane went to her rescue, grabbing the chair for her.

"Tell me which hospital, damn it!" she said, her voice growing shrill.

There were tears in Donna's eyes when she ended the call. "I have to go."

"Is there anything I can do?" Jane asked, feeling helpless.

"No." Donna shook her head and ran out of the room.

CHAPTER THIRTY-TWO

As they drew nearer to New Haven, the stone sitting in her chest grew until Lacey could barely breathe. By the time they turned onto the street where Terri's apartment building was located, it felt like a meteor had lodged there, burning her alive from the inside.

Lacey stared out the side window and struggled to force air into her lungs. So far, she'd been able to contain the floodgate of tears. She didn't want to release them in case she wasn't able to stop.

"We should probably check in with the building super first," Gavin suggested.

Lacey nodded, scrambling out of the car as soon as he pulled into one of the visitors' parking spaces. Terri's face was etched in Lacey's mind. Her sister's words echoed from the not-too-distant past.

It's been okay living here. It's close to work. But it's never been home. It couldn't be. Not with you out west somewhere. How could it be home without my baby sis?

She leaned against the closed door of the SUV and raised her face to the autumn sun. A tear escaped. Another one followed.

"No, you don't," she muttered inaudibly, blinking and looking down at her feet where the runaway droplets stained the pavement.

The other door closed. Gavin's footsteps came around the SUV. He stood next to her and draped an arm around her shoulder, pulling her tightly against him. She pressed her head against his shoulder. She'd planned to come here alone. But now she was glad that he was with her. His presence forced her to stay in control, to go through with what needed to be done.

They stood there in silence until the loud muffler of a motorcycle racing by on the street jarred her back to the present.

"Would you like me to tell the super that we're here?"

She nodded.

"Do you have the keys?"

"Yeah, I do." She reached inside her bag for them.

"Would you wait for me here?"

She nodded.

He walked away, and Lacey took out some tissues. She wiped her face, blew her nose, and looked at her reflection in the tinted windows of the SUV. She could do this. She had to. She was here, and she would get this done.

On the drive down, she'd decided what to do with Terri's things. She'd give them away to a women's shelter. One of those temporary homes for battered women and their children. All her furniture, the clothes. Perhaps they would provide someone with the means to make a new start. She already had the name of the women's organization that she had used in Terri's obituary, asking for donations in lieu of flowers. She would ask them to arrange a pick-up.

Still, Lacey had to sort through everything today. The only things she wanted to take were family keepsakes. Photos of their grandfather. And those of their mother when she'd been a child. Lacey knew her sister had them. She'd seen them framed, sitting on the bookcases here.

The building super's office was on the bottom floor of the apartment house. Lacey saw Gavin come back out and then stop.

The headline of a newspaper in the box on the sidewalk had grabbed his attention. He searched in his pocket and put money in, taking the paper out and reading whatever it was.

When he started toward her, Lacey knew there was something terribly wrong. She could see it in the darkened expression, in the set of his shoulders. He had the paper folded and tucked under an arm.

"He says there was a courier delivery for Terri that he accepted last week. He has it in the mail room. He'll bring it up in a few minutes."

"What was in the newspaper?" Lacey asked.

"Nothing." He started leading her to the building. "It's not about anybody you know."

"Please, Gavin. It's bothering *you*. I'd like to know."

There was a sense of tenderness in the way his gaze caressed her face. He stopped by the door and unfolded the newspaper. He pointed to a small article in the right column. The body of a Black girl from the city had been found near the train station in South Norwalk.

"I have a bad feeling that I know her."

"I'm so sorry," she said softly. "One of your cases?"

"No. Someone Terri was working with. She was trying to help this kid out of a real bad situation." He tucked the paper under his arm again. "The girl called me last week. She had no idea about Terri's death. I made some calls. I thought I put her in safe hands."

The words were drawn out, like he felt sick even saying them. He opened the building door, not giving Lacey a chance to ask any more questions. She followed, struck by the horror of what he'd just said and by the realization that she was about to enter her sister's apartment.

Lacey had been so consumed by her own grief that she hadn't given much thought about others who had been affected by her sister's death. Terri wasn't a person who did things half-assed. Once she latched onto an idea, or undertook a cause, she became consumed by it. She did everything in her power to make things happen.

Another life had been lost. Perhaps it had not been caused directly as a result of her sister dying, but maybe it had.

They reached the second floor and she found herself staring at the welcome mat of her sister's apartment.

"I can do this," she whispered under her breath. Forcing her hand to stay steady, she pushed the key into the lock. She succeeded on the first try. A turn and a second key, and she pushed the door open.

The stuffiness of a closed room greeted her. It was the smell of abandoned homes. It was the familiar scent of a dozen places that she'd lived in. From the threshold, she could see the kitchenette and the vision of Terri greeting her.

So, what do you think? I've been living here two years and never turned on the oven.

Lacey took a couple of steps inside and stared at the kitchen counter. A five by seven picture of the two of them sat next to a newly purchased silver frame. One of the guests at Jeannie Bond's wedding had taken their picture. They'd worn the same dark green shirt and matching color skirt. Their hair had been the same style. Many had commented on how alike they looked. Lacey had given a copy of that photo to her sister just a few days before she died.

This is my favorite picture ever. The Watkins sisters. Look at it. We're together and both smiling. We're happy. When was the last time that happened?

Lacey leaned against the wall, overwhelmed with the rush of emotions. Her throat burned. She felt the touch of Gavin's hand on her back.

"Can you give me a few minutes?" she managed to ask without turning around.

"I'll be in the hallway," he said softly. "I have to make some calls."

She heard him move away. The door thudded against the latch

he'd thrown to keep it open, and only then did she allow the tears to break free.

We've always been together. In our thoughts. In our hearts. And no matter what happens in the future, we will be there for each other.

Terri's face and words danced in Lacey's head. Her sister's presence was all around her, inside of her.

You can *do this. You'll get through this. You have it in you. You just have to dig deep.*

Lacey pushed away from the wall and headed into the kitchen for the photograph. She stared at it through a thick sheen of tears.

We're the same, Lacey. We've been to hell and back. We're strong. We're survivors.

"We're survivors," Lacey murmured and looked around. What was left in this place was only stuff. Things. Sorting it out wasn't saying goodbye. Mourning her sister didn't start or end here. This was just another step.

The kitchen, a large living room, one bedroom, and three closets. She could do this. She could get through this.

Lacey turned on the water in the sink and splashed her face with the cold water, again and again, until her cheeks felt numb. She only had to sort the things she was taking. She could pay someone else to come later and box up the donations.

The kitchen counter was the best place to start stacking. Their photo and the frame were a start. On the bookcases in the living room, she spotted the family photos she'd seen before. She collected those too, and stacked them on the counter. She should have brought an empty box with her.

She checked the closet in the hall to see if her sister had stored any there. There were only winter coats and boots and a vacuum cleaner.

"Suitcases," Lacey headed for the bedroom.

Neat. Efficient. Everything put away. The orderliness of this apartment had always reminded Lacey of a hotel room. As Terri had said, it was never a home, just a place to stay.

Opening the bedroom closet's double doors, she knew immediately that something was not right. To the left of the large space, clothes were off the hangers and were scattered on the floor, exposing a three-drawer metal file cabinet tucked behind them. Lacey recalled seeing smaller keys on Terri's keychain. But the cabinet was unlocked. The top drawer was partially open.

She looked inside.

A three-inch space in front, the size of a fat file, sat empty. Behind it were names and dates that might have had something to do with cases Terri had worked on. Lacey recalled the paperwork she'd handed to the New Haven police after Terri's death. That was much thinner than what looked to be missing here. She was glad Gavin was only in the hallway outside. He could make sense of these things better than she could.

She opened the second drawer. Copies of income tax returns and bank statements going back ten years, filed neatly by date—very much in Terri-fashion—filled the drawer. She closed this drawer too, and crouched down, opening the bottom drawer.

The file in front had no tags, but inside Lacey saw newspaper cuttings. She pushed it open farther and the pieces of paper fell to the side, exposing the first article's headline.

Couple Found Dead in Murder-Suicide

CHAPTER THIRTY-THREE

Nick Riley's truck had ended up with a sizable dent in the front fender the same weekend that Terri Watkins had died in the hit-and-run incident.

The thought had crossed his mind that there are no coincidences, but the way his luck was running these days, he hadn't dared mentioning it to anyone. Stupidly, he hadn't even filed an insurance claim or reported it to the police. Now, five weeks later, it was coming back to bite him in the ass.

The two local cops who showed up at his house came under the pretense of only asking some questions. He'd gone to high school with Ned Schumer, one of the cops. They'd played football together. When Ned had started with the routine that I'm-going-to-pretend-there-is-no-history-between-us, Nick knew he was screwed.

"So, run that by us one more time? Tell me everything that happened on the weekend of September seventh."

Nick leaned a hip against the kitchen counter, nursing the same cup of coffee he'd poured for himself when these two had first arrived. The brew had turned ice cold.

"I was doing some painting at the health club on Friday the sixth. A couple of the guys picked me up after work, and we went to the stag party." He'd already given the names of people and places. Schumer knew them even though he wasn't going to acknowledge it now.

"Afterwards, the guys dropped me off here at home," he explained. "I use my car on the weekends, so there was no reason to go back for the truck. I was doing more work at the club on Monday anyway."

"Was anybody else here with you, say, Saturday morning?" Ned's partner asked.

"No, it was a stag. I got pretty hammered. I spent the morning in bed and then just hung out, doing stuff around here."

"When was the first time you noticed the damage to your truck?"

"Monday afternoon. When I was leaving the club."

"What did you do?"

"I mentioned it to Donna at the club. I figured it had happened in their parking lot. She suggested taking it to Ron Marteka's body shop to get an estimate." Frustrated, Nick left the cup on the counter and ran a hand down the back of his neck. They were moving into the realm of 'he said, she said' and 'I don't remember who the fuck said what'. He was no good at this game. "The truck has been sitting there for five weeks—supposedly waiting for parts."

"That night, where was the key and who had access to it?" Schumer asked.

"I keep one on my keychain, an extra is always hanging by the door here at the house, and I keep a third one in a magnetic box on the underside of the truck chassis."

"Who knows about the box?"

"In a town this small, probably everyone. I'm bad with forgetting my keys. I do the same thing with my car outside."

"Why didn't you call the police?" Schumer's partner asked.

"Why should I if the club is going to reimburse me for it."

"Did they agree to?"

"Well, we haven't talked the specifics, but that was the understanding. Ron and Donna were going to work the numbers."

Two accidents, with one of them totaling a car in the past three years. The insurance company would drop him like a sack of potatoes if he reported a new accident. Five weeks ago, Donna had tried to be nice by working things out...*unofficially*, as she'd called it. Now Nick would be putting her on the spot and she might just deny the whole thing.

"Now look, Ned," he said. "You know Terri Watkins was a friend of mine. I did plenty of work for her. There's no way my truck was the only vehicle in town that ended up with a ding that weekend."

Ned Schumer motioned to his partner that it was time to go and pocketed the small notebook he was writing in. "The State Police are towing your truck from Marteka's garage this weekend to one of their sites. They're going to do some forensic work on the vehicle. If there's any kind of match..."

The police officer let the unsaid words hang in the air between them.

Nick felt sick. Shit, what the hell was happening?

CHAPTER THIRTY-FOUR

HE'D FAILED HER, Gavin thought. It was as simple, and as tragic, as that. A young life snuffed out.

The call to the assistant chief confirmed that the body discovered in South Norwalk was Alisha Miller. John Trevor swore that he'd made the call immediately after he'd hung up with Gavin. By the time the Bridgeport cops had arrived, he said, there'd been no sign of the teenager.

There was reason enough to suspect corruption on the New Haven police force. It existed in every small and large city in the country. And Terri had been well aware of it. That was the reason she'd given his cell number to Alisha as the back-up. And Gavin had failed his old partner too. There was more he should have done. He could have gone down there and picked the teenager up himself, and gotten hold of whatever it was that she had for Terri.

Trevor was clearly upset with this turn of events. He was quite vocal about it on the phone. He assured Gavin steps were being taken to find out what had gone wrong.

After hanging up, Gavin made a second call to one of his contacts at the State Police and found out that the assistant chief had bypassed New Haven's Internal Affairs and requested a State

Police overview of NHPD department personnel. Trevor wanted someone from the outside to start digging into this.

That was all Gavin could get, though. Favors only went so far.

As he slipped his phone into his pocket, he heard footsteps on the stairs. Going to the end of the hallway, he saw the building manager coming up with a courier envelope in his hand.

"Please tell the detective's sister if she needs anything, I'm around," he said, motioning with his head toward the apartment as he handed Gavin the envelope.

Gavin looked at the return address. This was a benefits package. "Thanks."

He walked back to the apartment not really sure if Lacey needed more time to be alone or not. But he didn't want to risk having her out of his sight for too long. He wouldn't fail her. He couldn't allow anything happen to her.

The door was resting against the latch as he'd left it. He knocked once gently. "Lacey. Can I come in?"

There was no answer.

He'd been standing here the entire time with no one coming or going from the other apartments on the floor, but for a crazy moment worry sliced through him. He pushed the door open and went in.

"Lacey?"

A faint reply came from the bedroom. "I'm coming."

Gavin locked and latched the door. He'd been here only a handful of times during the couple of years that Terri had lived here. Everything was the same as he remembered. He put the benefits envelope next to some pictures stacked on the kitchen counter. Taking his jacket off and tossing it onto a chair, he wondered about the best way to help.

Lacey came out of the bedroom carrying some hanging folders.

Her nose was red. Her eyes were almost swollen shut from crying. She tried to keep her head down and inadvertently tripped on the corner of an area rug. She caught herself, but the files fell, and papers scattered all over the room.

"Let me help you." He crouched down to gather them and immediately realized what they were. Newspaper clippings, old photos, letters. Things obviously having to do with Lacey's and Terri's parents. He looked up and saw Lacey leaning against the wall, shaking as tears rushed down her face.

"Hey, Lacey," he said softly.

Papers and files forgotten, he pulled her into his arms. She came willingly, her face pressed against his chest as wave after wave of sobs wracked her body.

Gavin held her and uttered vague words of comfort, wishing that he could ease her pain. Never before had someone's grief affected him as hers was, buffeting his heart and mind right now. Whatever had pushed him before to protect her, now swelled to a driving need to help her through this morass of grief.

"I'm sorry. I'm so sorry." He stroked her back, his lips pressed against the fevered skin of her forehead.

When she stepped out of his arms, he felt a piece of him pull away.

Lacey glanced around and spotted a box of tissues on an end table. After she blew her nose and used half of the box to wipe the tears, Gavin sat on the sofa and took her hand, pulling her down.

"Come here. Talk to me."

She sat next to him, the box of tissues on her lap, her eyes fixed on the papers on the floor. He put an arm around her.

"I never knew Terri had these," she started. "Those files. Everything is there. About our parents. His birth certificate. Their marriage license. There's a picture of my father in his uniform and my eighteen-year-old mother looking up at him like he's a god. They eloped." She shook her head, hiccups and tears breaking up her words. "I guess she could never imagine that beneath that veneer of good looks was a disturbed and abusive monster."

She blew her nose again.

"There are articles on the murder-suicide. And letters. Letters our mother wrote to Terri after...after I was shipped to Connecticut. I destroyed the ones she sent me. Never read them. I didn't want to know why she'd betrayed me. But my sister kept hers."

He caressed her arm, holding her close, giving her a chance to let go of some of the pain.

"There's so much in there that I want to go through. But I don't know if I'll be able to. It's so, so sad. I don't think I want to. But I have to."

Gavin lifted her chin until he was looking into her eyes. He brushed a tear off the smooth skin with his thumb.

"You don't have to do everything in one day. There's no reason to mourn everyone all at once. Let's take those files back to Westbury and tuck them away. Go back to them in your own time. Do it in small doses." He leaned down and kissed her cheek, tasted the saltiness of her tears. "Don't do this to yourself. I can't take seeing you this sad."

She kissed him. A gentle brush of her lips against his. She pulled back, but his mouth followed, taking possession. The thought immediately ran through his mind that it was wrong. This wasn't the time or place, regardless of how much he wanted her.

But the two of them were locked in a contradiction of desire. Gavin backed away, but she came after him, deepening the kiss, until he was lost in her taste, in the erotic dance of their tongues. He pulled her tight against him. Her fingers were threaded into his hair, and he could feel the skin of her back hot under his hand. He couldn't remember ever wanting a woman as much as he wanted Lacey right now.

Even amid the blur of lust, though, he knew this was more than just physical need. Lacey meant second chances, healing, the prospect of proving to both of them that hope exists.

But suddenly, she tore her mouth away, though her arms *did* remain around his neck and her words were a shy whisper in his ear.

"Wait. Not here."

"Okay," he replied, his voice little more than a low growl. There was no hiding how aroused he was physically. She was intoxicating. He wanted more. But Gavin wasn't going to push her or do anything to make her afraid. "Give me a minute. I'll try to behave."

He stood up and headed to the kitchen. In his entire life, he'd never said that to a woman. Never had to.

He took a glass off a shelf, packed it with ice, poured himself a glass of water, and drank it down, keeping the kitchen counter between them when he finally turned back to her. She was standing by the sofa, her arms crossed, staring at the papers and newspaper clippings that were scattered on the floor between them.

He didn't think she was ready to touch any of that again today. Without saying a word, he went to the pile and gathered all the loose pages, putting them back in the folder and placing them on the counter next to the other items she was planning to take.

"Put me to work. Where can I start?" he asked, turning to her again.

"I'm only packing some of Terri's personal things. Photos and maybe some of her books and music CDs. But there's a cabinet in the closet in the bedroom. There seem to be some work-related files in the top drawer. You can start with those. Tell me what I should do with them."

Gavin motioned for her to show him the way. He didn't want to let her out of his sight. He wanted to be sure she knew that she was safe with him. And he needed to know she was safe.

"Also, if you could get me the two suitcases from the top shelf of the closet, I can pack everything I'm taking in them."

He followed her into the bedroom and pulled down the suitcases for her. All the drawers of the file cabinet were partially open. She tugged the top drawer all the way out and right away he could tell what it was in it.

"These are cases that she worked on." He thumbed through some of the papers in the middle of the drawer. They were filed chronologically. "She took notes, hypothesized, liked to gather unofficial and off-the-record documents that would never be allowed in any court. She had her own system of doing things. I recognize some of the names. I was her partner on most of these cases."

"Like keeping a diary," Lacey said, standing next to him. "In the bottom drawer, I found a notebook that she'd kept from the days when she was still living with our parents back in Cleveland."

"Same thing. She kept a written record of everything she did or thought. Some of these are cases that were never solved. Never closed."

"Do I have to return all this to the police?"

"I don't know. Let me go through the files first and see what's here."

She slid back the hanging folders. "There was an empty space for a thick folder in front when I first opened this drawer." She held her fingers up, showing him the size.

Her work with Alisha and the pimp's murder. Bratva. Those were the first things than ran through Gavin's mind. Terri would have had a file on them. He checked the folder behind where Lacey said the missing one should have been. A different case. One they'd started working on together on Gavin's last days at NHPD.

Nothing on Alisha. Nothing on Bratva. Nothing.

His eyes moved from the files to the lock on the cabinet. He looked closer. "This cabinet has been jimmied open. Someone has been in here."

CHAPTER THIRTY-FIVE

"WAIT FOR ME HERE. This shouldn't take more than ten or fifteen minutes," Kathy Green told her assistant, getting out of the car.

The driver opened the door for her. "Are you sure this is the right place, ma'am?" he asked, looking dubiously toward the decrepit cottage perched on a knoll overlooking the marshy end of a pond.

A battered white car was parked by an open shed at the end of the driveway. Trash bags, old appliances, and car parts littered the overgrown yard next to it.

"Yes, this is the place."

Hitching the strap of her purse higher on her shoulder, Kathy moved toward the cottage. She'd left a dozen phone messages, but Claude had refused to call her back. She had to talk to him this weekend.

The single-story, ramshackle cottage looked like it was ready to collapse in on itself. Kathy's gaze swept over the missing shingles on the roof and the closed shades in the windows. More trash was piled up against the house, blocking the main door.

Ten years ago, even five, she might have felt some sadness, some pity, *something*, at the sight of how her ex-husband lived. But no more. All of this was his choice. They had plenty of money. He had access to doctors, programs, medications that he could try. But he refused all of it. It was his choice to live like a backwoods hermit.

Getting involved with politics had given her a new perspective on the decisions the two of them had made since Stephanie's murder. Her life was focused on the future. Claude's was focused on the past. On some misplaced sense of guilt.

She knew who to blame and she wanted no part of this life.

Walking around to where the cottage faced the pond, she noticed the newly replaced boards on the deck. This surprised her. Another door on the deck led into the cottage.

"Claude?" she called out from the bottom step. "I'm here, Claude. We need to talk."

No answer. She didn't know if he was home or not. He had no job. No friends. No country club where he could hang out. When she'd decided to run for office, she'd had him followed for a while. It was important to know all the skeletons in her closet. The report came back that Judge Green took walks. In the woods and cemeteries. He ate at fast food places. *When* he ate. That was about it. For the most part, he just stayed locked away in this dump.

Kathy climbed the steps and rapped on the door. "Come on, Claude. I don't have all day."

She listened. No creaking of the floors, no noise from the inside that said he might be home. Turning around, she studied the odd view of the pond from this angle. The dark water shimmered in the distance, but clumps of long, yellow marsh grass and swampy muck hugged the closest shoreline. Typical.

Kathy's heart leapt into her throat when she heard a creak behind her. He was there, on the bottom step. He was holding a black trash bag with something fairly heavy in it. She hadn't seen him approach. It was like he'd appeared out of thin air.

"Jeez. You scared me," she said, stepping back to give him room to reach the door.

The clothes he wore were older than anything Goodwill would give away. His thinning white hair hanging out below the ratty fishing hat was long and shaggy. The deep wrinkles on his face made him look twenty years older than he really was. He looked dirty and haggard and tired.

There was nothing left here of the man she'd been married to for eighteen years. Nothing but the eyes. They bore into hers with a coolness that made her shiver despite the thickness of her tailored wool blazer. As he reached the door, she glimpsed a patch of red wool peeking from under the collar of his coat. She recognized it right away. It was the scarf Stephanie had given him their last Christmas together.

"I've been trying to get in touch with you all week." She decided to lay it out for him. "The *New York Times* is doing a feature story on me. The reporter is planning to come to Connecticut next week. This is great publicity for my campaign, Claude. The trouble is that they want to talk to you too."

He looked at her for a moment, then slid a key into the door and unlocked it.

"So, here's the deal," she continued. "Obviously, I don't want them to come here. But a phone interview won't do, either. You need to clean yourself up. And I want to be present when you talk to him. We need to put up a united front. What I'll do is set up the meeting someplace public, like a restaurant or a library. Whatever you want. I can have my driver pick you up, and we'll bring you back her, afterwards."

"Go to hell," he muttered, pushing the door open.

"Wait a second. You owe me this," she snapped. "I haven't asked a single thing from you all these years. I've put up with—"

He disappeared inside, slamming the door in her face. She pushed it open, walking in behind him.

"Damn it, all I'm asking is for you to see this guy, to let the world see what those filthy bastards did to our family."

Claude disappeared through another door and slammed it behind him.

Kathy stopped. She was standing in a large kitchen space. The smell of mold and sweat and urine and paint and rodents all combined to turn her stomach. The counters and sink and stove were piled high with yellowed newspapers and magazines and other assorted junk. A kitchen table with three legs lay on its side by one wall and a single kitchen chair stood near it. Empty cans and scraps of rope and trash filled the corners.

Kathy's gaze fixed on the wall. Two spotlights, haphazardly nailed to the filthy linoleum floor, illuminated magazine and newspaper clippings and pieces of maps and photographs. They covered the wall from floor to ceiling.

Faces and headlines were marked up, underlined or circled in red. Whether it was blood or ink, she didn't want to guess.

And there was writing everywhere. Unintelligible words and symbols, as if written in code. Lines and arrows. She stepped closer, recognizing some of the faces. Others had pieces missing, eyes or a mouth gouged or carved out by a blade. The writing seemed to be gibberish, but as she looked closer, she recognized Latin words and scribbled curses.

Kathy jumped when Claude reappeared in the kitchen. He looked at the wall, then at her face. She saw then what she hadn't seen outside. His eyes were those of a dead man. And in his hand, he was holding a long kitchen knife.

Terror kept her frozen in place for an eternity.

"What, Claude? Why?" she managed to croak.

"I told you to go to hell."

She didn't have to be told again.

A moment later, Kathy was in her car, gasping and slamming the locks on her door and staring out the window at the cottage.

Claude Green was not only insane, but dangerous.

CHAPTER THIRTY-SIX

THE TWO SUITCASES lay open on the sofa, each only partially filled with Terri's things. Four stacks of books sat on the coffee table, the only ones Lacey had decided to take. She was done sorting for now. Gavin was speaking with someone at NHPD on his cell in the bedroom. He believed someone had gone through Terri's apartment after the funeral. And whoever they were, they knew what they were doing. Other than the signs of breaking into the file cabinet, there was no other disturbance.

Walking back to the kitchenette, Lacey caught a glimpse of Gavin's back as he stood in the bedroom. There was an immediate tightening deep in her stomach. Something was happening between them. In her. She was trying not to think about how alive she'd felt when his arms were wrapped around her and how the kiss had made everything that was wrong in her life disappear.

During those few passionate moments, she'd known that if they were to make love, she'd be a changed person forever. He wasn't like other men she'd known. Not in temperament, not in confidence, not in the way his simple glance melted her insides. He had a quality that Lacey recognized could wipe out any self-discipline she had left.

She tore her gaze away when he turned around. He was being a perfect gentleman and Lacey knew her limits.

The envelope the building manager had signed for was still sitting on the counter along with a half-dozen other pieces of correspondence about benefits and social security that had arrived for Terri over the past few weeks. She reached for this one and tore it open.

Pension information. She thumbed through it. Life insurance. Lacey's throat closed as her gaze fell on the benefit amount. She blinked back immediate tears. *Terri.* Even in death, she made sure that her sister was taken care of. Through blurred vision, she saw that Terri had taken out a million-dollar policy, with Lacey named as sole beneficiary.

"Damn it," she whispered. The tears were back.

The papers dropped onto the counter and she sank to the floor, her knees drawn to her chest, her face buried in a dish towel as she tried to muffle the sobs that shook her to the very core.

It was so wrong that her sister was gone.

Gavin found her a few minutes later.

"I can't leave you alone, at all," he said gently, crouching down in front of her. He brushed away the tears on her cheek. "I don't think it's such a good idea for you to be spending the night here."

She nodded, struggling to her feet, gratefully accepting his help. She headed for the bathroom to wash her face. He followed and planted himself in the doorway. She stole a glance in the mirror and was horrified by her reflection. Puffy eyes, red patches on her face, crazy hair coming out of the ponytail. She turned on the water and splashed handfuls of water on her face, too dejected to care that he was watching her.

"If you won't mind taking me back to New Milford to get my car, I can go back to my house," she said, grabbing a towel to dry her face.

"I don't think that's a good idea either. Not yet. There's no security system at the house and there's not enough time for me to hire someone to camp at your door around the clock."

"I really don't think—"

"I'm not going to leave you alone. So how about this? You come and stay at my apartment tonight."

As soon as she opened her mouth to object, he raised his hand.

"I have no ulterior motive. I just want you to be safe. I'll come out and stay with you in Westbury if that's what you want, but there are a few things that are coming to the surface here in New Haven. I might be close to figuring out who broke in here. And who took Terri's badge."

"You asked about her badge the first night you came to the house."

He nodded. "I found it in the possession of a local thug this past week. I've been trying to figure out how he got it."

Lacey needed him. And Gavin was doing exactly what she hoped someone would do, solve her sister's murder. And it *was* murder.

"Can you talk about it?"

"I need you to show me her keys first."

Lacey left the bathroom and he followed. Terri's keychain was on the kitchen counter where she'd left it. She handed it to him. He studied the keys.

"Is this the only set?"

"The only one I found."

"Whenever she was off duty, Terri kept her badge and weapon in her locker at work," he explained. "She often left her second set of keys in her desk. It was a duplicate set to this one. Except for these two keys."

Lacey looked down at the keychain, and at two identical keys he was holding.

"My guess is that these open that file cabinet in her closet," Gavin explained.

She frowned. "So, you think someone you worked with did this?"

"Someone who had access to her desk and the second set of

keys could also have had access to her badge. It would have been very easy for them to walk right in here."

"But then they would have had to break into the file cabinet."

He nodded. "I just spoke with my old boss again. Terri's desk was cleaned out after the funeral. There were no keys in there. So, yes, somebody in the department could have taken them."

Lacey didn't have a high opinion of police officers. Her sister had always been an exception. And now Gavin.

"Why would this person give her badge away to some criminal?"

"Not just *some* criminal. The mope who was carrying it is part of a larger organization and that missing file that is about them."

"I still don't—"

"There's a lot these guys can do by flashing a detective's badge."

Lacey thought for a moment. "This narrows things down, doesn't it?" she said, for the first time hopeful that he might be close to finding an answer.

He looked at his watch. "I'm meeting with one of the other detectives at five o'clock at a restaurant not far from here. Jake Allen worked with Terri on a couple of cases after I left. He's enough of a busybody to have ideas about who in the department is spending more than their paycheck these days. And we've been friends long enough that he'll answer some of my questions off the record."

"But do you trust him?"

"Everyone's a suspect. Jake has three kids, but his wife works too, and brings in a good paycheck. And even though that doesn't let him off the hook, it's worth seeing him."

Lacey understood this was Gavin's business. "I can wait here until you come back."

He shook his head. "I don't want you out of my sight. I want you to come with me."

CHAPTER THIRTY-SEVEN

LUKE BRANDT SAT in his car on Ferry Street, staring across the dirt and gravel lot at the dockside warehouse. He looked past the rusting blue structure to New Haven's skyline. Just below, the river widened into the harbor, and the red sun was about ready to crash and burn into West Haven.

Luke's stomach had been churning ever since he got the summons. It had been a good day until then.

After dropping off his daughter at his ex-wife's place, he'd been at the police station when his phone had buzzed.

He'd known who was calling. That phone was only used by Bratva's people.

Thirty minutes later, he was here, dreading what was ahead. This was the first time he'd been called to the warehouse.

Luke scanned the neighborhood even though he was certain no one was watching Quinnipiac Lobster, Inc. That was one of the things he was paid for, knowing and reporting what law enforcement was doing with regard to Bratva. And in spite of the fact that this was the center of Bratva's operations, no surveillance teams were deployed here or anywhere else to watch him.

He drove into the lot. There was a refrigerated truck backed up to a loading dock and three SUVs parked in the shadows cast by the building. As Luke pulled in beside them, one of Bratva's soldiers—dressed in yellow rubber overalls and black rubber boots—appeared by the back of the truck, eying him warily. There would be more of them around, with enough firepower to hold off an entire SWAT team. That was the way Bratva did things.

"Okay," Luke muttered to himself as he opened the car door. "Let's do this."

On the loading dock, he let Bratva's man pat him down.

"Where's your gun?"

"Left it in the car," Luke replied. "I know the rules."

The man shrugged and jerked his head toward the door.

The door opened, and Luke went into the dimly lit warehouse. The smell of seafood and salt water slapped him in the face as soon as he entered. It was ten degrees cooler than the October afternoon outside, but three of Bratva's men were standing around in short sleeves.

Behind them, four aqua blue tanks—three feet high and twelve feet long—were filled with water. In them, about a thousand lobsters of all sizes moved like a brown mass at the bottom, climbing over each other and going nowhere.

Along the bulkhead wall that cut the warehouse in half, four more blue tanks were stacked, one on top of the other, held up and separated by huge blocks of lumber. Water cascaded in a measured flow from each tank to the one below it.

One of the men pulled open a heavy, sliding wooden door beside the stacked tanks.

"In," he ordered.

Luke went through and the door slammed shut behind him.

A single light in the back corner illuminated this half of the warehouse. Four overhead doors were shut and the two skylights in the high ceiling had been painted over, making it even darker.

Luke was vaguely aware of more stacked tanks and a catwalk overhead. It was the pool-sized tank in the center that held his attention. That...and the naked, bleeding man, trussed up with duct tape and dangling from a hook above it.

"Detective."

"Mr. Bratva."

Luke looked at the crime boss. Middle-aged and balding, Bratva still had the lean, solid look of a man who did hard physical labor for a living. And wiping his hands on a bloody towel, he might have been filleting fish at a supermarket. There was an aluminum chair and a rolling table beside the tank. In his hand was a curved cutting tool. There were others on the table.

Bratva was wearing the same rubber overalls and boots as his warehousemen, but his were shiny with blood. The same blood that had created pools on the concrete floor around him. Next to his foot, a white bucket appeared to contain pieces cut from the bound victim.

On the far side of the tank, one of his men held the controls of the electric hoist.

"Come here, Detective," Bratva said quietly. "I want you to see something."

Luke moved reluctantly toward him. He knew that if he made a run for it, he was dead.

Bratva tossed the blade onto the table, and the man above the pool started to regain consciousness. The victim tried to scream through the layers of duct tape, but only a low strained moan could be heard over the rhythmic sound of the water pumps.

"I think you know him." The accent was distinct.

Luke nodded. A collector for the local branch of the Gambino Family. Before Bratva had absorbed their operation.

"I was expecting that you would already have my list." Bratva gestured to his man, who lowered the frantically squirming victim several feet closer to the water. "You know this is what happens to people who don't give me results."

The dorsal fin broke the surface and Luke realized what was in the tank. A shark was circling and cutting through the spreading cloud of blood that was dripping from the suspended victim. It was like a bad movie.

Except this was really happening.

"I'm on this, sir," Luke blurted out. "I've been following every lead."

"But are you committed to finding it, Detective?"

"You know I am. I brought you Watkins's badge from her locker, didn't I? I wanted you to know that I'm turning over every rock." He felt sweat beginning to run down his back. "And the files from her apartment. The ones that she'd been putting together about your operations."

"I don't care what you have already done," Bratva said calmly. "I only care what you have failed to do. And there are consequences for failing me, Detective."

Without taking his eyes off of Luke, the crime boss gestured again to his man.

The victim was not even completely submerged in the tank before the shark began to hit him. Luke watched in horror as the thrashing predator ripped pieces from the body.

"Are you committed, Detective?" Bratva asked.

"I am. I'm committed." Luke fought back a wave of nausea. "I'll find that list, sir. I won't sleep until I get it."

"Death happens to everyone. We both know that." Bratva moved to the table and picked up a plastic bag that sat on top with the knives and other tools. "What happens to us in the process of dying might bother us, but the end result is the same."

"I get the message, sir. I'll find it."

"Yes, I know you will." He reached into the plastic bag and pulled out a small, royal blue shirt. Holding it up, he turned it so that the number on the back was visible.

It took a moment for Luke to realize what it was, but then the blood drained from his body.

It was his daughter's soccer shirt.

"Nothing and no one is beyond my reach, so do not think of betraying me."

Bratva tossed him the shirt.

"In two days, I'll be feeding my fish again. You have two days to bring me that list."

CHAPTER THIRTY-EIGHT

THE MEETING with Jake wasn't a total waste of time. Still, the problem was that New Haven PD had too many new faces. He could provide no concrete leads about who might be on Bratva's payroll these days. Still, Gavin walked away with a list of the personnel changes in the department since he'd retired and that was more than John Trevor had been willing to share.

Back at his apartment, Gavin turned on the lights. He was relieved the place didn't look too bad. He came back to Lacey. "Let me give you the twenty-five-cent tour."

She was standing by the door, her purse and a small bag of overnight things she'd packed at Terri's apartment hanging from one shoulder. She'd decided to leave the two suitcases in his car.

"Coat closet on the right."

She dropped her things onto the floor and hurried out of her coat. He hung it for her. She was nervous, on edge. He understood how emotional the day had been for her.

At the restaurant while he'd been talking with Jake at the bar, she'd sat in a booth drinking coffee. She'd never been out of his sight. Afterward, she hadn't wanted to stay for dinner, so they'd stopped at a sandwich place, ordering takeout before coming here.

"Bedroom on the right, bathroom behind it," he said, taking her into the first doorway.

As she glanced around, he tried to see it as she would. Dark blanket, no bedspread. Basic furniture. Very different from the feminine bedroom he had seen out in Westbury.

"You can sleep here."

"No," she responded. "I'm not going to take your bedroom."

He took the overnight bag from her and tossed it onto the bed. "Too late. The bed is yours."

While she was recovering from her surprise, he went down the hall and motioned to a second, smaller bedroom.

"I use this one as an office. But the sofa doubles as a bed and it has its own bathroom through that door. With all my work stuff here, you'll be better off in the other bedroom."

He continued on into a large open space. "Kitchen, dining area, living room, and the balcony's out there. The view of Long Island Sound is great; you just have to look past the highway." He opened the shades.

"You weren't kidding," she said, dropping her purse onto a chair and walking toward the double glass doors. A dozen shades of red streaked through the rapidly darkening sky, bleeding their colors into the blue gray waters to the south. "This is beautiful."

He opened the sliding door. Nineteen floors up, the shore breeze enveloped them as they stepped onto the balcony. Lacey moved to the railing, looking, lifting her face to the sky.

Gavin watched as the wind danced through her hair, freeing some of the curls from the ponytail and molding the shirt against her body. His gaze swept over her, admiring the pebbled tips of her breasts, the curves in her jeans. She seemed lost to the world for a few moments as she stood there.

"What a spot." She smiled at him.

She was too beautiful. He had to do something, say something, to get his mind off the single track it was traveling on.

"Food. Sandwiches. What do you want to drink?"

"Coffee?"

"Not a good idea. You've probably had, what, twenty cups today?"

He backed into the apartment, and she followed, closing the balcony doors behind her.

"How long has it been since you had a good night's sleep?"

"Sleep is way overrated."

Gavin looked at her, searching for some hidden suggestion in her response. He wanted to say sleep wasn't the only option, but he kept the comment to himself as she walked to the bookcase.

He went around the high counter and into the kitchen, taking plates out, arranging the sandwiches. He grabbed a beer for himself.

"What makes you think I'd be able to sleep in a strange bed the first night, anyway?" She studied the line of framed photos on his bookcase. Suddenly, she looked up, blushing. "Do you mind that I'm being a busybody?"

He did actually, but he didn't say anything. He rarely had visitors, but it had been a conscious decision to have family pictures all over the apartment. He wanted to have those reminders all around him. He didn't want to forget.

"Your parents?"

"Yeah."

He grabbed napkins and silverware, bringing the plates out to the dining table.

"You look like your mother."

He did look like her. So did Elsie. He went back to the kitchen, searching in the fridge for something non-alcoholic to pour for her. "Ice tea, water, or cranberry juice?"

"Water, thanks," she told him, still consumed by the photos. "What a strikingly beautiful young woman. She has to be your sister."

Even though he knew it was coming, the sharp stab still hurt him. He filled a tall glass with water and brought it with his beer to the table.

She'd have questions. And then more questions. She was

Terri's sister so she wouldn't give up. In the past, people he worked with or socialized with would back off after a polite inquiry. Terri had had to keep digging until she had answers. Families mattered, she'd always said.

"Where is she now?" Lacey asked.

He decided to cut this short. Grabbing his beer, he took a long swig and walked over to her. More than a dozen pictures sat among the stacks of books. The collection covered Elsie's life. The oldest photo had him holding his new baby sister in the hospital.

"My mother died of breast cancer twenty years ago this past June. My father is retired. Lives in Florida." He gestured to a picture of the four of them, taken at his high school graduation. His sister was wearing his cap and holding Gavin's diploma. "My sister Elsie. Died when she was fifteen. The women don't seem to fare too well in my family. Dinner is served."

He walked back to the table. Absolute silence filled the room for a few moments. She finally joined him, taking the seat across the way from him. He waited for the questions to come, but she seemed lost in her own thoughts as she played with the food. The silence stretched.

Gavin had to remind himself that she was her own person. Lacey and her sister had shared a troubled childhood, but they'd traveled different routes since then. He reached across and tapped her glass with the bottle. She looked up.

"I'm sorry I was a grouch just now."

"You weren't. I'm fascinated by family pictures. I love seeing a perfect moment captured. Happy lives." She glanced over at the bookcase. "People can't help but smile when someone is taking a photo. They almost always show the best of themselves. I think that was why I was drawn to doing what I'm doing right now." Her green eyes met his. "And you've seen me in action. I don't do well when strangers ask me about *my* family."

"But you're not a stranger," he told her.

"Really? Not counting the funeral, we only met three days ago."

"I've been hearing about you for ten years," he admitted. "I feel like I've known you for at least that long. Terri always had stories—especially about when you were really young."

"What kind of stories?"

"About you taking your first steps and walking straight to her. And how you were a late talker, and the first word you spoke was her name. You called her Teddy. About how, when you were little, you always cried on the first day of the school year because you couldn't go with her."

"She spoiled me rotten. She was everything to me."

"She also talked about how she felt when she arrived at the hospital in Cleveland and found you unconscious and busted up after your alleged *stumble* down the stairs."

Lacey's chin dropped to her chest. He tried to lighten the mood. "Whenever your sister was talking her way through a decision, she would always say, 'Now, what would Lacey do?'"

"Will you excuse me?" Lacey asked, standing up. "I'm really tired."

Not waiting for an answer, she took her food into the kitchen, grabbed her purse, and disappeared in the bedroom.

He knew she was crying. "You really have a gift with women, MacFadyen," he muttered to himself, finishing his beer.

CHAPTER THIRTY-NINE

BENITA GOMEZ GOT the news that Michael Phoenix had attempted suicide, and a couple of phone calls later she knew where they'd taken him.

It was mid-afternoon when she arrived at UConn Medical Center. Benita thought about how timing was everything in her business. And Michael's timing couldn't have been better. His suicide, whether he lived or died, would add so much dramatic punch to the articles.

Phoenix had always provided an enigmatic element to this story. He was the brain behind the premeditated murder of Stephanie Green. He was the one who'd cut her throat. The others had been happy to turn on him to avoid the death penalty and he'd ended up with the longest sentence. From all the photos Benita had collected from the time of the murder, Michael was the James Dean of the sleepy town. Incredibly handsome, cool, smart, and dangerous, he was the kind of bad boy that drew teenage girls like proverbial moths to the flame. One of those girls had been Stephanie Green, but another had been Denise Geller.

Denise hadn't been at the lake that night, so she had avoided the glare of the ensuing investigation. But she had never dropped out of the picture entirely. And when Benita found out that she continued to visit Phoenix every week after all these years, she put Denise on the list of people to talk to. The faithful, long-suffering girl still carrying the torch.

And with this suicide attempt, the people closest to Phoenix would be called to the hospital. Denise had to be here.

As Benita stepped out of the elevator on the prisoner's floor, she spotted two police officers. Down the hall beyond them, a woman was haranguing a nurse about Michael's condition. She was crying and angry and apparently inconsolable.

And Benita recognized her immediately.

CHAPTER FORTY

THE HOT WATER pounded her skull. The shower steam filled the room. But the chill was slow to drain out of Lacey's body. The past was fused to her like a second skin, enveloping her with sadness.

She and her sister didn't have memories of their childhood, they had nightmares. Their mother had taken beatings when their father was drunk. She'd taken more when he was sober. She'd taken them when he'd left the service and couldn't find a job. She'd taken more because he felt like it. She'd taken the beatings so her daughters wouldn't have to.

That had only lasted so long.

When she was in high school, Terri had tried to kill him with his own shotgun, but she'd missed. Right after that, she'd been sent to live with their grandfather in Connecticut. She'd gone but had never forgotten about Lacey. The ties had always been there.

To hear the stories from Gavin made her realize once again how much she missed Terri. Everything she'd been able to repress for the past five weeks was coming to the surface today. Her shield was gone. She was exposed, and Lacey felt for the first time that she'd really started to grieve.

Surprisingly, she didn't feel vulnerable having Gavin witness it.

He let her be. He respected her need for privacy. She was lucky to have met him. In addition to everything that he was doing for her, he brought Terri's memories back to life.

When it came to family, he too was alone. He too was hurting. She saw it in the guarded expression he pulled over his face like a mask. She understood and respected him for the way he dealt with it.

Stepping out of the shower, Lacey was surrounded by his scent. The shampoo she'd used. The smell of his aftershave on the counter. She breathed in and felt a craving take hold deep in her body. She was so attracted to him that it was terrifying.

But she was not running away. Instead, she was staying here, of her own free will, under his roof. Open to whatever the next step might be.

The pair of flannel pajama pants and T-shirt she'd taken from Terri's dresser were hanging behind the door. She pulled them on. Wiping the steam from the mirror, she looked at the pallid woman looking back at her. The shower had helped put some color back into her face, but she still looked washed out.

She peeked inside the bathroom cabinet for moisturizers. There were none. But seeing a box of condoms brought a blush to her cheeks. Towel drying her hair, she let the curls hang loose and stepped out of the bathroom.

Lacey had remembered to grab Terri's charger out of the apartment. Now she plugged her sister's phone into the wall next to the bed. There was a faint sound of music drifting into the room. She looked at the bedside clock. It was only a couple of minutes past eight. Her stomach growled. She thought of the sandwich she'd left in the kitchen.

She left the bedroom. The music was coming out of the adjoining room. The door was open.

Gavin was working at the desk, going between his laptop and a PC, taking notes. The music blared from an iPod.

His hair was wet. He'd taken a shower too. He was wearing jeans and a white T-shirt. His feet were bare.

"You have a great shower."

He swiveled the chair around, and his gaze caressed her face, her loose curly hair, before traveling slowly down her body, pausing at certain points, making her skin tingle and come to life.

"Feel better?" he asked.

She nodded, feeling his scrutiny deep in her belly. More than anything else, she wanted to go to him, to wrap herself around him. She wanted to pick up where they'd left off this afternoon in Terri's apartment.

But, instead, she tried to lighten the mood to save herself the embarrassment of doing the unthinkable.

"I'm sorry I'm such a horrible house guest. I left the table after all your hard work preparing that delicious dinner."

"It took hours."

"Did you save my sandwich?"

"No, I tossed it out."

"Why?"

"Fish. I'm allergic to it."

"Really?" she asked, seeing the devilish look in his dark eyes.

"Absolutely."

"I know you're obsessed with feeding me, so there must be something in that kitchen."

He stood up. "Yeah. There must be something."

She hurried ahead of him and found her plate covered up on the counter. She picked it up and turned around when he followed her in. "You saved it. Thank you."

He looked much more appetizing than what was on the plate. Still, she lifted the cover and took a bite of the tuna wrap, savoring the taste. She was hungrier than she'd thought.

He leaned forward and brought her hand up to his mouth, taking a bite.

"Didn't you say you're allergic to fish?"

"What can I say? Some things are worth dying for."

He wasn't talking about sharing food. This was foreplay and she knew it. He smelled great. Looked great. Her fingers itched to touch the contours of his neck, the hard muscles so well defined under the form-fitting T-shirt. She was so out of her league.

Lacey took another bite of the sandwich and offered him one too. The way his dark lashes lowered, his eyes watching her mouth, made her insides turn to liquid heat. She was excited. More than anything else, she wanted his hands on her.

"Can I make coffee?" she asked before taking another bite.

"Sure, you can handle it?" He leaned down, tasting a piece of tuna that had overflowed from the wrap onto her finger.

The heat of his mouth burned her. She had to put the plate down on the counter for fear of dropping it. The only barrier gone, she was cornered by the cabinets and his body.

"I can handle it. Where is it?"

"Behind you."

Lacey turned around. The coffee pot sat on the counter. There was a coffee grinder next to it. She should have figured he'd have discriminating taste. She wanted for him so badly to touch her. To take charge of what she hoped would happen next. "And the beans?"

"In the cabinet above."

She opened the door. The beans were within her reach. He didn't touch her, but she could feel his heat. Her heartbeat was picking up speed. The anticipation made her deliciously warm.

"Can you get them for me?" she asked quietly.

He moved against her, and she hid a sigh of pleasure as she felt the hard bulge in his jeans press against her hip.

She leaned back as his hands wrapped around her. He slid the shirt against her skin, slowly, deliberately, moving gently until he was cupping the weight of her breasts in his palms. His lips sank to her neck, kissing her. Every inch of her body ached, crying for more.

The soft moan escaping her throat seemed to belong to a stranger. She turned in his arms. One strong hand slid upward on her back, and the other moved down to her bottom.

Then she was kissing him.

Lacey became lost in him. She curled into him, her hips arching upward, wanting more. She soared to the deeply passionate play of lips and tongue. She had no choice but to hold onto his neck while her body surrendered wholly, ultimately wanting the release that was within his power to give.

His hands moved inside her pants, kneading her bare buttocks. She continued to kiss him, too afraid that he'd stop taking her on this glorious climb. Her desire caught fire when she felt the fabric slide down to her knees.

"Step out of them."

Mindless with passion, she did so. She gasped when he slipped his fingers into her. Their mouths kept up a relentless duel while his fingers teased her wet folds.

She felt herself rising, carried breathlessly higher with every stroke of his fingers. And then she came, climaxing wildly within the protective circle of his arms. Wave after wave washed over her, but he gave her no time for any retreat to sanity. He would not allow embarrassment or common sense to take charge.

She clung to his shoulders when he picked her up and she circled his waist with her legs, his mouth never breaking the kiss, engaging her in an erotic dance as he carried her through the apartment.

He eased her onto the bed, peeling her shirt off as he pulled away.

She breathed deeply, her eyes half-closed, still high with the throbbing ache of passion. Watching him undress, she wanted him inside of her. She had never hungered for someone as she did now. The power of her need surprised her.

He was large and beautiful. Her heart pounded violently against her ribs when he climbed onto the bed on top of her. She wrapped her hand around him and he pulsed in her grip.

"Not yet."

He took hold of her wrists and pinned them beside her head. He took his time looking her over. Her nipples drew into tight buds under his inspection and he smiled.

"Did I ever tell you about our sessions with Dr. Ruth?"

———

Lacey's dark curls spilled onto his arm and pillow. The touch of a smile kissed her lips in the aftermath of their lovemaking. Her eyes were closed, and her naked body lay safely in his arms.

Gavin fought the knot that was rising in his throat. He'd savored every taste, every touch, every sigh. She belonged to him at this moment, but the thought of ever not having her again scared him—and he wasn't a man to let fear rule him.

He buried those thoughts. He'd have her again. She'd be his. She couldn't *not* be his.

Making love to her was something special. Their past, their futures, their joy, and their grief were all part of the moment. As she'd clung to him, he'd clung to her. She needed him and... as much as he'd never thought he'd need anyone, he needed her.

Her eyes opened and she smiled. "Have you ever had a feeling that you wanted to stop time, to preserve the moment and make it last for eternity?"

"Yeah. Right now."

She brushed her lips against his. He let his fingers trail over her silky skin, along her arm, down the side of her body, over her hip.

"I'm embarrassed about the scars." She pulled the sheets up over them. "They're so ugly."

Tightness gripped his chest. "They are part of what makes you so beautiful." He kissed her, gathering her tighter to him.

She came to him, let him hold her. She was silent for the longest moment, her face pressed against his chest. Gavin felt the dampness of her tears.

"I'm sorry for all the pain, for what happened to you. And I'm sorry I reminded you of it earlier."

She shook her head. "It wasn't you. It was my mother's letters."

"Talking is healing. Or so I've been told," he whispered, recognizing his own weakness. But this was her time. Her grief. And perhaps her chance to unload some of the pain. He kissed her hair, caressed her back. "What happened after Terri left Cleveland?"

She waited a couple of heartbeats and then words tumbled out. "After my sister was gone, my father checked into some kind of program. I don't know what it was or where it was, but he wasn't around for a few months. And when he got back, he was different. Subdued. Slept a lot. There were no crises to speak of. My parents seemed to be getting along."

"You must have been missing your sister."

"I was, but I was old enough to understand that she was in a better place. And she could never come back. We talked on the phone when we could. I knew she was safe." Lacey rolled onto her back, staring at the ceiling. "And I learned to be a good liar. When my father had a meltdown, I wouldn't mention it to Terri. When my mother's front teeth were knocked out, I kept quiet."

"You were just a kid and you had a lot to deal with," Gavin said.

"I didn't feel so young. But I was a survivor," she told him. "I stayed out of my father's way on his bad days. I had my hiding places. I was a master at zoning out, and I counted the days, thinking someday, when I was seventeen or eighteen, I could move to Connecticut like Terri did. But I couldn't last that long."

She pulled the sheets up to her chin. Gavin propped himself on an elbow, holding her.

"It was the night of my fifteenth birthday. My father was drunk, tearing into everything and everyone. My mother was pushing me to go out to a movie with some friends. She wanted me out of the house. But I only made it as far as the front door. I heard him beating her. Punching her. I went back in."

She stared at the ceiling, reliving the horror.

"I don't remember much of what happened after I went back. Head injuries with a concussion, broken bones, a shattered hip.

Somehow, I had fallen down the stairs from our kitchen to the basement. I think he beat me with a bat at the bottom of the stairs, but my memory of it was wiped away. The doctors told me later that it was a miracle I survived."

"Only the worst kind of man would do this to his own child, to anyone," Gavin said angrily.

"That's true. But the worst of it all for me...and for Terri...was that our mother never told the police. She chose him over me. She lied, saying I slipped on the stairs. That it was an accident. He wasn't going to contradict her. And then he took off."

Gavin clenched his jaws tight against the words he wanted to say. Terri had told him how she'd gone to Cleveland after hearing the news, ready to kill the bastard. And she said she would have succeeded this time if she'd found him. But he'd disappeared.

Lacey batted away her tears with a vengeance. "So, I did get my wish. I was shipped off to Connecticut. But I arrived here a broken person. Not just in body, but in spirit. And that was when I started doing alcohol and drugs and getting into trouble."

That was when the murder at the lake had happened. Life had turned its back on her.

"You know I spent three years in the prison after Stephanie Green's murder? While I was there, my mother sent me dozens of letters. But I didn't read a single one. I didn't want to read any excuses or explanations. I knew they were back together. And I knew she didn't love me."

Gavin pulled her back into his arms. He wiped away her tears that were flowing freely.

"I was still in jail when they died. She took his shotgun and she didn't miss. She killed herself a minute later. So, by the time I got out, it was too late. Too late to change my mind. Too late for anything. I never had a chance to make peace with her."

CHAPTER FORTY-ONE

NOTHING COULD PROTECT HIM. Running away only meant certain death. And not just for him.

Luke Brandt had no idea whose names were on the list everyone was after. But he did know that Bratva was a fucking butcher, and he'd die before he'd let the bastard get his hands on his daughter.

Alisha's pimp had supposedly stolen the list and was trying to use it for some blackmail scam. He'd been killed. Alisha had gotten hold of the paper, thinking it gave her some kind of protection. She was dead too. Terri Watkins was the only one that the thirteen-year-old had trusted. It was logical that she'd have possession of it. But that was hard to know since she was out of the picture. But he had to find the damn thing.

It'd seemed so simple when Watkins got dusted. How many places were there to hide the thing? Luke had searched her locker and then her apartment. The only loose end was the mail that was later forwarded to the sister.

He'd even dug up files on Lacey Watkins and done his research, finding out everything about her past. If the sister now had the list, she'd been awfully quiet about it so far. Still, it was time for a visit since there was nowhere else left to look.

Westbury was the kind of town where nothing happened, even on a Saturday night. This was a good thing. He didn't want to be running into anyone.

The flip side was that Lacey Watkins might be home. He had to get his story straight. Play the good cop, her sister's friend, running an errand for the department. She might just hand the sister's stuff over. That is, if she was alone.

At the station house, he'd overheard that Gavin might be hanging around Lacey these days. That was not good. Also, this afternoon Jake had been meeting Gavin for beers. That was bad too.

But at least Jake had no filter. All Luke had to do was ask a straight question, and the moron would answer.

He drove past the house where Lacey lived. Everything was dark. From what he could see, no cars were parked in the long driveway. He pulled his car to the side a couple of houses away and parked, shooting Jake a text message.

What's Gavin doing with Terri's sister?

He didn't have to wait long when the text came through.

Fucking her from what I can see. Nice piece of ass too. She was with him this afternoon in NH.

That was just what Luke needed to know. Leaving the car where it was, he walked down the driveway to the house.

CHAPTER FORTY-TWO

IT WAS a night that defied time. Defied everything that she knew.

Lacey lost track of how many times they made love. For the first time in her life, she felt cherished, trusted. Complete. Over and over, her body merged with his in a way that she'd never thought possible.

He'd held her so close that they might have been one entity, and she felt safe and protected.

But the first rays of dawn streaking into the room cleared the rosy haze from her head, and the old fears emerged once again.

She had to act, run fast and far, get away before she had to look him in the face and actually voice her fears.

Something very different occurred to her this morning. Something new. Lacey realized that she was afraid of herself. She was her father's daughter. She had demons that haunted her. She was unpredictable. Changeable. She made bad choices and people got hurt because of her.

And she was a coward.

She crept out of the bed while he slept. Throwing her clothes on, she picked up her purse and slunk like a thief out of his apartment.

It was easy to find a cab in New Haven even at that early hour of the morning. The fare was steep to New Milford, but she didn't care. And she managed to keep up the pretense of detachment while the cab driver chatted endlessly about anything and everything that was wrong with New Haven.

Paying the cabbie when they reached the police station, she got behind the wheel of her car. That was when the hard reality of what she'd done rushed back. Sometime during the night, they had each spoken about their past. Gavin had told her about his sister Elsie.

Overwhelmed with emotion even now as she drove, his pain had touched her heart. The responsibility that he felt for not being there for his sister was even more intense than the guilt wracking her over Terri's hit-and-run. Elsie had been only fifteen. She'd been expected to make smart, rational decisions and take the right path to recovery after their mother's death. Another lost teenager, different dangers, a bad decision, and so much more had gone wrong.

And Gavin had shared this piece of himself with her last night.

After a lifetime of repressing her emotions something had changed in Lacey since yesterday. She couldn't hold back. The pain couldn't be buried. The tears were free to fall.

Memories of that night at Sherman Pond came back to her. She'd called her sister, but she'd been too late. Stephanie had already been dead. But those boys at the lake hadn't been beyond killing Lacey too, if they'd thought she'd act against them. Her attorney claimed that Stephanie's murder had been premeditated by the rest and Lacey would have been another corpse in that lake.

And what was it that Gavin's sister had gotten herself into? Was it love that had made her run away? Had she been kidnapped? Had there ever been a time when she'd realized the danger and wanted to call her brother? If so, it had never happened. She hadn't trusted him enough or there hadn't been the chance. And that was another reason why he harbored such pain after so many years. Even as a cop, he hadn't been able to do anything to save her.

Elsie would have been thirty-four if she were still alive. Only three years older than Lacey. Now she understood the bond that Terri and Gavin shared. Now she understood why he was committed not to fail again.

And what had Lacey done this morning? Run away. Again. And in doing so, she was destroying the slender threads of trust that they had spun last night. She was proving how easy it was for him to fail again.

She was too upset to get out of the car when she pulled into her driveway. Sitting behind the wheel, she forced herself to think rationally about their situation.

Her heart ached for him. She was far from ready to admit it, even privately to herself, but she was in love. Love as she'd imagined it. As she'd seen in the movies. As she'd read in books. Flawed people, perfect chemistry, indescribable physical attraction, great sex. Together they could conquer worlds.

It'd always been a dream. Men like Gavin didn't exist.

Gavin proved her wrong.

What mattered now was that she couldn't hurt him. He didn't deserve to be treated the way she'd treated him this morning.

She took her cell phone out of her bag to call him. There were already six missed calls and four voicemails—all from Gavin's number. She'd shut off the volume.

She listened to her voicemail.

"Lacey, where are you?" His voice was deep, furious.

The next call.

"Lacey. Please answer your cell phone."

The next.

"Lacey, are you okay?" he sounded worried.

Her cell phone vibrated, indicating an incoming call before she could listen to the next voicemail. She stared at his number and took few unsteady breaths, forcing herself to remain calm and coherent.

"Hi. My ringer was off. I'm fine," she told him.

"Where are you?"

"I had to pick up my car." She didn't want to tell him that it had taken her as long as getting back to her house before common sense prevailed.

"Where exactly are you now?"

"Sitting in my car, behind the wheel, with the doors locked. I'm not driving at the moment." She tried to inject a note of humor into the words. "Paying one hundred and ten percent attention to this phone call."

"Why did you leave?" He wasn't buying into it.

Lacey thought about her answer for a moment. "I was being childish. No excuse. Listening to an old voice in my head. But I realize the voice was wrong."

"I'm coming to get you," he said softer, much gentler. "Right now. Where are you?"

"No need." She envisioned the tender way that he would pull her into his arms. How his wide shoulders would protect her, block everything that was wrong in the world. "I'm coming back."

"Now? You're not stopping anywhere?"

Lacey looked at her front door twenty feet away. There was a change of clothes, toiletries that she should pick up from the house. But then she thought of the person who was so bold as to leave dead animals on her welcome mat. She wouldn't take the risk. This wasn't *only* about her safety.

"Yes, right now. I'm coming."

"Lacey, last night was amazing. But this morning when I woke up and you weren't here, I..."

The missing words hung in between them, his pain transparent.

"I know. I'm sorry. I'll be there soon."

Ending the call, she refused to even glance at her front door. No more temptations. No mistakes, no hurting people that she loved. She turned the car around and started back to New Haven.

CHAPTER FORTY-THREE

DOWN THE STREET, Luke watched the curious episode. He had been camped out in front of Lacey's house since last night because there was no place else left for him to go.

Using Terri's keys, he'd gone inside. He'd spent hours combing through every piece of mail, going through the files and drawers. He'd searched through bookcases and behind pictures and even the basement. Nothing.

This narrowed everything down to one lead.

Gavin MacFadyen.

He'd been the one Alisha had called to save her sisters. And she'd called him again before Bratva's men had picked her up in Bridgeport. He was Luke's last resort.

Of course, he was also the most difficult one to crack. Luke already knew the guy couldn't be bought, and he was too damn smart to trust anyone like him.

He thought about what Jake had mentioned in his text about these two.

Starting his car, he followed Lacey at a safe distance. She might just provide the influence he needed.

CHAPTER FORTY-FOUR

GAVIN HAD NEARLY GONE into panic mode when he'd woken up this morning and found Lacey missing. His first thought was that someone had taken her. He'd searched the apartment. He even called the front desk, making sure that she hadn't left the building accompanied by anyone else.

Afterwards, the thought that Lacey had run from him almost crushed him.

Their night together had been epic. He'd pushed their intimacy to the deepest level. There wasn't an inch of her body that he hadn't touched or kissed. He felt like he was twenty years old again, staking his claim on her in a way she wouldn't easily be able to dismiss. He'd expected her to be a little nervous, maybe shy, even feel a touch of vulnerability after talking of their pasts. He'd felt that way. But even if she had, that hadn't prevented her from sharing herself with him. From sharing her past and her scars, both internal and external. And that took a kind of bravery she probably didn't realize she had. But he did. And God, he loved that about her as much as everything else he knew about her.

He wanted her, not only for today or tomorrow.

The realization was jarring. And exciting. But he had to play his cards right because he knew her history. Corner her and she would make a run for it. He just hadn't thought she'd run so quickly.

This morning, he'd been ready to go after her, to find her wherever she was. He wanted her to see him for who he was. He'd given her no reason to think of him as another guy like her father and the kind of man he'd been.

It was such a relief when she'd finally answered her phone. She was safe. She was coming back. Willingly, she was coming back to him.

Gavin could breathe again. He took a quick shower, straightened the bed, though he was looking forward to bringing her back to it.

The cell phone charging at the bedside caught his attention. It had to be Terri's. He sat on the edge of the bed and started going through the dozens of new messages left on it.

A number of them were from Alisha. He went through them all and listened to the last one twice.

"I hate your fucking voice mail. But this is it. I'm leaving town. So, listen. I promised you this fucking envelope. I got it and they want it bad. And I didn't peek at no names. What if they can find me because I got the stuff in my head? Look, I'm going, so here's the deal."

There was a pause in the message. Gavin listened carefully to the station announcements coming through the line. There was more he could have done that night.

"I got no money for stamps or nothing," she continued. *"So, I'm leaving the thing here. But I gotta talk to you. Make sure you know where. So answer your fucking phone if you want it. I'm calling that other guy, the one you gave me his number. He dope. He found you last time. And...thanks for getting my sisters out. You down for a cop. Okay, I'm out."*

CHAPTER FORTY-FIVE

LACEY WAS DRIVING SOUTH on Route 8, just past Waterbury, when Gavin called her again.

"Where are you?" he wanted to know. She could hear the anxiety in his voice.

She gave him the exit number she'd just passed.

"Everything okay?" he asked.

She looked in the mirror. Traffic on Sunday mornings was practically nonexistent. Just a few cars in sight. No one seemed to be in any hurry.

"Yeah. Everything okay with you?" she asked, sensing there was something on his mind. Something had changed since the conversation they'd had not even a half hour ago.

"When you come to my apartment, just wait there for me. I had to run out, but I left a key at the front desk. There won't be any visitors, no one doing repairs. No one. So you shouldn't let anyone come in for any reason while I'm gone."

"Yes, Detective MacFadyen," she said, teasing him. "I know how to be careful."

"I know you do," he said gruffly. "But I'm afraid that you matter too much to me."

There was a gentle tug at her heart. She couldn't wait to see him, to press her face against his chest and just hold him, and to apologize for running away this morning the way she had.

"I should be back in a couple of hours."

"Where are you going?"

"Bridgeport Train Station. That's where Alisha, the teenager Terri was helping, last called from. I went through the voicemail on Terri's phone. I want to take a look around the bus and train stations myself."

"Please be careful."

"I will," he said.

Ending the call, Lacey couldn't put her finger on it. Something wasn't right. This was the same feeling in the pit of her stomach that she'd had the morning Terri had left the house to go jogging.

Lacey had had three back-to-back appointments scheduled that day. Group and individual pictures for a kid's soccer team. A christening in the afternoon. A meeting with a restaurant owner two towns over who wanted new photos for his takeout menus.

Five weeks had gone by, but it still felt like yesterday. All that terrible day, Lacey had felt this same queasiness, but she'd still gone from appointment to appointment. It wasn't until hours later that she realized her sister hadn't returned from her run.

Recognizing the same feeling now, she knew she couldn't simply pace the floor of Gavin's apartment, waiting for him. She decided to go and wait for him at the train station in Bridgeport.

CHAPTER FORTY-SIX

THIS MIGHT NOT BE WATERGATE, and Denise Geller might not be Richard Nixon, but Benita knew how Woodward and Bernstein felt.

Leaving the hospital yesterday and being up all night, she had found more than the leverage she'd gone looking for. She couldn't wait to confront Denise with it.

Michael Phoenix's girlfriend had been a student at the same high school. They'd started going together early in their senior year. But she'd transferred out to a private school before the Christmas holiday. That was why she hadn't been implicated in Stephanie's murder.

More important to Benita, that was why Lacey Watkins didn't know her. Lacey had transferred in after Christmas. The teenagers' paths had never crossed. But now, they could see each other all the time in Westbury and Lacey would never have a clue that Michael's girlfriend was watching her, waiting for her moment.

If Denise Geller could hold a torch for Michael all these years, she could also keep the fires of revenge burning.

The hospital elevator seemed to crawl interminably upward toward the prisoner's floor.

That wasn't all Benita had been able to dig up. This morning, she'd stumbled on something quite unexpected. A couple of years ago, Denise had been charged with possession of a controlled substance with intent to distribute. A first-time offender with a good lawyer and parents who pulled every string they could get their hands on, she had received a suspended sentence on a lesser charge, with five years' probation.

And Fay Stone was Denise Geller's probation officer.

Benita had the scoop of the year, and she couldn't wait to talk to her.

When the doors finally opened, she knew immediately that something was wrong.

With the shift change, a different nurse was manning the station, but there was no one else in sight. No police officers and Michael's hospital door was open.

Walking to it quickly, she went in.

Three people were working inside. The glass in a picture on the wall was broken, and shards were still visible on the floor. The large plate-glass window had a bulls-eye crack at one end, as if something heavy had been thrown at it. A broken wooden chair with a splintered leg and a life support apparatus with twisted tubes and wires lay in a jumble in a corner.

"What happened here?" Benita asked.

An aide straightened up, holding a pile of linens. "I thought I've seen everything before. But this is bullshit. People don't grieve like this."

The janitor sweeping the glass gave Benita the straight answer. "Woman came back this morning, and they told her the boyfriend was dead. She did all this. Guess you could say she lost it."

CHAPTER FORTY-SEVEN

Travelers going between the bus and train stations in Bridgeport had a choice: they could take an elevated walkway that ran along the tracks, or they could go down the stairs and use the sidewalk on Water Street.

As Gavin walked both routes, he looked for anything that might provide a clue.

The Sunday crowd at both stations was light. Families, mostly, and college kids heading back to school.

Gavin wasn't sure if there was an envelope here or not. There was no way of knowing whether the people who'd snatched Alisha had gotten the list at the same time or not. But he had to find out. He wasn't leaving anything to chance anymore. And he didn't trust any cops in New Haven or Bridgeport to check into it.

He'd never investigated any cases here. He was only familiar with this station from taking the Metro North train back and forth to New York City. The bus station was more exposed. There were ticket and newspaper dispensers. No place where a teenager could safely hide anything.

He recalled the phone conversation he'd had with Alisha. The background announcement on the PA system told him that she had still been at the train station. The sidewalk on Water Street was the most likely place for her to get snatched. An abduction would have attracted too much attention any other place.

If the envelope was still here, it had to be at the train station.

Going back along the elevated walkway, Gavin tried to look at the place through the eyes of a thirteen-year-old. Again, he went through the station lobby. With its ticket window, manned concession stand, and rows and rows of benches, it also was too exposed. And for now at least, he rejected the idea of Alisha leaving the envelope in the bathroom. Daily cleaning made it unlikely that anything would still be there.

He walked out onto the track, looking up and down at the line of benches. On this side there were two more newspaper dispensers and no good hiding places.

Alisha would have taken a Metro North train from New Haven to here, he decided, envisioning her movements. She would have stepped out of the commuter train on this side of the tracks.

His eyes focused on the platform for the eastbound trains across the tracks. Directly in front of him, he could see the small, glass-fronted platform entrance. An indoor staircase and an elevator opened into that space. Inside, he could clearly see a line of vending machines.

Small, private, safe.

He went back inside and took the stairs down to street level. A tunnel under the tracks led to the eastbound platform. Taking the stairs two at a time, he knew he was in the right place as soon as he stepped into the room. Very few chairs. Lines of tall vending machines. People didn't seem to pause as they came up the stairs, but went straight out onto the platform.

A young man had the front of one of the snack units open, restocking it.

Gavin examined the machines. Each unit was butted up close to the next but there was certainly enough room for someone to slip a piece of paper or an envelope between them.

Alisha said she'd call Terri and tell her where to look for the envelope.

Gavin crouched down next to the vending guy, looking.

"Can I help you?"

Gavin reached inside his pocket and took out a business card, handing it to him. The young man looked at the card, at his face, then back at the card.

"Are you a cop?"

"No," Gavin knew this was the right answer in Bridgeport. "I do private work. Working the case of a missing thirteen-year-old. Last anyone heard from her, she made a call from here. She had an envelope that she might have hidden here. Maybe slipped it under these, or between the machines. Looks like they'd be tough to move."

"Yeah, they weigh a ton." Reaching into a box of tools, the young man pulled out a long stiff wire with a hook on the end. "But maybe you could use this."

CHAPTER FORTY-EIGHT

LACEY FOUND Gavin's car parked behind the bus terminal at Bridgeport's Transportation Center. Pulling into a nearby space, she turned off the car and took out her cell phone to send him a text message.

She knew she'd been impulsive coming here. Most likely, she would be adding to his stress. Still, she wasn't going to get out of the car and wander around. She'd wait for him here.

He wrote right back.

Getting close. Might have it. Stay there. I'll be down soon. Lock your door.

Lacey double-checked the lock on the door. She didn't know what the *it* was that he was getting close to, but whatever it was, it had to be important.

She'd been on a mad dash since opening her eyes this morning. She checked her reflection in the mirror. She needed a shower. Her hair was a crazy mass of curls. But there was a spark in her green eyes that reflected what was in her heart. She'd spent the night with Gavin and, ignoring a couple of hours of panic, she was happy. Satisfied. Hopeful. She couldn't wait to have him holding her again. He made all of her worries, everything that had ever gone wrong in her life, seem manageable. Almost distant, somehow.

Her thoughts turned to Amy. She hadn't spoken to her since Friday night. Lacey dialed Amy's number, but she didn't pick up. When the voice mail kicked in, Lacey left a message.

Her friend had promised to ask Nick to stay with her overnight. But what about the rest of the time? Or the second night? She wished Amy would answer her phone.

Lacey's understanding was that Gavin was working one of Terri's cases. But this wouldn't provide answers to who had sent those photos of Terri and Fay. And what about the dead animals around the property?

Lacey hadn't checked her email for two days now. What if there were pictures of another victim?

The worry was back.

She searched her list of contacts for Nick. He'd know where Amy was and if she was okay.

No sooner had she found Nick's number when there was a soft tap on her window. Startled, she looked up at a man with dark sunglasses. His shaved head gleamed in the morning sun. Polo shirt, a light windbreaker, wide shoulders, medium height. There was something vaguely familiar about him. He motioned to her to lower the window.

"Can I help you?" she asked instead. Her hand moved to the ignition key.

"Lacey. We've met before. I was friend of your sister Terri. I just saw you in the parking lot and stopped to say hi."

Warning bells rang in her head. He was standing too close to the car. She couldn't see his right hand. He was a cop. He was one of the faces at Terri's funeral.

Lacey turned the key in the ignition, starting the car just as her window was exploded, smashed from the outside. She had no chance to even scream as she was showered with glass and his hand reached inside and wrapped around her throat.

CHAPTER FORTY-NINE

GAVIN LOOKED ALMOST in disbelief at the paper that slid out from between the vending machines.

The dirty envelope had been used and folded and discarded and used again. He turned it over in his hand. The name and address of the person who'd been the last recipient was crossed off. Just above it, in childish handwriting, Alisha had scribbled Terri Watkins.

She'd done it. Alisha had left the list.

"Is that what you were looking for?" the vending machine attendee asked.

"It sure is." Gavin pulled a ten out of his pocket and tipped the young man.

"You don't really have to do that," he said, pocketing the money with a shrug and putting the tool away.

Gavin knew he was tampering with evidence when he decided to open the envelope. At this point, he didn't care. It was more important for him to have a back-up of the contents rather than hand off the information and having it possibly disappear.

Lifting the flap, he took out three folded pages that seemed to have been ripped out of a notebook. Names, phone numbers, method of payment, dates of visits, amounts paid. He immediately recognized some of the people. Politicians, city officials, media people. The list covered who was comped and who paid.

The list wasn't nail-in-the-coffin evidence, but important nonetheless. Investigating the credit card transactions alone would provide vital details on the trail of Bratva money. Knowing how the organizations worked, Gavin was certain Bratva had started covering his tracks as soon as he knew these pages were missing.

But the list could be used to expose quite a few people, and the public loved seeing the high and mighty humiliated. And there was enough drama packed into this document to affect the election next month. Some of the names on this list were on those ballots.

Gavin wondered if Bratva's clients were aware that this list even existed, never mind whether it had been stolen.

Other than his helper by the vending machine, there was no one else in the room. He placed the pages down on a chair and quickly snapped pictures of them on his phone, sending them to his agency email. He also sent Lacey a quick text.

I'm done. Coming.

As he put the pages back in the envelope, a text came back from Lacey's phone.

Did you find the list?

Gavin stared at the message, suddenly feeling sick. Lacey had *not* sent that text.

She didn't know anything about the list. Someone had her.

Every nerve in his body went on high alert. He had to get to her. But what was to stop the people who had Lacey from finishing the job in the parking lot? He had to give them some incentive to keep her alive.

He wrote back.

*No games. I have Alisha's list. I'll exchange it for Lacey, ALIVE, on east-
bound train platform. Come up now.*

He had to get them up here in the open, where cameras
captured everything. Where transit cops might catch wind of a
problem.

Neither of them would have a chance in a quiet parking lot.

Gavin had no idea how many people were out here. Bratva's
men traveled in packs.

He was wearing his gun, but that didn't mean anything. Lacey
could easily get hurt in the crossfire. He couldn't trust the locals,
not after what had happened with Alisha. He quickly texted
Trevor and the State Police hotline, briefly explaining the situation and requesting help. He turned to the young man at the
vending machine.

"Anyone comes out of the elevator or the stairs, you tell them
to stay inside."

He nodded, looking at Gavin's side where his pistol was now
visible.

"Do you have a number for the station lobby?"

He nodded again.

"Call them and tell them there is going to be hostage situation
here."

Pocketing the envelope, Gavin stepped out onto the platform.
He had no doubt that in about a minute there were going to be a
dozen transit cops and Bridgeport police bursting onto the platform across the way ready to open fire. Everybody with a uniform
was ready to be a hero these days, and Gavin was just a PI with a
business card. As a target, he would look no different to them
than Bratva's mopes.

But that was okay as long as he could get Lacey clear before
the shooting started. He didn't know how quick Trevor would be
arranging back-up, but he doubted Bratva's men would wait.

Just then, the PA system announced the Amtrak train from
Boston would be arriving in four minutes on the westbound plat-

form. He looked behind him. An elderly couple sat on a bench. He caught the woman's eye and motioned to the room where the vending guy was on the phone. Somehow, she understood. Exchanging words with her companion, they both hurried indoors.

People were just starting to filter out onto the platform across the way. There was nothing he could do about that. The bus station was on his right, and thirty yards along the platform, stairs came directly up from the street. Lacey and company had to be coming from that direction.

He moved toward the stairs. When he was clear of the building, he stood against the railing and waited. The seconds ticked.

Two transit cops appeared on the platform across the way, Gavin heard someone coming up the stairs from the street.

Turning, he saw Luke Brandt appear. What was he doing here? Trevor couldn't have gotten one of his own men here so fast. Seeing Lacey at Luke's side, however, demolished that possibility.

Luke was not here to help.

She was bleeding from a cut on her forehead. Pieces of glass sparkled in her hair and covered her coat. Luke held her snug against his side.

"Give me the list, MacFadyen."

They were eight feet from each other. Gavin watched Luke's gaze sweep past him to the transit cops across the track before pushing his jacket back, making the badge on his belt visible.

This was no exchange. Luke looked like a crazed man. And Gavin figured that he and Lacey were about to become collateral damage right now. Luke could not take that list and let them live. They were dead, for sure, whether it was Luke who shot them or the cops across the way.

"I've got the list right here in my pocket. Let her come to me first."

"No chance. Take it out of your pocket nice and easy, put it on the ground, and step back."

In the distance Gavin could see the headlight of the approaching train.

"I don't give a damn about this list, but I'm not going to give it to you until she is standing next to me."

More cops came into his peripheral vision on the platform across the way. Their guns were drawn. More witnesses.

"You're pissing me off now," Luke said under his breath. Turning his head slightly, but never taking his eyes off Gavin, he yelled. "New Haven PD. This man is armed. He tried to kill this woman in the parking lot. Call for back-up."

At that moment, Gavin realized how Brandt was going to play this. Right now, his pistol was aimed directly at Lacey's back. As soon as Gavin drew his gun, Luke would shoot her. The cops across the way would open fire, and he'd be gunned down. Luke would then just grab the list and be home free.

Gavin's gaze fell on Lacey's face. She looked as cool as any veteran cop.

The squeal of the approaching train's brakes drew Luke's eye momentarily to the track. Without any hesitation, Lacey kicked him in the shin and dropped to the ground.

As the train pulled into the station, blocking the cops on the far side of the tracks, Gavin charged.

Brandt was younger and had more muscle packed into his shorter frame, but Gavin delivered a right that sent him sprawling. Still on his back, Luke raised his gun to shoot, but Gavin fired first.

CHAPTER FIFTY

THE BONFIRE at the edge of Black Rock Lake had been burning for some time. Dead branches, broken pieces of appliances, newspapers, plastic bags with unknown contents had all been feeding the flames. The smell was hideous.

Judge Green couldn't contain his excitement.

Today was the day.

No more watching. No more standing by, passively observing. The Lord had spoken, given him the sign. Just a few hours ago, he'd found a note taped to his door.

I'll bring her to you.

He had read the message repeatedly. Its meaning was clear. She was coming.

And this meant he had to be ready. The moment had arrived.

Vengeance is mine, saith the Lord.

"And I will be your instrument, Lord," he said aloud.

Judge Green went back inside the house and into the bedroom. The box lay next to the mattress. He had put it there the first day he moved into this cottage. Every night, he'd opened the box and touched the smooth cool steel of the pistol's barrel.

He'd dreamed of the day when he would hold it in his hand and point it at her face. And then she'd be dead.

That day had finally come. The Lord had spoken. Today was the day of vengeance. Judge Green was ready.

CHAPTER FIFTY-ONE

"EVERYTHING IS GOING to be okay. I just have to go to the station and answer some of their questions."

Lacey didn't want to let Gavin go. She'd been taken to the parking lot where EMTs had seen to her cuts. They'd suggested she might want to go to the hospital for stitches for one deeper cut under her left eyebrow.

No one was taking her anywhere.

She'd stopped bleeding. She needed a change of clothes. But she was staying right here.

Now Gavin had to go away again.

"I want to come with you," she told him.

He touched her face, looked tenderly into her eyes, and smiled. "I love this. *You* are volunteering to go to a police station." He kissed her.

She was clutching his jacket when he broke off the kiss.

"I've made arrangements with the State Police," he said. "They'll take you back to your house and stay there until I get back."

Lacey nodded. She wasn't worried about herself. She was worried about him.

Luke Brandt was a police detective. Gavin was officially a civilian and he'd killed him. She didn't trust law enforcement. She was terrified that evidence would disappear, and Gavin would be caught in a web of people lying to protect the reputation of the New Haven police department. He could end up in jail. She'd seen it happen.

"Lacey," he said softly.

She looked up into his dark eyes.

"This is routine. I'll be okay."

Reluctantly, she let go of his jacket. She brushed her lips against his again and stepped back.

"Just stay inside the house. Don't go anywhere. I'm the one who's supposed to be worried."

"I'll be okay." She painted on the best smile that she could muster. It was still pretty lame. Regardless of what he said, she was sick with worry.

She sat on the passenger side of an SUV driven by a female state trooper on her way back home. Turned out, the woman had known Terri, and she kept up a string of stories almost the entire trip to Westbury. Bridgeport police would return her car when they were through with it.

Twenty minutes north of Bridgeport, Lacey's cell phone rang. She was relieved to see it was Amy.

"I'm so glad you called. I've been worried about you."

"Same here," Amy replied. "You sounded stressed on the message you left me. Are you okay?"

"I'll tell you when I get back. I'm on my way home now."

"I'll come over."

"Wait until I get there. Someone is going to check the house first. They want to make sure everything is okay, that nothing happened while I was gone."

"You mean the police will be here?"

"Yes. Gavin wants me to be careful," she told her friend. "He's got some things he has to clear up in Bridgeport, so I'd love the company."

Lacey didn't feel like much talking right now, so she cut the conversation short.

"Listen, don't worry about MacFadyen," the trooper said reassuringly. "He's an old pro. Everybody knows him and everybody respects him. He'll be fine."

CHAPTER FIFTY-TWO

JOHN TREVOR MADE a statement that Gavin had been called in and was assisting with Alisha Miller's murder investigation. This simplified everything considerably.

There was still a mountain of paperwork to do. They were far from getting a clear picture of Luke Brandt's involvement with organized crime. The fact that he wanted the list linked him to Bratva, but why he was so desperate that he was ready to kill Lacey and Gavin was still a mystery. They found Terri Watkins's second set of keys in his possession. They would be checking to see where he was the day of Terri's death.

Still, Gavin knew he wouldn't be totally in the clear until a complete search of Luke's apartment, bank accounts, phone records, email, and other personal items were completed. But he wasn't worried. He knew how the process worked.

He was still in Bridgeport talking to John Trevor when he noticed his answering service calling. He took the call.

"I have a reporter named Benita Gomez on the line. She says it's absolutely critical for her to speak to you."

Gavin was annoyed.

"She says the information she has is crucial for the safety of Lacey Watkins."

Common sense prevailed.

"Put her on the line," Gavin said. He could draw no ties between what had happened here in Bridgeport and the deaths of Terri and Fay Stone so Lacey was still in as much danger as she'd been before.

"Mr. MacFadyen."

"This better be legit," he told her.

"It is. I've been trying to call Lacey Watkins all morning to warn her. But her business number doesn't answer and I didn't have her cell phone. So, I tried yours."

"Why do you need to warn her? About what?" he asked.

"Michael Phoenix died this morning. At the hospital I saw his girlfriend from high school, from the time of the Stephanie Green murder. Her name is, or was, Denise Geller. She's been visiting him in jail practically every week since day one. And you won't believe who this woman is."

"Go on."

CHAPTER FIFTY-THREE

Lacey couldn't stand being cooped up in the car for one more minute.

Getting out, she sat on the steps of her front porch while the trooper checked the house. The air had become heavy with the threat of rain. The temperature seemed to have fallen since this morning too.

She needed a shower badly. She wanted clean clothes. Or better yet, pajamas.

But far more important than those things, she wanted to hear back from Gavin. No, she wanted him *here*.

The trooper came out of the house. "All set. I'll be waiting in the car on the street."

Lacey wanted to say that she didn't need this kind of protection, but she held her tongue. Gavin had asked for this, and the State Police had agreed to do it. There was some concern about Bratva's people and about the possibility that Lacey could now be a target because of what had happened in Bridgeport.

"My friend, she's my tenant, she'll be coming over. She's blind. You'll recognize her when you see her."

When the trooper left, Lacey started turning on lights. The house was cold. She had not yet flipped the switch on for the furnace. She guessed it might be a bit more complicated than that. This would be her first fall and winter in the house.

She was going to stay in Connecticut. She wanted to give a relationship with Gavin a chance. He was the best thing that had ever come along in her life. But at the same time, she had to learn to take care of herself first. She wouldn't allow him to move in and just take over. She wanted to be with him, but she needed to be a woman who could stand on her own two feet.

Lacey already had plans for the money Terri had left her too. She'd give a lot of it to causes that had always been important to both of them. She had to do some research first. Perhaps programs that helped women or juveniles coming out of prison. Or shelters for battered women and their children. Or job training. Lacey was excited to think of the ways to put that insurance money to good use.

The phone was blinking with messages. She turned on the lights in the office but refused to start the laptop or pick up the phone.

"Coffee first," she whispered under her breath, going to the kitchen.

She stopped as she went in. Amy was sitting at the kitchen table.

"Hey!" she greeted her. "How did you get in?"

CHAPTER FIFTY-FOUR

THE INDUSTRIAL SOUNDS had begun again. She tried to identify the heavy engine roaring and grinding and humming, the sharp shrieks of metal colliding and banging sharply between loud crashes.

She knew what it was. She was being kept in a junk yard.

Donna Covington dropped her forehead onto her knees and rocked back and forth. She'd given up screaming for help; she was empty from crying. No water. No food. No place to relieve herself. Yesterday, she had been thrown into this metal container pod with no windows. The walls, the ceiling, the floor had been painted in shades of gray. In the roof, a rusted hole near a seam was the only way she knew if it was day or night outside.

Ron.

Donna still didn't know if he was alive or dead. She'd been told over the phone Ron was in a car accident. He was hurt and had been taken to the hospital. She wondered if his wife Veronica had been in the car.

Maybe she'd been killed, Donna thought hopefully.

Leaving the meeting with the other district managers, she'd rushed to Waterbury hospital. But she'd never gotten past the parking lot.

The black SUV had appeared out of nowhere. Two bruisers had grabbed her and stuffed her into the back seat. She thought they were speaking Russian or something. They'd jammed a bag over her head, and after that her only struggle had been to get enough air to breathe. Whether the ride was twenty minutes or an hour, she didn't know. But at the end of it, Donna was shoved into this box. And that was the last time she'd seen or talked to anyone.

She had no idea what they wanted with her. Yesterday, last night, while she still had a voice, she'd yelled out, offering money. They could have her sports car. Later, she'd cried out for anyone to just talk to her, to tell her what she'd done wrong. She'd help them, give them whatever it was they wanted.

No one answered. There was nothing but the sound of machines. The next day—drained, all hope gone—she'd wished they would just crush the box and kill her.

Sometime later, Donna was shocked to have a door swing open. Her eyes blinked in disbelief when she saw Ron materialize in the doorway. Her heart soared. She struggled to her feet.

"Ron. Oh my God. Ron, you're okay."

"Stop right there," he ordered.

Donna was weaker than she'd thought. She leaned back against the rusty wall, staring at him without understanding.

"What's this about? Did your wife order this? I told that bitch everything. I went and I saw her. I explained to her about us."

"Just shut the fuck up," he yelled sharply. "You are the stupidest bitch on the planet, and you're here *because* of your own stupidity. Not because of Veronica. Not because of me. Because of you."

"But Ron, I never—"

"*Shut it!*" He took a step closer, and she could see the fury in his eyes. "You wouldn't hear me. You had to go off half-cocked, running your mouth and lying to Veronica."

"I didn't lie, Ron. I thought I was pregnant. Honest to God. I did one of those pregnancy tests at home. Our baby. We were going to have a baby. And I knew...I knew it was only because of your wife that you wanted us to break off what we have. So, I met with her. What was I supposed to do? She had to know."

So, she *had* lied about the pregnancy. So what? At first, she'd been so sure. Yes, it had turned out that her period had been late, but what was the big deal? If it hadn't been this month, it would be next month. She'd stopped taking birth control pills, and it *was* going to happen.

She *wanted* a baby. She wanted *Ron's* baby.

But that spoiled bitch Veronica was in the way. She wouldn't divorce him. He'd told her that himself. So Donna had taken things into her own hands. She'd met with her, woman to woman. She'd told Veronica that she was already carrying Ron's child.

"Ron, I love you. We're so good together. You don't need her. You should be with me. And she was fine with everything. She didn't cry or say anything. She'll divorce you. I know she will."

He shook his head in disgust and turned toward the door.

"Wait. Where are you going?" She cried out. "Wait!"

He stopped and looked back at her. "You should have kept your mouth shut and listened to me."

Then he was gone. Donna couldn't believe her eyes. He walked out the door and was gone. She started after him.

Before she reached the door, another man appeared in the doorway. She didn't understand.

"Where's Ron going? I need to talk to him."

Without a word, he raised a pistol and pointed it at her face.

CHAPTER FIFTY-FIVE

HER EYES FOLLOWED Lacey's steps into the kitchen.

Amy could see.

The realization was sudden and should have frightened Lacey. No one lied like this unless there was an ulterior motive involved. Instead, she tamped down her fear, pushed aside her questions, and tried to figure out her next step.

A dish towel lay on the table in front of Amy, covering her hand. Lacey guessed that she was holding a gun or a knife under the towel.

She was too far into the kitchen to back up.

"I didn't hear you come in," Lacey asked calmly. "Want some coffee?"

She walked to the counter where she kept the coffee pot. The backdoor of the kitchen was partially open. She usually kept it locked. Amy had a key and had used it to get inside after the trooper had left the house. There was a pantry right next to the back door. Lacey reached into the cabinet where she kept the coffee. The can was half full.

"Well, this one is all used up." She tossed it in the trash. "Good thing I always keep an extra in the closet."

She started toward the door.

"Stop." The command was sharp.

Lacey looked over her shoulder. Amy was standing, holding a gun and pointing it at her.

"You are self-centered and arrogant, but you're not stupid," she said tensely. "The only reason you know I can see is because I wanted you to know."

The cell phone in Lacey's pocket started ringing. She reached for it.

"Don't," Amy ordered.

A couple of seconds later, the phone started ringing again. Lacey guessed it was Gavin. If she didn't answer, he'd be calling the trooper in front of her house.

"We're taking a walk," Amy told her, motioning to the back door. "Leave your cell phone on the counter."

As she put the phone down, Lacey saw the text message on the screen.

Amy is Denise Geller. Michael Phoenix's girlfriend. Go to the trooper.

Concrete stairs led from the kitchen door to the backyard. A soft drizzle had begun to fall, making the ground slippery. There was no way the trooper would see them leaving, but she knew Gavin would get hold of her.

She didn't know Denise Geller. Lacey didn't recall any mention of the name at the trials. She didn't even know Michael Phoenix had *had* a girlfriend.

This all made Amy a very dangerous person.

"Where are we going?" Lacey asked, looking behind her, gauging the distance. They were the same height, though Amy was thinner. She could knock her down if there wasn't a gun between them.

"To the lake. Seems right. You ruined my life at a lake."

"I don't have a car. Isn't it a little too far to walk?"

"Black Rock will do."

Lacey thought walking into the woods was good. There she

would have a better chance of hiding behind trees. Her limp was a huge disadvantage, but she still might be able to get away. The path to the cemetery split off to another trail that led toward the lake. The distance was probably a couple of miles.

Her mind teemed with thoughts of how little she'd known about Amy during the few months she'd been her receptionist. She'd trusted her completely.

Lacey had accepted Amy or Denise (or whatever her real name was) at face value. She'd never doubted anything she'd told her about her other jobs or her family or where she went on certain days. Lacey wondered now how much Nick had been part of this ruse. But knowing how his family was woven into the fabric of Westbury, her guess was that he was as clueless as she had been.

"Why are you doing this? Why all these lies about being blind?"

"Do you really have to ask that?" she asked in an amused tone. "Do you know your sister rented me that apartment without ever checking any of my references or ordering a credit report? She didn't even ask for a photo ID."

Amy had preyed on them, somehow knowing that the two sisters would be sympathetic to any woman who was trying to make a new start. Even more so in this case because of the disability.

Lacey led the way through the dense woods. Wet leaves covered the narrow path. A couple of times, if she looked around for a place to make a break for it, a sharp poke in her back warned her that Amy was keeping a close watch on her.

"What did I ever do to you? Why are you doing this?"

"You didn't keep quiet. You ratted them out. All of my friends. Even Michael. You ruined the well-planned execution of a slut who deserved to die. Stephanie Green was supposed to die; she was supposed to be buried right in that lake. No corpse, no crime. There was nothing that would have tied her to Michael and the rest of us. Nothing. Except you."

"But you weren't there that night. How do you know what was supposed to happen?"

"Michael and I planned it, step by step," Amy told her. "We had everything figured out. Even what to do with you. I mean you or whoever Michael found to help get Stephanie out of her house. Oh, yeah, you should have worked out fine. You would have ended up dying that night of an overdose of some bad shit. Instead, you've been living for the past sixteen years on borrowed time. You're already dead."

Lacey could only recall bits and pieces of everything that had taken place at Sherman Pond. She'd been stoned. She would have taken anything Michael had handed her, even wondering if it would kill her. Eternity in a void, with no memories of the past, would have appealed to her then.

It would have been so easy for them to get rid of her that night.

"If you hated me so much for all these years, why didn't you just take care of it right after you found me?"

"Because I wanted you to feel pain the way I have been feeling pain."

Lacey stopped and turned around to face Amy. The path had widened and the lake was not far away. The rain was falling harder now.

"Terri's hit-and-run. Was it you?"

Amy nodded. "*Road Kill.* Wasn't it clever leaving reminders of that around the property? On your front step?"

"But how did you do it?"

"Nick's truck. Another trusting moron, like you and your sister. I took it. Killed your sister. Used one of *your* cameras to take the pictures. By the way, that will be the next thing. The police will find that camera, with pictures of Terri and Fay Stone still on the memory card. I would have loved to see how you'd sweat through that one. But you won't be around, unfortunately."

Somebody else was here. Lacey sensed it. She glanced around, but she couldn't see anyone.

"Why Fay?"

Amy shrugged. "We had some history between us. And then one day she called you. She was coming over to have some holiday pictures taken. She would have recognized me. I wasn't about to let the fat bitch ruin my plans."

She looked into Amy's face and motioned to the gun. "You kill people. You cover your tracks. You try to set me up. So why all of a sudden now? Why the change of plans?"

"Because Michael is dead. He died last night. He...he couldn't do it anymore. He broke his promise to me. He killed himself." Her voice shook. The hand holding the gun came up. "*You* killed him."

Lacey knew she had to stall her. She searched desperately for something to say. "Why didn't you kill me at the house? Why here? We're not even at the lake."

Amy laughed. "That's the only good part of this. I'm going to get away with punishing you. I'm walking away from your dead body and from your miserable life. I never saw you. I never came to your house today. I don't have to kill you. He will."

Lacey saw him, the old man from the cemetery. He'd stepped out of the woods. He was walking slowly toward them. He was carrying a gun, and he raised it, pointing it at Lacey as he came closer.

Amy kept talking. She was enjoying this. "You stole their innocent daughter out of their house. It was because of you that Stephanie died. You are the liar. You are the evil one."

Lacey stopped listening to Amy. Instead, she focused on the old man. Now she knew who he was. He was Judge Green, Stephanie's father. During the trials, she'd felt sorry for him and his wife. At that moment, she realized that she still felt sorry for him. The tortured expression of his face belonged to a father who loved his daughter. And all these years later, he was still suffering.

No one had ever loved her and Terri like that.

"You're finally getting what you deserve." Amy lowered her gun and stepped back.

Time slowed to a crawl. Lacey watched the old man take another step closer and stop. She was staring into the muzzle of the gun, unable to move her feet.

At that moment, she realized she wasn't mourning the loss of her own life. She was sad about what was going to happen to Gavin. How was he going to take the news? It wasn't his fault, but he would blame himself. There was nothing he could have done that would have changed this.

Lacey wished that she had told him that she loved him.

Then, something in Judge Green's face changed. The gun swung in a short arc until it was pointing at Amy's head.

And he fired.

"Thank you, Lord, for bringing Denise Geller to me."

CHAPTER FIFTY-SIX

SITTING ON HER FRONT STEPS, a blanket draped over her shoulders, a coffee cup in her hands, Lacey absently watched the movements of the law enforcement types doing their jobs inside her house and around the property.

After the shooting, Judge Green had disappeared into the woods. He hadn't uttered another word. Lacey hurried back to the house. There was already a fleet of police cars there. Bringing them back to where the body lay in the woods, she could see that Denise Geller was dead. Minutes later, the Judge was picked up by police by the lake near his cottage.

Lacey should have felt safe. The nightmare was over. But she was far from being able to shake off the sadness.

Thankfully, Gavin was here. He answered questions, directed people, showed them the way, filled in the many blanks that were necessary for the investigations. Afternoon was folding into evening when he finally came and sat next to her on the steps.

"They're done inside your house. But they still have some work to do in Amy's apartment." Gavin rubbed her back, placed a kiss on her forehead. "You're cold. Why don't we go in?"

She nodded, leaning against him as they walked into the house. She turned toward the living room, not ready to face the kitchen and the memory of Amy holding a gun on her there. Not yet. She curled up in a corner of the sofa, wrapping the blanket around herself.

Gavin locked up. Taking her coffee mug away, he disappeared and brought back a cup of hot chocolate a few minutes later. Then he sat down and gathered her into his arms.

"Nick Reilly was picked up this afternoon too."

"Poor Nick," she said. "He was sideswiped by Amy too, just like Terri and I were. I don't know why it never occurred to me to question anything about her. She played a part and I fell for it. Even when my computer was hacked, I defended her." The woman was dead, and Lacey was still angry.

"Her real name was Denise Geller."

"So, who was Amy? And how was this Denise able to get a job at the health club using that name?"

"The real Amy Powell lives in California. She's from Fairfield, originally. She was her college roommate before Geller dropped out. She used the woman's social security number. The rest was just good acting."

"And I assume she didn't really have a job at the adult daycare facility?"

"No. Visiting hours at Somers. She saw her boyfriend on Wednesday mornings."

There were so many questions that she still had about Denise. But Gavin told her that the police were just starting to dig into the layers of lies that the woman had built up over the years. It could be weeks before all the information would be out.

"I'm worried about Judge Green. He saved my life," she told him. "What now? Murder charges? Will they lock him up?"

"He's had years of establishing himself as insane. Also, he's got a lot of money. I wouldn't count on him serving any time," he assured her. "Interesting thing I heard from the State Troopers, when they went into his cottage, they found a wall covered with information on his daughter's murder and on everyone involved."

"He'd been watching me. I saw him before. When I walked in the cemetery, he'd often be there."

"Actually, the centerpiece on his wall was Denise Geller. He'd been keeping a close eye on her, and probably you too. But it was her that he was after."

Lacey put the cup on the table and laid her head on Gavin's chest. She could hear his heart beating.

"I suppose it would be too much to ask that the Green family could ever forgive me, no matter what comes to the surface now."

"Kathy Green strikes me as a woman who follows the polls. She'll forgive you if the media decides to smile on you." He rubbed her back. "As far as Judge Green goes, I think it's not about whether he forgives you; it's about him being able to forgive himself."

CHAPTER FIFTY-SEVEN

Two months later

BRATVA'S OPERATIONS had taken a bump, but the investigative teams had a long road ahead of them before they could put him out of business, never mind behind bars.

Kathy Green lost the election, but her concession speech held all the promise of someone who was already planning a comeback.

Meanwhile, the promotional package Lacey had put together for Gavin was working too well.

Six new cases of missing persons, both in-state and out. The most interesting one involved a client in Cleveland, a guilt-driven millionaire who had winged a Jane Doe with his Mercedes, leaving her with no memory. And Gavin had a dozen other requests for meetings. And this was on top of the security jobs. He was already busy enough to expand his business.

But the first step was to get his top recruit to accept the terms of his offer. Unfortunately, Lacey was playing hardball.

She was against them moving in together. Lacey seemed to have a clock ticking in her head with an alarm that went off any time they spent more than a couple of days in each other's company.

She admitted they were in love. They said how they felt, showed it, and proved it in a ton of ways. They had amazing sex. And often. But most nights, she packed him off for New Haven or got in her car and drove back to Westbury. She insisted that she was not ready to live together.

And Gavin wasn't going to screw things up. He'd bide his time for as long as it took to win her over.

For the past couple of months, Lacey had been doing contract work for him. Promotion and advertising, research, and even some client interviews. She was great with all of it, but when it came to dealing with potential clients, she was an ace. Gavin had plenty of law enforcement expertise, but Lacey saw things with an empathy that made people insist that they take their case.

So, he offered her a full-time job at his agency. Gavin figured this had to be the next step in their evolving relationship. With a bit of trepidation at first, she'd finally accepted. But she was putting herself on a probationary trial period, and today was their first day.

Gavin pulled into her driveway at 9:00 a.m. They had an interview with a family in Danbury at 10:00. As he got out of his car, he admired the oversized green wreath sitting on the porch. He thought that she'd want it hung above the garage doors, but he'd been here yesterday, and she hadn't asked him for help.

There was one week left until Christmas.

This was just one more thing that she would insist on doing all by herself. And it was exactly the kind of thing that he was so impatient for. To be here all the time and to decorate for holidays. To have her give him To-Do lists and order him around.

The front door opened and she stepped out, closing it behind her. He laughed.

"What's so funny?"

"You." He studied her from the bottom step. She was wearing a leather jacket of exactly the same style as his, dark gray pants, black shoes, black scarf and gloves. She had on the same sunglasses. "Well, at least people will know we're on the same team."

"That's kind of nice, don't you think?" She pushed the glasses on top of her head and took her time coming down the steps.

Before she even reached him, Gavin was beginning to think about postponing this morning's appointment. He gathered her into his arms and kissed her.

"I've missed you," he told her.

"You only left here seven hours ago."

"Yeah, but it was seven *long* hours ago," he said, kissing her again. His hands found their way under the coat and the soft sweater until he could feel her bare skin. He played with the clasp of her bra.

Her arms were wrapped around his neck. "You can't undress me on my front steps."

"Is that a challenge?"

She smiled. "How about this? Let's put in our day's work. Then we have an errand to run at the airport."

"What kind of errand?" he asked.

She looked him straight in the eye, never letting go of him. "I hope you won't be mad."

"What did you do?"

"We're picking your dad up at the airport."

Gavin felt a pleasant kick inside. He talked to his father every couple of weeks or so. The old man knew about Lacey, and he was happy for Gavin. But Gavin only visited him if there was a business trip that took him to Florida.

"It was supposed to be a surprise, but I'm terrible at keeping secrets," she said, kissing his chin.

"We won't advertise that on the business flyers."

"So how about this?" she said. "You two MacFadyen gentlemen come and stay here at the house for the Christmas holiday. Just the three of us. What do you say to that? Can you handle it?"

He raised a brow. "It'll be more than two days. Can *you* handle it?"

"I think I can, considering we'll have a chaperone."

Gavin smiled, glad that he'd never told her how deaf his father was and that he slept like a dog.

Thank you for taking time to read *Road Kill*. If you enjoyed it, please consider telling your friends or posting a short review. Word of mouth is an author's best friend...and much appreciated.

And please page down to read the included preview of Trust Me Once.

TRUST ME ONCE

A woman runs through the glittering streets of Newport with killers on her trail.
She needs help. She needs someone she can trust...

Attorney Sarah Rand returns home from abroad to discover that she is a dead woman. In shocked disbelief she realizes the murder victim mistakenly identified as her was really her best friend. No one knows that Sarah is still alive—except the killers still hunting her down.

Alone and on the run, Sarah desperately searches for answers. Why has her boss and mentor, a prominent local judge, been arrested for the crime? What does she have or know that's worth killing for? And what are the most powerful people in exclusive Newport—a senator, a dying professor and his embittered wife, a top-notch security expert and a cadre of criminals—determined to hide.

With danger closing in, Sarah must turn to a man she barely knows—Owen Dean, a Hollywood celebrity with dark secrets of his own...

*Get **TRUST ME ONCE** from your favorite retailer*

AUTHOR'S NOTE

After more than two decades of writing and publishing, we've come to respect and accept the time each story needs before it is ready to be presented to our readers. Each novel follows its own timetable. Some of our books have taken six months to write. Some have taken a year. *Road Kill,* and some of the upcoming tales we intend to weave for Gavin and Lacey, have been in the works for ten years. Over the course of those years, this novel has been shaped by news stories that continue to haunt us. Many 'what if' conversations have taken place at our breakfast table.

So, we hope you have enjoyed this first book in our Gavin MacFadyen and Lacey Watkins series. We hope you're interested in reading more about what lies in store for them.

Road Kill is part of a series of award-winning and bestselling novels. Hope you'll check them out:

Trust Me Once - Sarah Rand returns home from abroad to discover that she is a dead woman, mistakenly identified as a murder victim. No one knows that Sarah is still alive except the killers still hunting her down. Alone and on the run, Sarah desperately searches for answers. With danger closing in, Sarah must turn to a man she barely knows—Owen Dean, a Hollywood celebrity with dark secrets of his own...

Twice Burned - A man awaits execution for a murder he did not commit. A woman returns to a place of scandal and death to save her brother. A small town's smoldering secrets are about to ignite in a blaze of suspicion and deadly retribution. Sarah and Owen (Trust Me Once) play a role in this Hitchcock tale.

Triple Threat- Just weeks before Independence Day, the president is nearly assassinated by a powerful financial cartel plotting to destroy the American dream. Now, only two people stand between a national catastrophe and a glorious celebration ... and time is running out.

Fourth Victim - After surviving a cult suicide as a child two decades ago, a young woman tries to make the best of her life. But when her past threatens everything she holds dear, a determined police officer with personal connections to the tragedy risks everything to keep her alive - and this time there's nowhere to hide.

Five in a Row - A brilliant hacker with the ability to control cars from his laptop is obsessed with Emily Doyle, a beautiful computer engineer. Now he'll do anything to get her attention. People are dying, and the attacks appear to be random. But when she realizes she is connected to the victims, she teams up with an investigator to unravel the mystery. Emily's family is in the killer's sights, and as the body count rises, a twisted mind moves from virtual reality to international terrorism.

Silent Waters - A nuclear submarine has been hijacked by armed terrorists. The target: New York City. Fighting for their lives aboard the submarine, Commander Darius McCann and Ship Superintendent Amy Russell have only one hope for

survival...they must stop the terrorists. On land, two NCIS inves-
tigators are working feverishly to follow a trail of secrets as
dangerous as the silent weapon aimed at the heart of America.
With the lives of millions at stake, they must all play a dangerous
game of cat and mouse where failure would mean certain death.

Cross Wired - America is gripped by the shocking crimes: "good
kids" who are suddenly, inexplicably killing their classmates. Lexi
Bradley's son is one of those killers. Ten years ago, Secret Service
Agent Bryan Atwood became an expert on adolescent violence.
Now the nightmare is back. Just as he is assigned to this new rash
of killings, an MRI of the boy's brain reveals what must be pure
science fiction. With Lexi's help, Bryan is determined to unearth
the truth before more children die, but investigating a cross-
country trail of buried horrors casts them both into a dangerous
world where corporate greed can lead to sudden death.

The Janus Effect - An Iraqi scientist has been wrongly held in a
CIA "black site" for over five years. Now, as cases of unexplained
deaths—marked by rapid decomposition—are cropping up across
the U.S., Homeland Security Agent Austyn Newman is willing to
bend any rule to find the source of the deadly infection, even if it
means resurrecting the "dead" female scientist. Now, with a
biochemical plague about to decimate America, the two must
make their way through war-ravaged Iraq and Kurdistan...for the
answer lies at the end of her journey home.

The Puppet Master - The Scientist...on the eve of a new satellite
launch, the fiancé of NASA project manager Alanna Mendes is
apparently killed in a fishing accident, only to be spotted six
months later in Silicon Valley. The Computer Genius...four years
after being caught by Homeland Security hacking into NASA's
mainframe computer, Jay Alexei is still blacklisted from the top
colleges and computer companies. Now a changed man, he is
desperate for a second chance. The Financial Wizard ...once a

successful international banking CFO, today David Collier is a broken man who can't afford the expensive treatment for his daughter's rare kidney disorder. The tech mogul...when a terrorist group abducts the son of billionaire Steven Galvin, no amount of money can help him awaken from the nightmare.

Four lives are unraveling...and one person is holding the strings.

Blind Eye - Scientist Marion Kagan is the sole survivor after gunmen attacked the facility where her team was working on a top-secret project. Wounded and trapped, she must stop radioactive testing samples from leaking out and killing millions. In a hospital two thousand miles away, Marion's twin sister, who has been in a coma-like state for years, begins to thrash violently in her bed. When an experimental program is used on her to read the images of her brain, researchers are shocked at what they find. An American army veteran is searching for direction in his life. As he watches the news about the research facility explosion, he is unaware that fate has just chosen a direction for him—straight into a deadly game of international corporate intrigue...

Road Kill - Haunted by the ghosts of a murder two decades ago, Lacey has returned to this place of scandal. With nowhere left to go, Lacey is struggling to build a life as a photographer...until her sister is found dead. When crime-scene photos of two murders are discovered on her computer, Lacey suddenly finds herself at the center of a police investigation...and the target of a killer's obsession. Her only hope is ex-Detective Gavin MacFadyen, who is starting a new career as a private investigator. But when his ex-partner is killed in a suspicious 'hit-and-run', he is pulled back into that world of corrupt cops, child prostitution, gang murders, and crime bosses who litter the shore with headless corpses. Gavin has secrets of his own, but Lacey needs an ally, now more than ever...because the murderous fury of an avenger is about to destroy them both.

When the Mirror Cracks - Christina Phillips, grieving after a personal tragedy, leaves California for Istanbul, hoping the exotic sights and sounds and smells of the ancient city will help her heal. But when she finds herself being stalked by a young Kurdish woman and threatened by a driver who seems to know all about her family and her life, she must correct old injustices by unraveling family secrets before tragedy strikes once again. Zari Rahman fled the bombs and chemical warfare of war torn Kurdistan, seeking safety and a new life for her newborn daughter. In Istanbul, homeless and desperate, she receives an unexpected kindness that comes at a soul-crushing price. The lives of these women collide in the city where the East meets West, where together they must travel a perilous path to justice and redemption.

Omid's Shadow - Two women are caught up in revolutions thirty years apart. A third woman—the woman who connects them— carries the scars of loss that time has not healed. Weaving together the past and the present, two storylines tell the life of Omid, the daughter of one revolutionary and the mother of another. This is the tale of two periods of crisis in a woman's life: as a seventeen-year-old struggling to cope long distance with her rebellious mother's situation...and thirty years later, as a mother herself, agonizing over the news of her own daughter's arrest, escape, and the aftermath.

Jane Austen CANNOT Marry - Nadine Finley is a Scribe Guardian from the future who must play 'un-matchmaker' to Jane Austen, a British naval officer, and the romance that jeopardizes literary history. Xander is an American billionaire who accidentally follows the woman he loves back to Regency England...and may just be sabotaging her entire mission.

Erase Me - In the sun-soaked streets of a California beach town, two strangers' paths collide, sparking an unexpected and fiery connection. Avalie and Reed are covert agents, each possessing the power to alter the course of history. Sparks ignite with every moment they share, yet their hearts and loyalties are divided. They find themselves ensnared in a whirlwind of deception, and their missions pit them against each other. Trapped in a perilous game of cat and mouse, trust is scarce, and betrayal lurks around every corner.

As authors, we work hard to write stories that you will cherish and recommend to your friends. If you liked *Road Kill*, be sure to leave a review. For news updates sign up for our newsletter and follow us on BookBub.

Peace and Health!

You can visit us on our website.

PREVIEW OF TRUST ME ONCE

Adult Correctional Institute, Rhode Island
August 2, 2001

THE BLACK MERCEDES rolled to a stop in front of the gray stone building. The driver of the car lowered the tinted passenger window and stared across thirty feet of concrete at the armed guard, who was frowning with scarcely veiled disgust from behind bulletproof glass. Sweating profusely, the driver flipped the air conditioner to high and turned his head toward the line of concrete barriers leading from the prison's gate to where he sat waiting.

Moments later, a heavy door swung open, and a tall, athletic man in jeans and a black polo shirt emerged. The driver, grunting as he leaned his ponderous body across the center console, pushed open the passenger door, and the inmate climbed nimbly inside.

In a few minutes, the Mercedes had passed beyond the outer gate. Frankie O'Neal, his sausage-like fingers wrapped around the wheel in a death grip, kept glancing into the rearview mirror as he picked up speed. They passed the sign pointing toward the Interstate and made the turn.

Letting out a half-sigh of relief, the driver wiped away the beads of perspiration from beneath his lower lip before lighting a cigarette. He looked over at his passenger. "How much time, Jake?"

Jake Gantley's eyes flicked toward his cousin. In a single motion, one hand went to the power window button while the other snatched the cigarette from between Frankie's lips. Jake crushed the cigarette in his fist as he tossed it out of the car.

"This stuff will kill you, Frankie. Don't you watch TV...or read?" His mouth turned up in a half smile. "And secondhand smoke is even worse, you know."

"Stop screwing around, Jake." Frankie's eyebrows, already a straight line connecting above the bridge of his nose, bunched up in agitation. From the driver's side control panel, he rolled up Jake's window and glanced nervously again at the mirrors. "I asked how much time!"

Jake Gantley glanced into the back seat and smiled. "You brought my suit." He reached over and pulled the plastic-wrapped garment onto his lap. "And you had it cleaned."

The driver banged a heavy hand against the steering wheel. "Come on, Jake! Of course I brought your suit. You never do a fucking job without wearing your suit." He put another cigarette to his lips, then immediately raised a hand protectively. "And you mind your own goddamn business about my health. Now, are you gonna tell me how much time we have or not?"

"Look at you, Frankie. You're a fat pig. You smoke. And you worry too much, besides. Last month's *New England Journal of Medicine* had an article about stress. I'll send it to you."

The driver rolled his eyes and gnawed at a sore on his lip while his passenger changed his clothes. A few moments later, Frankie watched his cousin knot his tie in the mirror.

"Listen, Jake. This is important. I need to know when you hafta—"

"Have you collected?"

"What? Yeah, of course. Half the full amount. As usual."

Frankie glanced over and found himself begin to relax. All dressed up—his thinning hair combed back, his tie in place, the gray eyes in that cold squint—Jake Gantley had finally joined him. Frankie leaned forward and ran his fingers along the side of the center console until he felt the button beneath the carpeting. As he pressed it, a panel behind the gearshift popped open, revealing a hidden compartment. He pulled out a leather case and handed it to Jake. "How much time?"

"Five hours." Jake unzipped the case, slipped the chrome-plated 9mm handgun from its holster and ran a hand over the gleaming metal. Laying the weapon on the floor, he attached the holster to his belt. Then, with movements that were slow—almost reverent—he picked up the pistol, slid in a cartridge clip, and placed it in the holster.

"So we have to leave Newport no later than quarter after four." Frankie was still counting hours on his watch. "Jeez. Five hours furlough? That's not long enough."

"That's plenty long enough for this little lady, Frankie." Jake turned his cold smile on the driver. "We'll have time to kill."

The rambling Tudor mansion stretched out atop its perch of grass and rock in the attitude of a lion, lazy and regal, its face raised in the afternoon sun as if testing the breezes for a scent of supper.

Beneath the rocky bluff that dropped off fifty feet to the Atlantic Ocean, waves crashed in between massive boulders. The salty wind, cool and refreshing in spite of the blazing sun, swept over the gray slate roof of the mansion, past the dozen chimneys and on across the lawns of Astors and Vanderbilts and Whitneys. No force of nature on this day could disturb these century-old monuments to bygone elegance and power.

Inside, at one end of the Tudor estate, in a spacious apartment looking out over the sea, the sound of surf was drowned out by the hammering beat of Pearl Jam. The music, loud enough to vibrate the neatly arranged prints of Cézanne and Cassatt and Van Gogh, emanated from speakers tucked amid the books lining several walls. Oblivious to the volume of the music, a young woman came down the stairs to the ground floor, her body moving to the beat as she descended.

A step from the bottom, she halted, switching the phone from one ear to the other. She looked impatiently at her watch and shook her head.

"Come on...come on...come *on*!"

She caught her reflection in an antique mirror hanging on the wall opposite the stairs and scrutinized her image.

"Come on, lady. I have places to go. People to see."

Placing the phone in the crook of her neck, she ran a hand through her crop of short blond hair and then stepped closer to the mirror. She tightened the back of a gold loop dangling from her earlobe, and brushed her fingers across her cheeks to blend in the blush she'd just applied upstairs. A moment later, satisfied with the face staring back at her, she pushed open the kitchen door. A voice crackled through the phone, and her body tensed.

"Yes! Of course I'm still on the line. For ten minutes I've been holding. No, I can't hold another—"

Banging the phone on the counter, she frowned and took a deep breath as she was again put on hold. Glowering, she yanked open the door of the fridge and took out a Diet Pepsi. Kicking the door closed, she stalked into the living room, soda in hand.

Her eyes scanned the room, coming to rest on a large mahogany desk in the corner. A few reference books sat beside a felt desk blotter, and the answering machine at the other end was partially obscured by newspapers and some ten-year old photographs in a variety of silver frames. She had no sooner reached the desk, when a voice again issued from the telephone.

"I'm here, and don't you put me on hold again. Wait a minute, I can't hear you." She plunked the can of soda on the desk and hurriedly crossed to the stereo receiver, twisting the volume knob.

"Okay, go ahead. No response to the page? Okay. Are you absolutely certain she'll get the message? You're sure?"

As the voice on the other end spoke briefly, the blonde-haired woman frowned again.

"Okay. Maybe it's still too early for her to be there. Just have her call me. Yeah...no, I'm not going anywhere. Just be sure the message says it's important. Good! Thanks a lot."

Punching the button on the phone, she tossed it onto a chair. She was clearly thinking of other things as her fingers automatically cranked up the volume on the stereo. Crossing the room to the desk, she reached over the newspapers and picture frames and switched off the answering machine.

"This next call is for me, honey." Picking up the can of soda, she was again halfway up the stairs when the sound of the doorbell spun her around.

"Thatta girl. You found it." She bounced down the stairs to the front entrance.

As she pulled open the door, two telephones—the one on the desk and the one on the chair where she'd dropped it—started to ring. She turned her head in surprise, but then looked around at the open door as a man stepped across the threshold. She took an involuntary step backward into the room.

"Just a sec..."

Her eyes widened as he lifted the muzzle of a pistol to roughly a foot from her nose. There was no time for thinking—never mind reacting—before he squeezed the trigger, firing two bullets in rapid succession into what had once been a very pretty face.

Preview of TRUST ME ONCE

CHAPTER ONE

Rhode Island

August 16, 2001

Out of nowhere, the headlights appeared behind her, blinding Sarah with their intensity. Blinking her eyes against the glare, she tilted the mirror and hit the rear defrost button again.

"A lovely night for tailgating," she murmured, cracking the driver's window.

Sarah fished into her bag on the floor of the passenger side and pulled out her friend Tori's wallet. Flipping it open, she held it up into the light from the car behind her as she glanced again at the contents. The money, the credit cards, the California driver's license were all there. A pang of guilt settled in her stomach. She could just imagine all the trouble the young woman must have been through over the past two weeks. Sarah knew first-hand what a pain it could be, replacing all this stuff.

Wind-driven rain continued to slash at the windshield, and Sarah peered through the darkness, trying to ignore the vehicle on her tail.

It was easy to see when it had happened. Earlier on the same day Sarah had left for Ireland, she'd picked up Tori at the airport. She remembered watching her friend sling the purse into the trunk.

Sarah dropped the wallet on the passenger seat and tightened her grip on the wheel as her car hydroplaned around a bend in the road. A truck passed in the opposite lane, buffeting the sports car with wind and spray.

Letting out a nervous breath, she turned up the volume on the radio to hear the weather report of the storm that was punishing the coast. The heavy rains were likely to continue through the night. She turned off the radio and focused on the road ahead. This weather was not part of the cheerful welcome she'd been envisioning for the past two weeks. Well, at least she was home. The worst was behind her.

She tightened one fist on the steering wheel and tried to make herself believe that.

Fighting back the sudden pooling of tears, she tried to erase the image of her father as the dark-suited corpse she'd seen in the open casket. John Rand was no longer the tall man with dancing green eyes and the powerful laugh.

It was the laugh she would make herself remember, and not the arguing before the separation. She would force out the memories of those nights as a child when she had prayed aloud and buried her head in a pillow. No, she would remember his laugh, and his eyes, and his warmth as he cuddled her on his lap and held her close to his heart.

The rain was coming down even harder now, and she flipped the wiper blades on to full speed. The high beams reflecting in her mirrors were as unrelenting as the sheets of rain.

She had no clear memory of the day he left. She knew she didn't want to remember it. And maybe someday she would forget the bitterness that had lived in her mother's eyes and put the edge in her voice to the day she died.

Sarah shook her head. As for herself, she would just remember him as John Rand. Maybe even as the father he never was. Just green dancing eyes and a laugh.

The car behind her edged closer. The high beams glared threateningly in the side mirror.

"And can I help it if there's no passing zone?" Sarah sped up a bit.

She glanced at the clock on the dash. Ten thirty eight. Not too late to call Hal again when she got home. Sarah had left him a message, but she knew better than anyone his penchant for checking them about once a week.

She was bone tired. The flight from Shannon had been long. And the wait at JFK for the connecting flight to Providence had seemed even longer. But there was too much on her mind, and she needed to talk to someone. Someone who would listen. Someone who had recently gone through what she had just gone through. Someone like Hal.

Sarah glanced again in the mirror and frowned at the headlights of the car behind her. There wasn't another car on the road. She pressed her foot on the accelerator, and her sports car gained some ground. The gain was only momentary, and the headlights closed the distance.

"Ass." Sarah pressed her foot to the floor. Her effort was in vain as the lights again slithered up behind her.

The shoulder widened, and Sarah pulled the car off the travel lane. Slowing down, she glanced back for the driver behind her to make his move past her.

The other car pulled onto the shoulder, as well, staying on her tail.

Sarah tried to swallow the sudden knot of fear that rose in her throat, and reached for the lock button. She pressed it hard and tried to get a look at the driver beyond the blinding high beams. But there was nothing she could see—nothing but the lights' fierce glare piercing the driving rain. Pulling back into the travel lane, she looked at a passing speed limit sign. Forty-five.

"You're in no danger," she murmured, trying to ignore the cold pool of liquid in her belly. With the exception of that truck, the road was deserted because of the weather and the hour, but she was only about three miles from Wickford, if she needed to get to a town.

The sudden dimming of the headlights behind her and the appearance of flashing lights on the dash of her pursuer elicited a gasp of relief from Sarah. She immediately eased up on the gas. Again there was no shoulder, but she pulled to the right side of the road to allow the unmarked police car to go by. The large sedan stayed behind her, though, lights flashing.

"You *scared* me into speeding."

She slowed and stopped.

As the police car halted behind her, a dark figure emerged from the passenger side. Then, to her surprise, the vehicle pulled around and angled in front of her, effectively blocking the car.

"Oh, brilliant. Just what I need. Officer Overkill makes the collar!" She reached for her license and registration, keeping an eye on the driver of the unmarked car. He was just stepping out. His flat-brimmed hat was covered with plastic, and he shrugged into a raincoat before coming around his sedan.

Before she got a good look at his face a flashlight was shining in her window, drawing her attention. The officer kept the light directly in her eyes, and Sarah lifted a hand to block the glare.

He was standing close to the car, and she glanced away from the light. Dark gray pants flapped in the wind, and large black shoes reflected the red flashing light of the police car. The two policemen didn't appear to be concerned with the driving rain, and the driver of the unmarked vehicle was now flashing his light into the car from the passenger side, covering every inch of the interior.

Before the officer could say anything, Sarah had her driver's license and car registration sticking out of the small opening of her window.

"Lovely night, isn't it?" she asked, watching him flash his light on her license. The brim of the hat obstructed her view of his face.

"So what have I done wrong, officer?" Suddenly, it struck her as odd that at least one of them wasn't returning to their car to run a check on her license. The wind pushed at the raincoat. She hadn't even seen a badge.

A small noise to her right brought her head around. The passenger door was locked, but she was certain the second man had tested the door.

"I'd like to see some identification, officer." She could hear the hint of a quiver in her voice. He ignored her request. "Excuse me..."

"Switch off the car, Ms. Rand, and step out, please." The flashlight was blinding.

"I'm an attorney in Newport." She forced herself to stay calm. "I'll be glad to follow you to the station, but I believe you are required to identify yourself."

Sarah tried to see the license plate on the police car, but the angle of the vehicle prevented her getting a clear look.

"Step out of the car. *Now!*"

Squinting her eyes, she turned her head fully into the glare of the light. "Officer, you know that I am within my rights to ask to see—"

The shattering glass of the windows on either side of her showered Sarah with glittering pebbles.

She barely had time to let out a scream before the man's hand clamped around her throat.

It was adrenaline. It was panic. It was the sudden terror of knowing she may have just taken her last breath. Rather than clawing at the man's brutal fingers, Sarah's hand reached for the center console of the car, and she blindly yanked the gearshift into Reverse. Slamming her foot on the gas, her body jerked forward as the car leapt into motion. Sarah found her throat still caught in the man's grip for an endless moment, before he finally let go and stumbled into the middle of the road.

Fifty feet away, she came to a screeching stop and, still gasping for breath, stared in terror at the two men advancing toward her, their drawn weapons pointed at her windshield.

There was only one thing to do.

Putting the car in drive, she jammed the accelerator to the floor. One of the men jumped directly in the path of her car, and Sarah jerked the steering wheel in an attempt to miss him. She felt the body of the other man bounce off the side of the car, and a split second later the sports car wiped out the tail light of the unmarked police car as she sped past.

Glass splintered around her as the windshield became a lacy mass of crystalline webs.

They were shooting at her.

She quickly left them behind. But as she tried to peer through the shattered windshield, a cold fear flooded her with the realization that at any moment her assailants would be coming after her.

Sarah's body began to shake uncontrollably.

Acting on impulse, she suddenly yanked the wheel to the right. The car responded and plowed through a gully of water onto a gravel road. In an instant she was out of sight of the main road, following a narrow track of gravel and mud and flooding rains.

The rain lashed at her face, but she continued on until the low-slung automobile suddenly dove into a water-filled gully. The vehicle lurched out of control and entered the woods. Sarah felt the car bouncing through the undergrowth as she frantically jerked the wheel right and left in an effort to dodge larger trees. In seconds that felt more like hours, she managed to bring the car to a shuddering halt between a pair of scrub pines.

Wet branches jutted in through the open spaces that had once been windows. Her breath was still coming in gasps, her body shaking as the adrenaline continued to pump through her. Sarah shut off the headlights and listened to the rain falling in waves on the car's roof. Protected as she was by the surrounding trees, the sound of the wind and the storm seemed so distant. Then, the vaguely ominous scent of pine and wet earth enclosed her, and real fear began to steal into her bones, cold and numbing.

She had to get out. Grabbing her bag off the floor, she pushed the door open against the weight of the trees and shouldered her way out. Branches and needles scratched at her face, soaking her clothing, and a shard of broken window glass, jutting up from the door, cut the palm of one hand, but in a moment she was standing in the semi-darkness behind her car.

Lightning lit the forest floor with a ghostly flash, and a thunderous crack rocketed through the woods. She didn't know where she was. She had no idea where she was going. But she knew she had to run.

That is, if she wanted to stay alive.

The room had all the warmth of an empty art gallery.

Owen Dean placed his wine flute on an angular glass shelf and excused himself from the pair of chatty socialites who had cornered him there. Ambling past a bored-looking string quartet, he climbed a wide set of stairs to a loft-like area and paused at the top. He looked out over the rail, letting his eyes wander over the room.

Frank Lloyd Wright had to be the coldest, most academic stiff ever to sit at a drawing board, Owen thought, eyeing the sharp, sterile lines of wood and stone and glass.

"Quite a place, isn't it?"

"Yeah, I was just thinking that." Owen turned and looked at the speaker. Tall, middle-aged, tanned, with the build of a former linebacker. He'd been introduced to Senator Gordon Rutherford earlier in the evening.

"This house of Warner's is quite a showpiece. Though, to be honest, my taste runs more to Middle Georgian architecture."

"Actually, I'm more an Early Ski Lodge type, myself."

"Are you?" Rutherford flashed a mouthful of square, well-cared-for teeth and waved off his minions hovering in the background. "May I call you Owen, Mr. Dean?"

"Of course, Senator."

"I have to tell you, that show of yours, *Internal Affairs*, is one of my guilty pleasures."

Owen cocked an eyebrow. "Well, I'm glad to hear that you're a satisfied viewer. But why guilty, if you don't mind me asking?"

Rutherford looked down at the glittering crowd of guests below. "I've built my political career on being a law-and-order man. If it got out that my favorite TV series portrayed the police every week as a bunch of corrupt self-seekers, with moral standards that often sink beneath those of criminals on the street, how would it look?"

Owen mulled that over for a moment. "Hmm. I see what you mean. But I like to believe we simply tell it like it is, Senator. After all—regardless of profession—none of us is perfect. And, in the case of this show, our premise is that police have human failings, just like everybody else."

The senator smiled again and accepted a drink from a passing waitress. "Right you are, Owen. And who knows about human failings better than a politician these days?"

Owen let the comment hang in the air as his attention drifted down over the railing. His gaze immediately lit on Andrew Warner, distinguished-looking beneath a shock of white hair. Andrew was lighting a pipe and speaking to two deans from the college. Outside the large windows, lightning briefly illuminated a rain-drenched scene of fenced fields bordered by woods.

"This is your fifth season, isn't it?"

Owen accepted a glass of champagne from a passing waitress as distant thunder rumbled. He turned again to the senator. "Yes, it's the show's fifth season."

"Ratings good?"

"Damn good."

"And if I remember correctly, you left a successful acting career in film to get into starring in and producing this TV show."

"Success is a relative term, Senator. I was ready for something different."

The politician laughed and shook his head. "You movie stars are hard to understand. I would have thought somebody with your screen appeal would have stayed in the fast lane—bigger movie roles, more money—instead of stepping back into television work."

"Stepping back?"

"Well, perhaps that's the wrong term. But here you are in Rhode Island, at Rosecliff College, doing God knows what for Andrew."

"It's called 'teaching,' Senator." Owen straightened up at the rail.

"Don't take me wrong, Owen. It's just that the way Andrew brags about you, a person would think Steven Spielberg sweeps out your offices. Just a little odd having such a big fish in our little pond." The senator leaned forward with a conspiratorial smirk on his face. "What does he have on you, anyway?"

Owen replaced his untasted champagne on a passing tray and looked the politician in the eye. "Extortion isn't the only way of getting a friend to help out, Senator. But maybe you need to get out of Washington more often."

Rutherford's perfect tan turned a darker shade. "No doubt about that, Mr. Dean. But an honest legislator's work is never d—"

A woman's voice floated in over the party noise as she climbed the steps. "Well, there you are. I'm glad you two got an opportunity to talk."

A flash outside the large, plate-glass windows was accompanied by a loud crack of thunder, punctuating the sentence of the small, gray-haired woman who joined them at the railing.

The sound of a man coughing cut through the guests' surprised laughter in response to the thunder. Owen looked over the railing and saw Andrew retreating to a corner, his shoulders hunched as he fought to control the hacking fit.

"Wonderful party, Tracy," Rutherford declared.

"Thank you, Gordon. It is a nice way for the college benefactors to get to know one another before the school year starts, don't you think?" She took Owen by the arm, pulling his attention back to her. "And this year they also get to meet our very own Hollywood celebrity."

"I'll only be teaching a course."

"Yes! And Andrew tells me you were at the college today, checking out the campus."

"I was."

"Dull place compared to what you're accustomed to, I'd wager. It will probably be a relief to get back to your very own exciting life."

"Not before the semester is over."

"But you must find the whole lot of us extremely boring." She winked at the senator and waved a hand over the guests. "Not a supermodel or a rock star among us."

From the first moment Owen had met Andrew's wife nearly thirty years ago, he had known that her resentment for him ran deep. He'd been too young then to attempt to understand her reasons. Later, he'd become too detached to care. He glanced at the fake smile Tracy had plastered on her face for Rutherford's benefit. Her eyes, though, were bullets.

"Well, Tracy, I'm glad to hear that I'm not the only one so thoroughly impressed with the presence of Owen Dean at Rosecliff College. We were just—"

"Senator." Owen cut him off, extending a hand toward the politician. "It was an experience meeting you."

"You're not leaving, Owen."

"Sorry to be a disappointment, but I have to run."

Owen put out a hand. Tracy took it and pulled him down to where she could brush a kiss across his cheek.

"Of course."

Turning his back on the two of them, Owen took his time heading down the steps. Andrew Warner, his face back to its usual color, his snow-white hair back in place, had returned to playing host by the far windows, joking with another group of the college's benefactors.

When Owen was a couple of steps from the bottom, Andrew glanced up, caught sight of him, and motioned for Owen to join him. Owen shook his head and pointed at his watch before waving and heading for the entrance hall.

He had only come out to the party as another favor to Andrew. But being a good ally didn't mean he had to put up with Tracy's subtle barbs.

The rain was falling in sheets when he stepped onto the porch. Even in the darkness, he could see that the gusts of wind were scattering leaves and branches across the yard and the gravel drive. Owen watched the storm for a moment as another bolt of lightning lit the sky, giving the scene a surreal look. The broad creek flowing into the pond at the far end of the field was a raging torrent. The crack of thunder that immediately followed was sharp and loud.

Taking out his keys, Owen turned toward the steps and the long line of luxury cars choking the circular drive.

"Last in...first out," he whispered into the wind, turning the collar of his sports coat up and running across the rain-softened drive to his Range Rover. The rain, changing directions with every gust of wind, had him nearly soaked by the time he climbed behind the wheel.

Putting the key into the ignition, he glanced at the brightly lit windows of the house. Through the large plate glass windows, the well-dressed crowd could be seen milling in small groups. Separating himself from one of them, a rather frail-looking, white haired man stared out into the storm for a moment before turning brusquely on his heel and moving away from the glass.

Owen turned the key. "What a waste. So little time."

The lightning was all around him. Owen headed down the long and winding drive that separated the Warner's house from the main road.

He was out of his element. He knew that. But teaching had nothing to do with it.

Before coming to Newport, Owen had considered the fact that in taking this one semester position at the college, he would once again be allowing his life and Andrew's to become enmeshed. He would be poking at old wounds. But when the older man had dropped the bomb on him about his illness earlier this summer, Owen's common sense had dropped out of the equation.

Owen had to be there for him, just as Andrew had been there for him so many years ago.

And Tracy's resentment of him was something he'd just have to endure.

A flooded section of the road slowed the Range Rover to a

crawl. The rushing waters of the creek had spilled over its banks, washing over the gravel surface.

Owen flipped on the high beams and answered the cell phone on its first ring. It was Andrew.

"What did she say to you?"

"Nothing." Owen frowned at the wheezing he could hear clearly through the phone.

"I warned her."

"You're jumping at shadows, Andrew. I was tired, that's all. Just not the party animal I used to be."

"You don't have to protect her, Owen. I'm not blind. Or deaf. Last Sunday at the brunch, I know she sent those damned reporters to our table. And then yesterday. That flu business. Canceling our lunch at the last—" The cough cut off the words.

Owen heard the sound of a drink being gulped down. "Andrew, it's not worth getting riled about."

"I won't let her do this. You're a son to me."

"Tracy's your wife. She's trying to protect you."

There was another fit of coughing. "Don't! Don't let her get to you. I'm telling you I want you here."

"I'm here." His head was beginning to pound. "I'll call you tomorrow night after that Save the Bay thing I got hooked into. Maybe we could meet for a drink."

"Good." Another pause. "We need to talk."

"Sure." Owen ended the call. "And it's about time we did."

Though Owen didn't like getting patted on the head, Rutherford hadn't really been too far off the mark. Owen had put his life on hold to come to Newport for these four months or so. But he had no regrets, so long as he and Andrew could finally resolve what was past. He was tired of playing the game.

A brilliant stab of lightning hit the ground somewhere to his right, illuminating a small river where half of the road had been just a couple of hours earlier. Jerking the wheel, he suddenly saw the woman appear in his headlights. Owen slammed on the brakes.

"Dammit!"

His reflexes were quick, but he couldn't be certain if he'd hit her or if she'd just fallen against the front of the car. She lay sprawled across the hood, her face resting on the metal, and he was out of the vehicle and at her side in an instant.

"Lady, you okay?"

She lifted her head slowly off the hood and tried to straighten up. Owen reached for her quickly as she wobbled a step.

"You stay right here. I'll call for an ambulance."

"No!" Her response was sharp as she looked up, clutching at his hand.

In spite of the dripping jacket and pants that at one time must have been tailor-made for her, the woman was a muddy mess. She was soaked to the skin, her hair plastered against her head. All in all, Owen thought, she didn't look like someone who should be wandering in the rain in the middle of the night.

"No," she repeated more softly, letting go of his hand and standing up straight. "I'm fine. It just...took my breath away...running into the car. I'm okay."

The rain was streaming down her face, and lightning continued to flash above them. Unconvinced, Owen held his ground and studied her in the glare of the car's headlights. Clearly distraught, she nonetheless turned her face away from him. Pretending to adjust the shoulder strap of the case she was carrying, she peered into the darkness of the woods she'd just left.

"Your car break down?"

"No...yes."

"Well, which is it?"

"I...I ran out of gas." With a scowl, she stepped around him, out of the headlight's beam, and pushed a lock of short wet hair out of her face. Again, she shot a glance into the woods. "I thought it would be safer passing through the woods than walking on the shoulder of the state road."

Owen stared at her in the darkness. She looked so familiar to him. A bit worse for wear, but she was well-dressed and well-spoken. But it was her face that was nagging at him. Oval-shaped eyes—he couldn't tell the color in the darkness. The high cheek-bones, streaked with mud. Or were those scratches? He tried to imagine how she would look cleaned up.

"Have we met before?" he asked.

"I don't believe so."

She shivered and transferred the long strap of her briefcase from one shoulder to the other. He spotted the dark stain by one sleeve. He looked down at his own hand where she'd touched him. There was blood on his hand.

"Did you cut yourself?"

She looked down at her palm and then pulled a folded wad of wet tissue out of her pocket. "I just fell back there. It's just a scratch. Must have done it on a rock or something."

A bolt of lightning struck close by, and she jumped back a step. Owen suddenly realized that they were now both soaked through.

"I'll give you a ride. Climb in."

She hesitated a moment and looked about at the storm-tossed woods.

"I would appreciate a ride to the closest gas station. I think there's one about a mile up the road."

He gave her another once-over look. "Okay. Get in."

Without another word, she moved to the passenger side, but then paused before getting in.

"I'm muddy and wet. I'll make a mess of your car."

"If it makes you feel better, I'll send you the cleaning bill."

Frowning, she hopped in and shut the door. Without thinking, he locked the doors. She immediately reached over her shoulder and unlocked hers.

He didn't blame her for being nervous. Running out of gas at this hour of the night, in this storm, and now getting into a car with a total stranger. Not a particularly comfortable situation. He turned to her. "Where's your car?"

"Just...just up the road."

"There's the phone. You're welcome to use it."

She shook her head. "No, I'll be fine when we get to the gas station."

"It'll probably be closed. It's late."

"It doesn't matter. I can call for a cab there."

He shrugged. "Okay. Where are you heading?"

"Newport."

Owen reached the end of the private lane and turned onto the main road. There wasn't a car in sight that he could see. Once he'd made the turn, he noticed she was glancing nervously in the passenger side mirror.

"I'm going to Newport. I can take you there."

Her eyes, dark in the dim light of the car, studied his face for a moment. He looked over at her and she looked away. "If you don't mind. I wouldn't want to put you to any trouble."

"No trouble."

He watched her attention turn to the outside mirror again.

"Owen Dean." He stretched a hand in her direction. She tucked her injured hand out of the way and reached over with her other.

"Sarah Rand."

He repeated the name in his head. Sarah Rand. Even her name sounded familiar, but he couldn't quite place it.

"Are you certain we haven't met before?"

She shook her head.

"What is it you do?"

"I'm an attorney," she whispered, pulling her briefcase tighter into her chest.

Owen swerved into the other lane to avoid a good-sized tree limb that had fallen into the road.

"What kind of law do you practice?" he asked, glancing back at the blackness of the road behind them.

She continued to stare out the window, obviously pretending she'd never heard the question. He let her be. Owen concentrated on his driving, but as the silence descended, he could feel the weight of her gaze occasionally on his face.

Owen found it curious that this woman hadn't once pushed down the visor to check her own reflection in the mirror. She didn't seem to care at all about how her short blond hair looked, plastered around her pale face. Or how the rain might have messed up her make-up. He glanced at her. Those *were* scratches running down her face, but she didn't seem to even notice.

He frowned and looked back at the road. Something was gnawing at the edges of his memory.

For the next ten minutes, they drove on without talking, with only the wipers and the wind-driven sheets of rain to break the silence. She appeared totally content to be left to herself. Glancing in her direction now and then, Owen found her face turned toward the passenger window, her hands tightly fisted around the handle of her briefcase. Only once did she move at all, bending down to fiddle with the heel of her shoe as a car passed, going in the other direction.

"You'd be better off calling tonight and having your car towed someplace safe."

"I'll take care of it." Her voice was distant, dismissive. She was looking ahead at the Newport Bridge, the top of which was enshrouded with rain.

But Owen was not ready to be dismissed. "Are you from around here?"

"You can drop me off by the Visitor's Center in Newport. I can get a cab there."

She was definitely dismissing him, working at a front of arrogance and coldness. This, however, only piqued his curiosity more.

"I'm an actor. And a producer," he said, shooting her a half glance. He knew he sounded like an arrogant bastard. "I've already told you my name is Ow—"

"Nice to meet you again, Mr. Dean. But I would still appreciate it if you'd drop me in front of the Visitor's Center."

"And I suppose you're one of those people who doesn't watch TV." Owen glanced at her and then looked back at the road. Her face would probably crack if she smiled. "What kind of cases do you handle?"

"Corrupt law enforcement," she said after a pause, this time meeting his eyes. "Racketeering. Murder. Substance abuse. Very realistic and often quite scary."

"Tough way to make a living."

That couldn't have been a smile, he thought. But her furrowed brow did open up for a fraction of a second before she answered.

"No, not me! *You*. That's what you do for a living. I know who you are, and I've seen your show, Mr. Dean."

"That's great. But you still don't think we've met?"

She shook her head more decidedly this time. "I'm positive, though we did come close once."

Owen watched her attention turn to a police car, sirens and flashers going, traveling in the opposite direction on the bridge. Here was something different, Owen thought. A woman not trying to hit on him.

"Please take the first exit after the bridge," she said. "If it's out of your way to take me to the Visitor's Center, I can get off at the gas station at the end of the ramp."

"It's not out of my way," he said gruffly, flipping on his turn signal.

When they stopped at the first light, he watched her for the first time running her fingers through her wet hair and pushing it behind her ear. A couple of pine needles dropped onto her shoulder.

She had a long, beautiful neck and a firm, well-shaped chin. Owen's eyes were drawn to her earrings. Very striking. Antique-looking. A large diamond, set in the star-like setting of smaller stones. Even her earrings looked familiar to him. He studied her profile once again. She was a classic beauty. Kind of a Garbo look to her. Lost in thought, she was looking straight ahead. Her eyes suddenly focused.

"It's green." She pointed at the light.

He put his foot on the gas and started down the road. Making the next turn, he frowned as they rounded the corner and headed downtown. The tent-like architecture of the Visitor's Center loomed just ahead.

Letting her just disappear seemed like the wrong thing to do. Of course, he couldn't force her to do otherwise. He pulled up to the curb.

"It looks closed to me."

Her look of disappointment was all too apparent. "I can wait here. I'm sure there'll be a cab coming soon."

He used her hesitation to his advantage. "It's raining. I can drop you off where you're going."

He pulled away from the curb before she had a chance to protest. After a short pause, she gave him an address on Bellevue Avenue.

"High rent district," he commented, continuing on America's Cup Avenue.

"It's not my place."

Then it must the boyfriend's, he decided, suddenly annoyed. He hadn't seen any wedding band on that fist clutching the briefcase.

He brought the car to a stop at a red light and turned to her again, almost in spite of himself. "I'm fairly new in town. Any suggestions on things to do for excitement?"

"The Visitor's Center has lots of flyers." A police car pulled up in the right lane, and the officer behind the wheel stared over at them. Sarah turned her face to Owen. "I...I'm sorry. That was rude."

"Okay."

"It's been a tough night."

For the first time, she looked unguarded. Even scared. Her eyes were riveted to his own. They were incredibly large. Beautiful. When her gaze flitted away, he looked again at the scratches on her face.

"Are you sure running out of gas was the only thing that happened to you tonight?"

The light turned green, and the police car beside them moved on. She turned her attention back to the road and nodded. "I'm sure."

The small gate where she had Owen drop her was on a side street off Bellevue Avenue. The granite walls that protected the mansion rose a good twelve feet above the street. He saw no plaques by the iron-gated side entrance.

"Thanks for the ride, Mr. Dean." She reached for the car door and opened it.

His hand shot out and took hold of her elbow. He fumbled in the pocket of his sport jacket and withdrew a card. "Here's my number. Call me sometime."

She hesitated, then took the card, staring down at it for a moment in the dim light of the car. "A local number. I thought you were new in town."

He shrugged. "A couple of weeks hardly makes you a native."

She gave him a polite smile and tucked the card in the pocket of her muddy jacket. "Thanks again."

She swung the briefcase over her shoulder and stepped through the puddles to the gate. Owen sat there and watched her search in the case for keys. The rain continued to pound his car, and he waited until she opened the gate. Turning, she gave him a final wave and disappeared inside the walls. He looked up at the darkened building.

"There resides a lucky man."

The irritation he could hear echoing in the empty Range Rover struck Owen as odd. As attractive as the woman was, Hollywood was full of beautiful women. They were always around and always very willing. How many years had it been since he'd made an effort to pursue a woman?

In a few minutes, the mansion was far behind him. Out on Ocean Drive, a sports car raced by him, going far too fast for the wet roads. The wind was steadier here, howling in off the

Atlantic, and he could feel it pushing his own vehicle. Involuntarily, Owen's mind again returned to Sarah and where he might have met her.

Considering the way she was dressed and the expensive earrings she wore, she could be any one of the 'trust babies' that spent so much time in this town. He might have seen her picture in the local paper, attending one of the society events. Something stirred at the edges of his memory.

He turned his car into the long drive of the converted mansion. Waves were crashing onto the rocky sea wall, and throwing up buckets of spray over the car. At the end of the spit of land, the stone, French-style chateau stood solidly against the battering winds of the storm.

Parking in the spot assigned to his apartment, Owen pushed up the collar of his wet jacket and took off for the main door. The place he was renting was on the first floor in one wing of the mansion and had a separate entrance off the stone terrace, but the large central hallway held the panel of chrome-faced mailboxes. Hauling out the assortment of mail, he headed down the hallway to the apartment.

A copy of the Newport Daily News lay on the floor. Owen picked it up, stuffed it under his arm, and unlocked the door. The apartment was silent, except for the sound of the rain beating at the windows.

Dropping his keys on the counter, he dumped everything else on the kitchen table. Opening the fridge door, he reached in for a beer...and froze in his tracks.

Whirling, he turned back to the kitchen table and studied the picture of the woman staring back at him from the right-hand column of the newspaper.

Of course he knew her. After all, Sarah Rand had only been dead for the past two weeks.

*Get **TRUST ME ONCE** from your favorite retailer*

ABOUT THE AUTHOR

USA Today Bestselling Authors Nikoo and Jim McGoldrick have crafted over fifty fast-paced, conflict-filled contemporary and historical novels, along with two works of nonfiction, under the pseudonyms Jan Coffey, May McGoldrick, and Nik James.

These popular and prolific authors write historical romance, suspense, mystery, historical Westerns, and young adult novels. They are four-time Rita Award Finalists and the winners of numerous awards for their writing, including the Daphne DuMaurier Award for Excellence, a Will Rogers Medallion, the *Romantic Times Magazine* Reviewers' Choice Award, three NJRW Golden Leaf Awards, two Holt Medallions, and the Connecticut Press Club Award for Best Fiction. Their work is included in the Popular Culture Library collection of the National Museum of Scotland.

facebook.com/JanCoffeyAuthor
x.com/jancoffey
instagram.com/jancoffeyauthor
bookbub.com/authors/jan-coffey

ALSO BY MAY MCGOLDRICK, JAN COFFEY & NIK JAMES

Scottish Relic Trilogy Box Set

Love and Mayhem

18TH CENTURY NOVELS

Secret Vows

The Promise (Pennington Family)

The Rebel

Secret Vows Box Set

Scottish Dream Trilogy (Pennington Family)

Borrowed Dreams (Book 1)

Captured Dreams (Book 2)

Dreams of Destiny (Book 3)

Scottish Dream Trilogy Box Set

REGENCY AND 19TH CENTURY NOVELS

Pennington Regency-Era Series

Romancing the Scot

It Happened in the Highlands

Sweet Home Highland Christmas *(novella)*

Sleepless in Scotland

Dearest Millie *(novella)*

How to Ditch a Duke *(novella)*

A Prince in the Pantry *(novella)*

Regency Novella Collection

Royal Highlander Series

Highland Crown

Highland Jewel

Highland Sword

Ghost of the Thames

CONTEMPORARY ROMANCE & FANTASY

Jane Austen CANNOT Marry

Erase Me

Tropical Kiss

Aquarian

Thanksgiving in Connecticut

Made in Heaven

NONFICTION

Marriage of Minds: Collaborative Writing

Step Write Up: Writing Exercises for 21st Century

NOVELS BY JAN COFFEY

ROMANTIC SUSPENSE & MYSTERY

Trust Me Once

Twice Burned

Triple Threat

Fourth Victim

Five in a Row

Silent Waters

Cross Wired

The Janus Effect

The Puppet Master

Blind Eye

Road Kill

Mercy (novella)

When the Mirror Cracks

Omid's Shadow

Erase Me

NOVELS BY NIK JAMES

Caleb Marlowe Westerns

High Country Justice

Bullets and Silver

The Winter Road

Silver Trail Christmas